Twenty Twenty Vision

by

Sue Coulton

**Grosvenor House
Publishing Limited**

Sue Coulton is hereby identified as author of this
work in accordance with Section 77 of the Copyright, Designs
and Patents Act 1988

The book cover picture is copyright to Kulbir Thandi

This book is published by
Grosvenor House Publishing Ltd
28-30 High Street, Guildford, Surrey, GU1 3HY.
www.grosvenorhousepublishing.co.uk

A CIP record for this book
is available from the British Library

ISBN 978-1-906210-57-1

Sue Coulton began her career as a journalist on a weekly newspaper in Devon, where she was born and brought up. After her first marriage to a fellow journalist, she worked as a freelance on magazines and newspapers while bringing up three children.

She worked in London as a press officer at the Royal College of Nursing before becoming Deputy Head of Public Affairs for the British Medical Association during the 1980s at the time of Margaret Thatcher's NHS reforms. In 1989 she returned to journalism and worked on the evening paper for South Devon - the Herald Express. In 1992 she was appointed to set up and run a press office for Exeter City Council. In 1994 she left to freelance but in the last six years she has determinedly worked on her own writing and has cut down on freelance commitments. This is the second novel she has written in the time.

She is happily married to Peter Hunt, an author, and lives in Devon. Soon after they met they back-packed the length of the Pyrenees from the Atlantic to the Med - a rigorous test for any relationship.

To my husband Peter who has given me every encouragement and support to write fiction.

I would like to acknowledge the help and constructive advice given by Dr Simon Knowles and Dr Ruth Knowles, and by Jimmy and Margaret Auld. I would also like to thank James Rushforth.

Book cover photographed and designed by Kulbir Thandi.

PART 1

Introduction

I knew three of the people involved in what became known to the general public as 'the death by numbers' scandal following revelations that the government tried hard to suppress. The pressure group formed to try and reverse the policy kept the issue in the headlines. One of the key people was Warne and I knew him, knew of him is more accurate, because Steph, the girl I was living with, had worked with him professionally. She is head of communications for the Medical Associations of England, Scotland and Wales. Ireland has its own organisation.

Recently I have been asked to sift through his papers. I guess I'm considered rehabilitated. God knows I've worked hard enough to give them evidence of my integrity and commitment throughout the whole of this cloning policy nightmare.

The 'they' are my employers ... the government of the day, the grey suits in Whitehall, the ministry of this, that and the other. I've shifted about a bit. One department after another. I had been singled out as a high flyer. Top economist. Very bright future. All that's gone out the window, of course, but maybe it will change. After all they want me to do the background papers and first draft for the Commission.

They have given me Warne's papers. I didn't spot it until Steph said 'typical doctor, writes like he's making a diagnosis. Takes him a long time to narrow down to a conclusion. And he's a bit Machiavellian. Wants it to be his view, his take on history and will connive at getting his way. I've seen him in action. He can be ruthless.'

She said most doctors had problems communicating but added, rather defensively: 'Warne was one of the good ones. Grasped the importance of getting to the point quickly in telly and radio interviews.'

Warne obviously intended to publish but events overtook him. He struck me as one of those people who have had a lot of options right from the start and would have succeeded in whatever field he entered. He probably took up medicine because he was a benevolent despot. There is a power thing with medics, controlling other people's lives and Warne was a complicated man. An ethical do-gooder, a bit of a saint but there was also the 'look at me' syndrome, a vanity which was difficult to identify. Control freak? Not quite. Steph was probably right. A caring sharing Machiavelli? It's odd that I think of him just by his surname. He was John Warne but somehow I only think of him as Warne and Steph only ever uses his surname.

He was a yachtsman and a good one, national standard, in his teenage years. He was probably a nightmare as a kid with all his talents. A school report, I think, backed up the theory about his controlling nature. Certainly not a bully but there was something. He didn't seem to have a lot of friends. He had a wife for whom I'd certainly have been prepared to do life. She was a prize cow.

He got himself involved in some very emotive issues. I've been charged with incorporating any of his material which is relevant. I'm going to have a hard job sorting it all out. The Commission wants my report in a month's time. It has another month before it must itself report, dealing with the wider issues. This will be its second report and this time it really intends to move things on.

The Commission's primary role is to contribute to population development in the longer term by providing an authoritative factual basis for policy-making and debate and setting new policy agendas and priorities. Nobody, however, is under any illusion what the intention is - legalise human cloning and retrospectively condone what has already taken place.

I'm hoping I can present a logical appraisal. Other reports in which I've had a hand have been received favourably. The chairman of a select committee once praised one of 'my' reports. I wasn't named personally, of course, but the mandarins were pleased.

I'm going to use some of Warne's material in this, my first brain-storming draft for my own use. Strictly for my own use. I don't want people seeing this material. I don't want anybody seeing this though I might just let Steph have a look. It is just to help me get my head straight about the sequence of events. It will need careful editing and I intend to insert, where relevant, other information, other people's records, diaries, reminiscence. They have given me Maeve Dunlop's diaries. She didn't give them up willingly and they threatened legal action but she obviously wants to stay on as a commissioner. Her diaries will help me cross-reference what Warne has written.

Quite a lot I know from personal experience because I became so involved. When I do the formal draft only the factual material will be left in. There will be statistics and I've got a team working on those. Then I'll go back over the whole thing and see how it gels.

I started off by saying I personally knew three people involved. Besides Warne, the other two were the couple who were living next door to me at the time. Fern and her husband Johnnie Purton. I should have counted Steph in, of course. That's four. Mac makes five. The baby, William, makes six. I paid very little attention to him at the time. I should have.

Via voice, James Fields, Department of Lifestyle, Monday, November 6, 2023.

Chapter 1

From Warne's manuscript

We had sat in committee all the day of Wednesday, November 16, 2019. There had been a couple of interruptions. During the afternoon session one of the press officers had come down with an urgent inquiry ... she'd opened the door quietly, rather obviously tip-toed up to the chairman, waiting for him to finish what he was saying ... she whispered but it was audible ... a story was breaking and Mike Tomlinson, who was in the chair, was needed to give a considered quote. He's a heart surgeon at the Brompton.

She was auburn haired with the unusual pale colouring that Highland Scots have, a dusting of freckles, probably not long out of university. I wasn't the only man who welcomed the break and speculated about the freckles. Things had got heated. Of the three women, two obviously knew and liked the girl and tried to catch her eye with their smiles, while the other, blonde and good-looking, a haematologist from Essex, pursed up her rosebud mouth. She presumably hoped it would be interpreted as resentment at the business being interrupted but I knew her too well. She didn't like any sort of competition. Pretty young red-heads weren't welcome.

Tomlinson smiled at us all urbanely, showing how relevant he was at the cutting edge, and left the room for a few minutes. The second time the girl returned to give him an update on what was happening.

The meeting had been acrimonious. Two of us vehemently opposed the recommendation. All the papers had been stamped highly secret and numbered and would be gathered in at the end. We had all been reminded yet again, at the start of the meeting, of the secrecy document we had signed on joining the committee.

I was the most vehement in opposition. I've done a lot in medical politics, risen through the ranks to become chairman of one of the key negotiating committees and I'll admit to being flattered to be invited to sit on this committee. Its original composition, several years previously, was solely of doctors - senior consultants in a number of specialties, some highly regarded public health doctors and one other GP but now the remit has widened. Two years ago three actuaries and the chief executives of two rival health insurance companies had been co-opted on.

I was wondering, yet again, if I should have refused. Another chap, public health consultant from Bristol, an Indian, was backing me but I was pretty sure that if the others got tough he'd cave in. The rest of the committee didn't seem to care much about what they were being asked to rubber stamp or maybe they did but weren't going to risk being chucked off. I'd had enough.

Tomlinson came back in and the meeting re-started. The administrator from the Medical Associations of England, Scotland and Wales was efficient at getting us back to the agenda. The organisation usually grabbed the secretariat positions on committees like this. It kept up its profile.

The proposal had to be voted on, but I managed to get an amendment, with Thandi's help. This was taken first. It fell, and the vote on the original proposal was taken. I voted against but Thandi abstained. The proposal went through. All the papers were immediately collected by one of the clerks.

Hart, the other GP on the committee, said: 'Difficult decisions, these days, I admire your stand, Warne, but ...'

I replied brusquely that I had to make the 5.35 from Paddington. I got the tram in Tavistock Square without any trouble but it still took longer than I thought it would, despite the almost empty streets. I was streaming with sweat by the time I reached the station. I rushed up the steps, stumbling and almost falling.

I was trying to do too much. We were short-handed at the practice again, despite the incentives. Two of the three women doctors were on maternity leave. Two of my partners shared a job, a husband and wife. God knows why they had qualified in the first place. They were far more interested in growing organic veg on their small-holding on the edge of the town.

Patients were beginning to complain and that meant more hassle. I remember thinking that maybe I should have voted with the committee; the proposal at least gave a degree of power back to doctors over life and death. It would shake up the patients a bit knowing who held the balance of power and maybe stop the constant whingeing and threats to sue.

I settled into a first class seat; the committee members were entitled to claim first class travel arrangements. A lot of them were flying down to London now but the train line from the west wasn't too bad.

As the train pulled out, I felt a numbness where I had fallen, in my left leg. I sat rubbing it for a while.

The ethics of what the committee had just done was getting to me. The part we were discussing today had been non-intervention, withholding procedures which cost a lot and giving more palliative care. I was aware there was another committee which was considering the medical implications of other population issues but it was even more secretive than the one I was on. My area of expertise has been in geriatrics and that's why I justified my place.

Today's meeting had been about the target-setting. 10,000 heart and stroke patients and 30,000 cancer patients among the over 75's in the individual regions in any one year. They weren't called targets, of course. This was something more complex but it was an astonishing leap from the trial programme which had now been running for three years, road-tested in two areas in north east and south east England. They could wrap it up in committee speak as non-intervention as much as they liked and say that doctors had always made these decisions but we all knew it was part of a population manipulation programme. The ultimate QALY - that stands for Quality Adjusted Life Years. If the patient doesn't meet the criteria then their chances of getting treatment to prolong life are slim. Patients who are smokers, excessive drinkers and the clinically obese have very little chance.

I'd had nothing to do with the original decision. That had already been in place when I joined the committee and when I realised what had gone before I became increasingly antagonistic. Mine was a lone voice. It wasn't what my training had taught me and I was now sure that I had been asked to sit on the committee as a piece of window dressing. I've had what has amounted to a subsidiary career in television and radio discussion programmes and mine is the name the researchers inevitably turn up first, second or third when asked to find 'the perfect family doctor' for news and current affairs. I think they thought my name would add credence to the committee if things got sticky.

A woman, in the seat opposite, already bored with the journey tried to start a conversation. She had several Harrods bags on the seat beside her and was elegantly dressed. She had a broad Devon accent when she spoke and was a lot older than the facial window dressing and the short skirt suggested. She had been fiddling with a mobile internet link and said: 'I see they've put the price of beer, spirits and wine up yet again in the budget.'

She said: 'It'll put us all out of work.'

She said she kept a pub in Exeter. I asked: 'In the shitty shentre?' As I said it I realised I'd slurred my words. She gave me an odd glance but answered nonetheless. I didn't know it when she told me the name. 'Roughish place,' she said. 'But I don't stand any nonsense. The regulars know me and keep the rules. It's been in my family for over 100 years. My father was the licensee before me. One of the last of the free houses in the city.'

I was relieved when another man, sitting across the aisle, joined in the conversation, taking it over, expanding it. I could see from the landlady's face that she resented being upstaged but she never regained control. He had strong views on government interference in health issues. She kept nodding in agreement, trying to interrupt.

At last the train began slowing down for its stop at Tiverton Parkway. It was bitterly cold as I stepped out on to the platform and I knew the lanes were going to be icy. There was a half hour's drive through them before I got home to the isolated farm-house we bought when the money started rolling in after the practice went private. Recently the government had found ingenious ways of clawing more of the practice cash back. I wasn't nearly old enough to retire yet, only 48, so another 22 years to go if I was lucky. That evening it felt like a death sentence.

There were no lights showing as I swung down the rutted farm track which jolted the bruised leg and got me trying to rub it as I drove. Margaret was still out. I've told her again and again that it's an open invitation to thieves ... if they could ever find the place. I let myself in through the kitchen door, knowing the impossibility of a nice comforting casserole in the Rayburn. She'd soon got fed up with my irregular hours, night calls, interruptions to our social life. I only got into medical politics when she made it clear how the land lay. Margaret pursues her own interests. She's the only child of elderly parents, long since dead, and has never viewed our relationship as a partnership. She wants, needs, to be the centre of attention. Children might have helped us resolve some of our mutual difficulties. We both still grieve, I think, about the child that didn't make it.

As my salary increased she took up further education ... and embarked on a series of affairs. Her apparent indifference to men and her beauty present a challenge. I know she's involved with the lecturer on the post-graduate archaeology course.

We don't communicate much, rarely see each other except at the breakfast table.

I boiled a kettle, found a packet of soup and cut myself some bread and cheese, switched on the television. It was then the leg went completely numb. I slumped onto the sofa in the kitchen. I knew I should get help, phone 999. I closed my eyes then heard the sound of a car coming down the track. I looked at the clock ... after 12. I could feel my colour draining. Margaret found me slumped on the sofa when she came in. I said: 'I'm pretty sure I've had a stroke.'

She pursed her lips then said: 'I'll call the ambulance out. God knows what time they'll get here. You'd better have some aspirin.'

CHAPTER 2

James Fields, via voice: I have this diary entry from Maeve Dunlop for the day after John Warne had his stroke. She is a key member of the commission and was, of course, Warne's mistress.

November 17, 2019: I have found the whole day quite emotional. I wasn't expecting that at all. I was OK until I was waiting in the hospital corridor for Fay. She was inside the loo and I stared at the red occupied sign under the red handle for a long time before I tapped on the door. She was cross when I asked if she was all right. She is getting much angrier and very annoyed that she is having to rely on me.

When she came out she grasped my arm, holding so tightly her fingers pinched the soft upper part of my arm. She said that there was more bleeding and was cross again when I said, more brightly than I intended, that that was why we were here but she did mutter that I was to come in with her.

She had to do her attention-seeking thing of course in the reception area. I hate it. She said loudly that it must be an awful job looking up people's bums all day.

Nearly everybody looked embarrassed. They were already aware of her oddness, her non-conformity, and had steadfastly not caught my eye. They buried their heads in their magazines but one man laughed. Fay asked him what was wrong with him but he looked down at his magazine. I was relieved that the nurse came in at that moment and called us.

I got the feeling that the papers the doctor was shuffling on his desk when we went in were nothing to do with Fay's case. I let her do the talking. Have I ever been able to stop her? He spoke with a middle European accent and she was miffed when he called her Mrs Dunlop. She makes such a thing of it. *Ms Dunlop*. He looked at me and asked me who I was and was disconcerted when I said 'her daughter'. He then asked her age and she said that he must have it on his notes. She shot me a look of pure hatred when I said that she was 75 and he started to ask me the questions but I dealt with that.

I had anticipated what he was going to say. We both had but I think she was as shocked as me when he confirmed the diagnosis. Yes, there was a cancer in the bowel and the tumour was big. About four inches in, in the wall of the colon. The scans and tests had confirmed it. He showed us an X-ray; something fuzzy white among the blacks and dark and light greys and said they'd start the treatment soon. He said there was no need for surgery and Fay argued that there was. He said flatly that her heart would not stand it and the drugs would work well. Fay made him shake hands and the nurse who had been hovering behind us opened the door. In the corridor she said that it was amazing what they can do these days with cancer treatment and that it has come a long way. I could see Fay put her black mood face on. The nurse also said that we had seen the best man but I didn't believe her and did not trust him. Fay refused the offer of counselling which the nurse offered to fix for her. I'm going to make sure Rory knows that was her decision.

Coming home I said to Fay that I hadn't liked the look of the doctor and mentioned that he had misshapen teeth, jutting out at all angles, yellow coloured and that he looked like Plug in the Beano. She said the usual and I could have killed her. 'Stop looking for a man, you don't need one.' God knows how I'm going to cope with her through all this. What a bloody awful day.

□□□□□

James Fields - Via Voice

Steph had her own views on Fern Purton right from the start. She says she got her sussed when she was briefing Fern for the television interview. It was Mac, much later, who told me quite a bit about Fern's attitude towards the baby. He called her a selfish cow, totally self-centred and with a complete lack of any maternal attitude. Of course he told me that when things had got really bad between them so I can't be sure how much of it was his hurt talking.

I knew Fern before she had the baby but only to say hello to. I remember helping her put the recycling stuff out at the end of the path but I don't think I was aware that she was pregnant. She and her husband, Johnnie Purton, lived next door to me. They moved in when they got married. I remember seeing the furniture van. She was tall, blonde, very ... well, beautiful is not too excessive, with a figure like a model and I guess she was clever enough with her clothes to conceal the bump. The child was born ten weeks early on November 11.

I saw Johnnie a couple of days later and he was pretty desperate. He said the little boy was in the London Hospital for Premature Babies, a special hospital which has only been open about five years with state of the art equipment. The government are opening more of these specialist units through the country to try to ensure viable births and children surviving. This hospital is in Fulham Road, near Parson's Green. The baby had already had one operation since his birth and weighed just under a kilo.

I know I tried to imagine what a baby of that size would look like. Johnnie said that William was a little fighter. I remember being rather touched that Johnnie was already thinking of his little son by name.

It was Mac who told me how Fern had felt. At the time I wondered why he was so insistent on my hearing but he obviously wanted me to know what a shit she was. I didn't need convincing. He said that she had told him that she had hated every minute of her pregnancy. Once it was born and so ill she wanted it to die. She said that the nurses had kept trying to get her to bond with the baby but that had really pissed her off. Mac imitated her imitating the West Indian nurse. Of course this was a long time after and I could laugh out loud because by that time William was OK. 'We having a bad day? Don't worry, dearie, he fine, really doing fine. Doctor very pleased with him. A real little fighter. Prize man, bless him. I wouldn't be surprised if you weren't home with him in record time. Mind ... he got a lot ahead of him ... poor wee man.'

Fern told Mac she thought the baby looked like a bald pink rat and had hated everything about being pregnant, about the shock of labour, the heat of the prem baby unit, the precautions that she had to take to make sure no infection reached the baby, the tubes that linked him to all the machines. She hated her in-laws who kept turning up and asking questions, most of which seemed to imply that it was her fault that the baby had come early and was so undersized. They had accused her of smoking during the pregnancy and she was furious because she had really tried to give up. Her own mother had been as useless as usual, safe out of reach living in the South of France with the new husband.

Mac said that she had even gone on about the nurses making her express her milk. How she hated the smell of it, the smell of herself. Then there had been all the endless trips back and forth to the hospital once they had allowed her home.

I could well imagine how difficult she would have been. A high maintenance woman. I wondered then why on earth she became pregnant if she hated the idea so much. When I did see Johnnie he always seemed so affable and very pleased when I asked after William.

I'm really putting all this in as a marker for when everything began. November, 2019. I need to put in my own memories as prompts. I see Warne has dated his committee meeting as November 16, 2019. William was born on November 11. Maeve's diary entry is November 17.

I can date my first involvement. Involvement is too strong a word. It wasn't even suspicion. A hunch? Yes, that's better. I know it was just before I met Steph at that pre-Christmas dinner party. She keeps diaries and says the party was on December 10 in which case I remember the conversation in the office a couple of weeks prior to that.

I was deputy chief economist at the Department of Lifestyle. Aged 37, ear-marked for a really top position. The Department had taken over a number of other departments in recent years. Swallowed them up. We'd cornered the market in all things to do with global warming and the change in the atmosphere and the after-effects of the contamination as well as the old fashioned things like planning, transport and what was left of agriculture. We were very big on all things to do with population. We'd also commandeered areas which should really have been within Health's remit.

Lifestyle had become a very powerful ministry. One of the plum jobs for ambitious politicians. Almost up to Chancellor. Certainly better than the Foreign Office where careers foundered so easily in the volatile atmosphere of global politics.

There were far too many junior ministers wandering the corridors, poking their noses into things that didn't concern them but Lifestyle had a lot of status. The joke was that a civil servant in our department was worth the salaries of two at health and five at education on the same grade. We certainly had far better salaries than comparable jobs in the private sector and there still was a pension with the job. Competition was fierce for any kind of civil service job nowadays.

We started the day very early, getting in well before the commuter curfew. At about 9.30 we would stop for a coffee break. Jude, my PA, and my number two and the young lad from down the corridor, new out of university and tipped for rapid promotion, would gather in my office. We'd all have a go at the harder crosswords then move on to discussing the headline news.

I'd begun recently to scan the deaths column in the Times. Morbid? It caught my imagination. Little snippets, clues to people's lives sometimes, guessing which one would have an obituary in a day or two. Also, I'm afraid, beginning to realise I knew of, even had met some of, the deceased, the 'old' brigade of civil servants who had soldiered on to 70.

That day I remember saying to the others that the average age of that day's batch (dispatch?) was 73. On the other hand the births column was well-nigh non-existent.

I said: 'What happened to the octogenarians, the nonagenarians, the centenarians? They were always jumping out of planes, ballooning or bungy-jumping when I were but a lad?'

'Ah, that t'were trouble. They all went splat on the tarmac,' said my number two.

'Seriously,' said Jude 'it's pretty worrying. We ... well ...' she looked at the young lad 'our generation and old codgers like you two are carrying everybody. Health care, pensions, you name it. We're paying for everyone. It's getting serious. We'll be working until we're 100, they're bound to change the goalposts again ... 70's bad enough.'

I said. 'You're not going to get that far. The average age is 73. It's almost down to three score years and ten. Pension fund managers must be rubbing their hands with glee ... retire and die.'

Jude said: 'Three score years and ten was probably more like 40, anyway. The Bible's not the best authority on age related topics. It says Moses was 120 when he died. I can't remember what age Methuselah was when he kicked the bucket ... and women were having babies when they were definitely past their change.'

She had recently taken up religion of the clap-happy variety but she didn't go round trying to save people, thank God. Or maybe she didn't think us worth saving.

She said, rather pink in the face: 'I can't volunteer for baby duties, anyway.'

'That's the trouble with women nowadays,' said my number two, unmarried at 45 and with a string of broken relationships behind him. 'They think sex is just for fun.' Jude slammed out of the office and I raised an eyebrow and said: 'You stupid unfeeling cunt'.

'OK, OK,' he said.

If Steph is right, it was about a fortnight later that the subject came up again at that dinner party. I'm on the spare man list. I've always thought the conversation goes like this: 'Who can we ask who would do for ...?' I was the doopher. I guess it's worth mentioning that I had been married. To Rosie. All over years ago. Well, five years before the time I'm writing about. OK, five years, three months, 22 days. She left me. And not for another man. That was the hardest part.

I got to the terraced house in a road off the Fulham Road, nearer the Chelsea end. I was bang on the invitation time. I try not to be so prompt. I always am. There was a woman in the hall so not the first. Short, curly dark-hair. Plump rather than fat and I automatically associated jolly but really there was no reason to make that assumption. She smiled when we were introduced. So maybe jolly. On her own. My opposite number?

Stephanie, Steph Meadows, she said, holding out her hand. I shook it. James, James Fields.

She laughed and said: 'Wonder why they thought of us?' Our host, whom I did not know very well, muttered something about making hay while the sun shone. I managed to cram my coat onto pegs already filled with little woolly jackets. Children, obviously. There was a tricycle in the hall. We notice these things.

The host led the way upstairs. Sitting room on the first floor and a man and woman were already there. Introduced as a couple. Steph greeted them effusively. Old friends. I was glad to take the drink I was given and sink into a deep sofa. The host was called away almost immediately to answer the door bell again. No sign of the hostess. I can remember wondering if it was an eight seater or ten seater party. It turned out to be ten.

The last ones to arrive were two doctors, married to each other. They made an entrance. A statement on how important they were? Or thought they were. I took a bet with myself that one or other would get pulsed - the new techie stuff so much more discreet than the old style beep. She was a consultant in cardiology; he was in general practice, earning a fortune from his Kensington-based private practice clinic.

I knew two of the other guests. Another reason for my invitation? He's a friend of one of my university pals and I've played tennis with him quite a few times. We've made up a four on a private court. I've always fancied his wife. Vivacious blonde with the sort of legs that go on and on. She was wearing a short skirt. Delightful. I was pleased to see both of them. And her and her husband.

She was on my left when we sat down to eat. Steph was on my right. She didn't bother talking to me; deep in conversation with the GP. I overheard her say that she did the public relations for the MA. Now what did that mean? I hate people bandying initials. I heard him say he was a member. Medical Associations?

I got into deep conversation with Amy, the blonde. I was still talking to her when the hostess brought in the cheese. She'd decided on cheese before pud with minimum discussion. Obviously bought a lot and didn't want it to go mouldy.

Suddenly the meal was interrupted by the appearance of a small child. He climbed onto his father's knee and the mother fluted: 'Now Adam you know what we said ...'

'It's boring upstairs.' The kid had a moony face, very ginger hair, freckles. Amy said, bravely: 'You look just like your Dad.' He stared at her then past her – at me. 'Why that man not got no hair?' Bloody little moron.

Steph said quickly: 'Same reason you've got carrots on your head ... he's made that way.' Everybody laughed and the kid stuck his tongue out. The mother said sharply: 'That's enough. Back to bed, young man.' He went, protesting.

I remember thanking Steph. She said: 'The other kid's very handicapped. They've got a lot on their plates.' It was then I asked her about her work. She lowered her voice to say what a difficult bunch the doctors were to work for.

I said: 'They seem to be killing off most of their patients as far as I can see. The old ones, anyway.'

She looked startled. Asked me what I meant. I explained about my analysis of recent deaths columns. She said: 'Killing them off individually or in batches? There are all sorts of checks in place since Shipman on signing certificates and sudden, unexpected deaths and a lot else besides. The EPA does some good work and has been given some teeth to carry it out. Doctors do have some principles ... some ethics.'

Snort from me. 'I heard the EPA stood for Ease the Patients out Authority; nothing to do with Ethics and Principles. And the family doctors are screwing as much cash out of the government, insurance companies and their patients as they can. Your MA is the only trade union that's survived. And the toughest.'

Steph turned to the doctor beside her. Smarmy bloke. She said: 'James thinks the doctors are in a conspiracy to alter the balance of the population. Get rid of the burden of the ancient ailing.' Very quick on the uptake.

The doctor said smugly: 'Bible says three score years and ten. I wish all my patients would conform to the good book. Mind you, my nightmare is all the buggers who use the internet to diagnose themselves; drives me barmy.

Worst thing is they're so often right. And then there are the others who believe all the complementary medicine crap and then expect us to sort out the problems.'

Conversation turned generally to health and how we financed ourselves. Nobody mentioned children; politics and religion were more acceptable than that.

When we were back in the sitting room, drinking coffee and liqueurs, an intellectual party game was threatened. Time to leave. I thought jolly old Steph might like games but she made excuses too. Chasing me? I remember feeling slightly flattered but she squashed that pretty successfully by hailing a cab, clambering in and waving me good-bye through the window. I caught the tram home to Putney.

□□□□□

Six months later, June 14, 2020. I'd woken and Steph was still asleep. I rolled over and curled myself round her warm back and buttocks, touching her to wake her up, rouse her. I won't go into details. It was warm, comfortable, lovely … we were in that transitional stage, almost past what my mother insists on calling 'the at-it-like-rabbits stage', mellowing into something much more companionable. Then the phone rang. She tensed.

I said: 'Don't answer it.' I watched her roll out of bed, grab some tissues and dab herself between her legs. I'd suggested a number of times that she should have the phone by the bed. Or just let it ring and let the answer phone deal with it. 'Can't do that. I'm paid to be on call. Anyway I need the walk to get my head straight,' she said.

I could only half hear the conversation. One of the health journos. She sounded relaxed, jokey. Then I heard her voice change. Press officer hat on. 'I'll ring you back. Promise. Got to talk to Hislop.' Hislop was top man, general secretary of the Medical Associations.

Bugger it. She said it. I thought it. Sunday ruined. She came back and sat at the end of the bed. 'This is going to be big. Nick's got hold of the wrong end of the stick but he'll worry away at it until he gets it right. Do you remember asking me when we met at that dinner party ... about doctors killing off patients to get the actuarial balance of the population right? Well, you didn't put it quite like that but that's what it's about. Not actually killing. Playing God. Deciding who's going to live, who they'll help. Who gets adult brain cell treatment. Deciding when to stop trying. Non intervention. And more than that. Withholding prolonged cancer treatment particularly for all those leukaemia and cancers related to radioactive fall-out, not operating in some cases; not operating on heart cases automatically. Big bad marks for any patient who smokes, drinks too much or is clinically obese.

'There is a committee which draws up targets. It's going to look very bad for the medics, bad for the government. Daft thing is this kind of assessment has been going on for years. When it started it was called Quality Adjusted Life Assessment Years. QALYs. Then it got more formalised after all the implant treatments came on stream. The results are only now beginning to show. Not so many in their late seventies surviving. And of course with people working until they are 70 more don't last so long when they do draw their pensions. Only the really, really healthy ones who escape the doctors' clutches. It ties in with ability to pay, too. Rich you live, poor you die. I've got to get hold of Hislop ... it's a question of whether he's at home or whether he's with Janet. Sunday probably means he's playing at home.' She went off to phone.

I curled up, knees warm against my belly, hands cradling the old cock and balls. We'd been planning a walk, picnic in the country, catching a train out of Waterloo. Damn and blast. To be fair she'd warned me what it would be like. Her line of work wasn't anything you could leave until the next day. Crisis tactics most of the time. This was going to be a big story. I heard her voice get into its stride. Hislop liked his women strong and sassy. Steph had him sussed and she was brilliant at not over-stepping the mark. She was back-pedalling subtly now. Trying another tack. She put the phone down so she must have won some kind of agreement.

'I've told him that I don't think Nick has got enough to run with the story for tomorrow's papers. We might have most of today to get things straight. He's going to have a word with the secretary of state and the chief medical officer. We're all going to have to pull in the same direction on this one. I can see this is going to ruin today. Do you want to duck out?' She meant get out. Leave now.

I quite liked her being bossy. I said I'd grab some breakfast and go. She was back on the phone by the time I'd drunk my coffee. She pulled my head down to kiss me and I slid my hands between her legs. She still hadn't got dressed. She gave a satisfying little gasp which she instantly explained away to the journo she was talking to. Nick again? I mouthed I'd phone her later.

I remember stopping on Putney bridge. It was a sunny June morning, promising heat but as yet just enough of a breeze coming off the river to make me feel glad to be there, looking down. The eights were already busy on the river. I rowed for my college but I'm not a sporty sort beyond the indifferent game of tennis. Neither's Steph. Says she has enough exercise belting up and down the corridors at MA house. She is plump, though. Mmm.

Rosie was skinny, almost anorexic. Into running marathons and picking at her food, leaving at least three quarters on the plate. It really irritated me. Irritated my mother even more, she couldn't bear to see 'good food going to waste'. I think she ate it up herself when she took the plates out to the kitchen. Steph's flesh on her legs presses together for about five inches below her fanny. Great. You really know you're wanted ... grips hard. Thin girls are OK to look at but you feel you might break them if you aren't careful. Steph presented a challenge and I felt I could rise to it and frequently did.

I thought about her handling the story that was breaking. She'd only know the half of it. Somewhere complementary policies had been developed. I could think of at least two in my department. Population initiatives were flourishing. Top of the pops. I think the Brown administration started them and then the coalition continued.

I wandered on, wondering if there was any way, officially, that I could help. Anyone I could contact. I knew some of the people at Health who were working alongside us. When I got to my house – I didn't really think of it as home because by now I was living far more of the time in Steph's flat – I was quite preoccupied and didn't see, at first, Johnnie and Fern carrying William out in his carry-cot towards their car.

I asked: 'How's he doing?'

Johnnie said: 'Brilliant, he's three kilos now.' I thought of a bag of potatoes and wondered if that tallied. Never have had much to do with kids.

Fern said: 'He's got to have another op next week. We're taking him down to see Johnnie's parents.' She sounded fed up. It was Johnnie who was fussing about, getting all the baby clobber into the car. She just got in and sat in the passenger seat. The baby started wailing. 'Oh Christ,' she said. 'Come on, let's go.'

Johnnie looked worried. Opening the driver's door he said: 'We've been meaning to ask you in ...'

'You've got enough on your plates. Hope all goes well next week.'

I was reluctant to go into the dark house with its curtains drawn. It smelled musty, unused. I had a suspicion there was some damp getting in somewhere but I really didn't want to investigate. It might be mice.

It would have been such a great day to go walking, have a picnic ... sod it. I hadn't brought milk. Drank bitter black coffee from grains in the jar that had solidified and went upstairs to the room I keep the computer in. I forced myself to start on the report that was outstanding and worked until 2. Then I phoned Steph. The line was engaged to begin with ... endless irritation of 'the person knows you're calling ...' and when I did get through I could hear her exasperation.

'It's bedlam. Somebody else has got hold of the story and it's likely to break on television today, later on. I've traced it back to some small paper in the north-east with a garbled quote from a doctor.'

I asked if she'd been talking to the department and got a withering reply. 'They're as enchanted with all this as we are. Caught on the hop over the week-end. They've had to rustle up a junior minister and brief her. She's not the brightest thing on two legs. God knows how she's going to come across.'

'This government is committed to reducing the elderly population ...?'

'Oh shut up, I don't need it.' There was silence for a minute then she said, trying it on me: 'This committee is regularising what's been going on for years. If you number crunch it, the proportion of people not being given treatment isn't so many more than it was ten, twenty years ago. It just seems there are a lot more of them because a much higher proportion of the population is elderly. It certainly isn't just one doctor playing God.'

'Why have I only just noticed the much higher proportion of people in their seventies dying, and hardly anybody in the decades above them?'

There was silence. Steph was groping for an answer. If it was good and I bought it then the minister might be given it. She rattled off an obviously rehearsed argument: 'Because this country has altered its attitude towards geriatric care. It was made clear at that general election when the Tories got in for that brief spell. Funding was switched and people voted for it. More was spent on saving young people; less on the elderly. People made it clear that they didn't want old people kept alive at all costs with no quality of life.

'The elderly ... the people who are really old now ... were fit and rich. They were the baby boomers, the just over sixties at the time of the millennium; they'd had good careers, good pensions; private health care insurance. They proved to government that they could take care of themselves and in the end government said 'well done, you've looked after yourselves all your lives, you're an example to us all' but secretly they were saying 'fine, you get on with it, one less problem for us'. They are the fit 80 plus people now.

'The over-80s do die but the worn-out seventy year olds die quicker and are getting assessed differently. And of course the illnesses triggered by the radioactive fall-out have made a difference. We're back to rationing, making decisions, because the last thing any government wants is to be spending enormous amounts setting up structures to keep a vast population of elderly people alive when at the other end of the scale there are so few babies being born. The contamination has had a catastrophic effect. An alarming percentage of babies that are born are handicapped in some way and will never be able to contribute.

'There aren't many of us workers left to support society with our taxes. There is a big imbalance. Far too many under 50's who can't or won't have children. Everything is being geared to the wage-earners and potential wage-earners. The new treatments are only being given to people under 65. They want us to be fit old people who can still go on working until we're 70, maybe even longer. There's already talk of upping the retirement age to 75.

'Government after government has made it clear there is only a finite amount that can be spent. ...' she faltered. It was something that had obviously been so well-rehearsed in the corridors of the Medical Associations that they'd lost sight of who they were preaching to, the general public. It sounded old hat to me.

I said: 'That may be true. Far too true. It won't wash. You can't have the minister saying that. It's like saying we're murdering our mums and dads, our grandparents. She'll be lynched.'

'I'm desperate.'

'The bit you said about stopping individual doctors playing God ... that's a better line; explaining that the numbers are probably the same as they've always been but it's part of clinical assessment. Play the population imbalance card carefully. You might get away with a bit of that. Put it back on the public. Tell them they took the decision to spend healthcare on the young ... the other side of the coin is rationing for the elderly. Ask the question ...you could show a baby who's had a lot of treatment to help him survive. Switch the emphasis. Actually, there's one next door. Well, he's gone to visit his granddad but he's bound to be home soon ... his mother looked very sour about the trip.'

Steph said: 'You should be doing my job.'

CHAPTER 3

Maeve Dunlop's diary: June 16, 2020.

The news broke about quotas for deaths today. Fay called from the study. She is now skeletal, big eyes staring from the pinched small face, lost in the single bed I've put in there. Ellen said when she came to sort out her drugs and give her a bed bath that it won't be long.

Fay asked me if I'd heard the news item. I said I hadn't. She said: 'They're killing me off. No treatment. All that rubbish about this contraption they've wired me up to. Coloured water probably. I heard them say it on television just a minute ago. 30,000 cancer patients not having the treatment they could. Depends how old you are. Over 75, no chance. Bastards.'

There was a junior health minister talking. The woman spoke fluently. Talked about decision-making and that for years doctors had been relied on to make clinical decisions 'in the best interest of their patients'. She spoke about resources, limited resources. What that meant 'in real terms'. She talked about all the work being done to ensure that babies, little children had the best care available. How precious their lives were when so few were being born. Each child, in good health or poor, must be nurtured. Society depended on them.

'Like this little chap ...' the camera zoomed away from her and onto a mother and child. Small baby cradled in its mother's arms. The girl was stunning and the baby was lovely, blonde like her. The interviewer asked her: 'Can you tell us what happened to little William, Fern?'

Fern said that William had been born ten weeks prematurely and that he'd weighed less than a kilo (shot of small bag of sugar). The London Hospital for Premature Babies had done everything possible to help him and now, although he needed more operations, he was well on the way to growing into a normal, strong little boy. He was now six months old.

The interviewer turned back to the Minister. 'So the government thinks it's better to spend health care money on the babies and children, and the old people are being written off?'

'No, that's not what I said.' I was amused that the minister looked flustered. She droned on about comparison lists, held regionally, to keep a record of how many people died, at what age and from what cause. She said these lists were being misinterpreted. They were complicated figures. They were discussed by local committees made up of doctors and laymen. The figures then went forward to the national committee.

The interviewer let her off the hook and turned to the general secretary of the Medical Associations, Stephen Hislop. I've seen him before. I heard him speak once at a conference I was at. I said to Fay that I'd met him - it wasn't strictly true but she likes to be touched by celebrity, however far removed. He's a middle aged man with white hair and a youthful bronzed face. He oozes charm. He talked about how doctors had always had to make choices. Talked about QALYs. He categorically denied that doctors were killing off, or deliberately not treating, elderly patients. The news moved onto something else.

Fay said: 'They can wrap it up all they like. What they're saying is that it's a straight choice. Keep the babies alive ... kill off the wrinklies. Culling us. But we're not old. Your grandmother had cancer at 70, lived until she was 87. I'm only 75. It's not old.'

I said: 'She had Alzheimer's. And she was in that awful home.' It stank of piss and made me gag.

'Alive though.' She sank back, exhausted, on her propped up pillows. 'I'm going to tackle that doctor ... that bastard in the hospital ...what did you call him? Plug?'

I made her take some more jungle juice. It's what we call the medicine which the specialist cancer nurse says she must take. Today she told me that it was something about not having 'complications'. A speedy and less traumatic death, I guess.

I wish Rory was nearer but he's 200 miles away with his jail-bait wife. He was definitely knocking her off when she was in the fifth form. He is a bastard. He rang today and told me I must get Fay to say who our fathers were before she dies. I'd pushed that to the back of my mind but now it's there again, big and nagging. Rory thinks his father was the husband of one of Fay's girl friends. I think mine was most likely a policeman or a security guard at Greenham Common. I will ask her before she dies. I almost did today. Why has she always refused to say? She'll probably lie.

Rory says all he can remember is the girl friends. He says it has screwed him up and that's why his life has been such a mess. It's a mess because of the drugs. God knows how that private school has given him a teaching job although marrying the boss's daughter may have helped. He's a sponger, sponged off Fay all his life. The wife must have some family money. Now he's put himself out of reach of day to day responsibilities but, like Fay, still wants to control me and he's five years younger.

Fay said again today when I mentioned how attractive the guy from the MA was that I must not make myself a door mat. She said I'd done that before, that I'd always done it. She mentioned Phillip. She's got this irritating habit of recalling every man she thinks I slept with. Amazing memory. It really bugs her that I'm not a lezzy. For God's sake, I'm middle aged, deputy head of Social Services for Bristol and may get another promotion soon but all the time she makes me feel a failure. She always puts me in the wrong. I can't help it but I'll be relieved when this is all over. WHEN SHE'S DEAD.

I watched the news again when she was sleeping, snoring loudly, her jaw dropping open. She looked appalling and for that I am sorry. She is my mum and she was very beautiful. There was television footage of her striding ahead of the other women, leading the protest. We saw it over and over again when we were growing up.

On the news the figures had been made into a clever graphic. There were some vox pop interviews and a professor of economics was taken through the well-rehearsed population projections which threaten the country, threaten the world. The interview with the mother and her baby was repeated.

Fay is probably right about the wrinklies being culled. She is usually right. If she wasn't dying, she'd be out on the streets, waving placards. She'd be making sure that old people had their rights ... the right to live, the right to receive the best treatment. Why do I hate her so much today? Everybody else thinks she's wonderful, a character, a fighter. They don't have to look after her and being nice to her is giving me ulcers.

CHAPTER 4

Warne's manuscript

My stroke was quite severe. I was offered a foetal cell
brain implant and agreed. I took my time convalescing,
enjoying the first long break in my working life. I told
the practice I wouldn't be back until the end of June.
Time is now running out and I view my return to work
with a mixture of enthusiasm, apathy and anxiety. I
suppose it's the first day back at school syndrome.

**(James Fields, Via Voice - Warne asterisked a note to
himself here 'I must sort out what tense I am going to
use. I realise I keep swapping from past to present,
using my diary for reference, but I'll sort all that out
later.')**

I now understand why Margaret wants to live in the
town. It's lonely in the country and the house, set in a
dip at the bottom of a Devon combe, is dark in winter
and loses the sun in early evening even in high summer.
No wonder the Swedes, Norwegians and Finns turn to
drink in the dark months. In the first two or three
weeks after my return from hospital I had visitors.
Even my sister made the effort, although that was over
the Christmas holidays when free food and drink were
on offer.

My partners came out to see me to begin with. Now
they only e-mail or, if driven to it, phone about practice
business. I soon realised how few friends we had
collected as a couple. My own friends, friends I feel I
can open up to, have dwindled to two people I knew at

medical school and one I'd met on the medical politics circuit, all of whom live too far away and are too busy to do other than telephone occasionally. I'm conscious of not imposing myself.

Two women, former lovers, drawn from the world of medical politics once Margaret had established, insisted even, that I was free to go my own way, were over and done with. Neither of them has remained a good friend. The partings were bitter. I remained stubborn on the divorce issue, not wishing to break their marriages or risk my own. I suppose there is still a strong remnant of my Catholic upbringing which I like to pretend I've abandoned.

For the last couple of months there have been no visitors at all and, apart from my medical check-ups, I have had practically nobody to talk to. Only Jo, the lady who cleans the house and in the holidays brings her little daughter, has been any sort of company. We have never really got to know the neighbours. Living so far out means the nearest is more than a mile away. Margaret leaves for the university early in the morning, gone all day, all night more nights than I want to think about.

Jo is endlessly cheerful but the conversation revolves around her elderly parents, the weather and, aware that I am paying her to work, I attempt to limit conversation to the compulsory coffee break. I liked it when she brought the little girl with her, Nicole, at half term and in the Easter holidays. She is a pretty little thing, fair-skinned, dark-haired and deep blue-eyed. I suppose Margaret must have looked a bit like her when she was a child with that same unusual colour combination. The Irish complexion.

I've taken up sailing again and bought a yacht. A 26ft Contessa, probably a bit big for me single-handed but I don't intend to do much more than potter along the coast. I used to have a 21 foot Westerly a few years back but I sold it when I got onto more committees. I keep it on the Torridge estuary at Instow. There is a certain amount of superficial contact with others. Like most sailors we spend more time tinkering with our boats than sailing. The late spring has been good and there have been beautiful days on the water.

I like the drive north going through the Devon lanes. The hedges were first speckled with primroses, then daffodils, then the bluebells and the beech green curling like lettuce on the spindly branches. Now the trees are in full leaf and the cow parsley bushes out into the lanes, brushing the sides of the car. I've spent the days tacking back and forth across the estuary, venturing over the bar where the Taw and Torridge meet, out to sea sometimes and up the coast towards Lynton or down as far as Hartland Point. When it has been too windy I have anchored in some quiet inland cove, the water lapping on the brown weed-covered, rounded stones at the edge and slapping my boat this way and that. I've done a lot of reading and caught up on the classics I always promised myself I would read.

I have been bored, though. I'm a political animal and I hate being out of things. The letter from the secretariat depressed me. It informed me that I was being replaced on the Population committee and thanked me for all that I've done. It hadn't occurred to me that they would act so swiftly; a previous personal letter from Mike Tomlinson had been kindly, inquiring after my health.

I miss the excitement of the television and radio interviews that frequently came my way. I had to get Margaret to refuse several in the early days when I was first recovering and realise now that I must have been crossed off the contact books. I don't like that.

The house move is on hold. Margaret is summing up the pros and cons of moving, less convinced that I will recover fully. Wishful thinking? Anyway she's decided that there should be no unnecessary expense at the moment.

I saw the news, of course. The death targets are out in the open and it serves the committee right for meddling with people's lives. There was some suggestion on one of the news channels that it was a doctor who had first pointed the finger at the policy. I instantly thought that they might be trying to make me a scapegoat. Paranoia? Not necessarily.

The junior health minister handled the questions well; so did the secretary of the Medical Associations, Hislop. I've always thought him too smooth for words but I have to hand it to him, he pitched it exactly right.

I thought that it was going to be the usual 24-hour wonder in the media; hammer and tongs at the story and then only to be revived if short of news, maybe in August. Figures and graphs didn't look as convincing as tiny premature babies and nobody seemed to have turned up any relations who would say that their late lamented had died of a QALY. Of course, that was a master stroke by Hislop. If in doubt, throw in an acronym and then explain it so obscurely that the audience loses interest.

I got up and switched off the television. My left leg is still a bit gammy and I limped out to the kitchen. Margaret, unexpectedly, said she'd leave some supper out for me. She'd gone off early in the morning muttering something about a seminar, but really she didn't need to make up stories at this late stage.

It wasn't time to eat and I remember thinking that one whisky wouldn't hurt though I've been told to go easy. Red wine is OK but it meant opening a bottle just for myself. The tastebuds aren't functioning as well as they might which is another side effect of the stroke. There's a bit more bite to malt and the peat smoke on my palate gives me a lift.

The June evening was warm, balmy, and I thought I'd catch the last of the sun before it went down and then watch the purple, pink and fiery red of the sunset which streaked our sky though the setting was masked by the western hill. My next house will have a view, be south or southwest facing. I hadn't realised until I'd been confined to the farmhouse how depressing a view solely of steep sided hills could be. When I was working every day I had been proud to drive away, leaving behind my own land as I steered the four-wheel drive on my own particular course of the rutted lane, the vehicle lurching left then right as I avoided the pitfalls for nearly half a mile.

I've worked hard at my recovery and I cannot fault the treatment I have received. The doctors and hospital staff have been excellent right from the moment I was admitted. I don't remember much about it, the first day at least. I knew it was partly because I belonged to the doctors' club, 'one of them', but some of the other patients on the stroke unit said the same. We were all well under 65. The cut-off age.

Since we went private the practice has refused to take further responsibility for after-care of patients with long-term illness. Again, it was a decision I was out-voted on. The policy is that it is the family's concern and they should liaise with other forms of private health care or with the community trust and social services. It is hard for those with no family to help them.

In my thirties I struggled with the authorities to get specialist drugs for certain patients, mainly for a number of chronic illnesses, particularly for diseases affecting the elderly, like Alzheimer's. In most cases I was refused because they were too costly. There had been some outcry among the medical profession, about it being the individual doctor's right to prescribe what was best for the patient but when the cost got re-visited upon their practices the battle was surrendered.

Some relatives complained on behalf of the sufferers but they rarely had the stamina to keep a long campaign going. The government of the time, a Labour government, was clever. They'd got the bill through parliament to allow stem cell research that promised cures for Alzheimer's and a number of other diseases affecting the elderly and they'd allowed multiple sclerosis patients to have cannabis.

Recently therapeutic stem cell treatment has been age-restricted as part of the policy that has just hit the headlines. That aspect of non-intervention seems to have escaped the media in the present furore.

I sat on the terrace until it got too cold, watching the shadows creep across the hill. It was still an effort to walk up the fields to look west across the rolling Devon countryside, towards the moors, and see the sun sink beyond the whirring wind turbines. When the phone rang I was in two minds whether to answer it or just listen to the answer phone. It could be my sister but even she'd break the monotony.

'Dr Warne ...BBC television ... Plymouth.' It was a young man's voice.

'Yes, it's John Warne. How can I help?' I knew my diction was just slightly slurred. I could hear the young man hesitate. He thinks I've been drinking.

'We've got your number as a good contact on medical matters,' said the young man. I was still on the books so that was good.

'Wondered whether we could get you in the studio for an interview on this story that's broken ...seems to be saying that doctors are setting targets to make sure older people don't survive cancer, heart attacks ... wondered whether you could maybe give some kind of reassurance ...'

I said: 'I'm recovering from a stroke myself ...' I could hear the young man begin to make apologies. I said quickly: 'If you sent a car for me ... I'm almost back to' ... I hesitated over the word normal ... said: 'I'm fully fit and certainly compos mentis.'

I needed the excitement of getting out and about. The adrenalin rush of appearing on television. I might be able to steer the debate and, after all, I was no longer on the committee. That was official.

The researcher was hesitating. I could imagine him, hand over the mouthpiece, asking someone else. Do we want a doctor who's had a stroke? His voice sounds a bit funny. He might not look too good.

I said: 'Well, if you can get someone else ... but in fact I was a member of the committee that drew up this policy. It is considering the actuarial effect on the country of the projected decline in population ... the QALY argument came into our considerations ...' I imagined the researcher's face. I had hooked him.

He said: 'Just hold on a sec, will you, Dr Warne ... please don't hang up.' I was put on hold for maybe three minutes. The answer was yes, they wanted me. In fact, they'd like to get me now and it would be better in the studio. There was one in Exeter. They could take me there and film. They'd send a car and someone would be back soon to fix it all up and get directions.

□□□□□

Maeve's diary

I watched the breakfast news with Fay. The item on death targets for old people was still going strong. They'd got a doctor on who'd been a member of the committee. He was being interviewed from a studio in Devon. He was very good. The sort of man most people would like as their family doctor. I have seen him before; they've used him a lot on telly. Dr John Warne. Soft, cream linen jacket, blue shirt, dark eyes in a lean, aesthetic face, strong chin ... curly greying hair but it must have been dark ... For God's sake.

He said: 'It's all about the treatment you get; it's not about killing people outright with some sort of injection. People must not be scared of that sort of thing. This is about decisions on whether or not to prolong lives that are going to end and making it sooner may avoid a great deal of pain and suffering. I am afraid that people do die. None of us can avoid it.

And with something as life threatening as certain cancers ...'

He was asked which. Lung. Bowel. Liver. Still too many kinds of breast. He went on to talk about heart disease. Then he dropped the bombshell. 'Of course, part of this non-intervention policy is that therapeutic stem cell treatment is now being denied at a certain age ... 65 is the cut off.'

The interviewer was clearly stunned. She made him repeat again what he had said. 'Were you offered a stem cell brain implant?' she asked.

'Yes, I was. I'm only 48. I had it.'

Fay was really excited about this. She said: 'Good man, now the shit's hit the fan. It's what I told you. They decide. Nothing to do with you. If you're a certain age and you're unlucky enough to get a terminal type illness they don't treat you. I want you to campaign on this when I go ... yes, I know I am ... not long now ... I want you to kick up a stink, get this changed. It's wrong. Criminal. Hiding behind statistics ...QALYs ... I'll quallie them ... not even letting us have treatment which might prolong our lives, might even cure some. I'd have anything they could dish out if it meant I was going to live longer.'

I switched off the television at the end of the item because Fay had gone a very funny colour. She made me promise to kick up a fuss and I promised. I phoned the nurse immediately and I am writing this while I wait for her to turn up. I have phoned Rory and he says he will come immediately. I'll believe that when I see him. I do not think it will be long. Fay is asleep, her breathing very deep, very noisy. Every so often her breath seems to have stopped and I think it is all over. Then she starts again.

CHAPTER 5

James Fields, via voice: Steph's put this bit together.

Hislop was livid that Warne had been interviewed. 'Who let that moron get on television?' He rarely loses his temper but he is deadly when he does.

I glanced across at Henry, Hislop's deputy, sometimes my ally when things go wrong. He kept his head down, doodling on a blank piece of paper in front of him. I said, in my best appeasing voice: 'Warne's been around a long time. The media all know him and have used him a lot as the common-sense doctor everyone wished they had. He must be on every researcher's contact list. He's usually very sensible. He phones the press office and asks us for advice when he thinks he ought to know the lines we are taking and doesn't want to say something that could cause the public alarm.'

'Well he's certainly blown it this time. Kept a story going which we'd nearly got dead and buried. How are you going to dig us out of this one, madam.' Hislop has a knack of shifting the blame, usually to me.

I thought quickly: 'Maybe we could field the chairman of the committee. They were after you to reply but let's distance ourselves. Mike Tomlinson can be good.' I knew it was a gamble. Hislop hates Tomlinson's guts. There is something in their medical political pasts which I have never found out. Somebody hinted at rivalry over a woman but I'm pretty sure it is more complicated than that. Probably back in their student days.

'God almighty, woman, that's just what we don't want. Bloody Tomlinson. I can imagine the kind of impression the public will get from that idiot. No, I'd better come back on this. Get me the secretary of state on the phone ... not that fucking stupid sidekick of a woman from yesterday ... and you'd better get on to the department's chief press bod and stitch something up with him. I want this wrapped up. And get me a list of all the interviews ... if the timetable won't work and anybody has to do the minor stuff Henry can.'

I caught the glance of pure loathing that crossed Henry's face. Being Hislop's deputy isn't doing his ulcer any good at all.

I left the room and Henry caught me up in the corridor. He was angry, wanting to order somebody about. 'I've got meetings to go to ... you're going to have to brief me properly and arrange a schedule that I can manage. I don't want a lot of obscure radio and television channels firing off damn silly, ill-informed questions. And I don't want that big fat bloke you've got in the office being my minder ... I want one of the girls who's a bit more intelligent. The red-haired one is good.'

This is so unfair on Steve who has only recently joined the staff and is still getting to grips with the politics of the organisation.

I remember saying shit, shit, shit ... it is going to be a hellish day ... probably week. I went back to the public affairs division and called all the press officers into my office, briefing and delegating work. The big board was filling up with requests for interviews, keeping everyone aware of timings and spokesmen being deployed. I asked Cathy to get hold of John Warne. I might be able to head him off ... I was prepared to buy him off, if needs be. I'd have given him a free lay if that was what was needed. Blow job. Anything. They were bound to be interviewing him again.

'I could only get his wife,' Cathy told me. 'She doesn't know where he is. Didn't seem to care much, either. If he phones she'll tell him to get in touch with you.' It was another bowel clenching half-hour of not leaving my office before Warne phoned.

'Where are you,' I asked.

'On the train to London ... they want me live on the lunch-time magazine programmes ...I think I may be up against your man Hislop.' His speech sounded a bit odd.

'Well, you've certainly stirred the shit on this one,' I said. I have always liked Warne – he is one of a handful of doctors on the same wavelength when it comes to handling the media. I was surprised when I saw him on the breakfast show and I realised that I hadn't talked to him since the stroke. I feel really guilty about that.

'Seems like it ...' there was a brief silence as the mobile lost contact then revived. 'Is Hislop going to talk QALYs ...I don't mind going along with a bit of that but I'm not going back on what I've already said. We shouldn't have medical committees involved in setting targets for population control ... the public equate that with killing people. But I'll agree with him that health has always been rationed ... even back before the very first health service when it was a case of who could pay and who couldn't.

'What people haven't fully realised is that we're back to that. The bright idea that compulsory insurance would cover the total cost was never going to work. All that happens is that the rich pay more to get the best service. The poor go on losing out. But the worst thing is this arbitrary age cut off for implant treatment. It's unethical.'

I said: 'I'll tell Hislop. Maybe we can widen this out a bit ...' I could sense Warne had quite a lot he wanted to say about health care in general.

Warne snorted. 'Up to your old tricks, eh? Clever move ... widening the issues.' He knew me too well. We've connived too often in the past to dig specific doctors, or the medical profession, out of holes.

I said: 'I'll be coming along with Hislop to hold his hand. We'll have a chat. I'd really like to see you again and I should have been in touch ... I don't know, we're kept pretty busy here with one crisis after another. I'm sorry. You're obviously doing really well.'

I got Hislop on the internal phone. 'I think I can get him to widen this into a health service debate. You know he's had a stroke ... not totally recovered yet ... still off work?'

Hislop was quick ... he often surprises me even though we have worked closely for nearly six years. 'Just a suggestion ...eh? Play on it a bit, discredit him ...yes, that might work ... his speech will be a bit slow ...clever girl. I want some good answers on the stem cell question, though. Bamboozle them with science if I have to.'

I knew he could do it. Hislop would look good, well cut clothes, good bedside manner, excellent television skills, concern oozing out for Warne. Warne would come across more as the country doctor, down to earth, bordering on blunt. I like Warne far more than I like Hislop but it is the Medical Associations who pay my salary.

□□□□□

Warne's manuscript

Margaret was at home when I got back. I was exhausted from the travel, the interviews, the waiting about.

Her first words were: 'Well, you've been making a bloody fool of yourself. I saw you and Hislop on that lunchtime programme.' It was the start of the first proper conversation that we have had for a long time.

I said: 'Somebody's got to speak up for the patients. Our customers.'

'And it had to be you?' She poured out a whisky for herself and, after a glance at me, another. 'Ice?' She knows I take ice.

'You can't tell people they're being bumped off when people like Hislop can so smoothly refute it; provide statistics that prove you wrong ... tell people how many lives are now being saved from diseases which were once terminal, thanks to all the stem cell developments. And he flattened you on the age question. And you didn't know about that piece of research that indicates that after a certain age stem cell treatment can do more harm than good. He had you there. 'Dr Warne, as a general practitioner, you will, of course be aware ...' You looked really stuffed.

'He made you look like some deranged medic that had a bee in his bonnet since he'd been ill himself. Someone who couldn't move with the times and kept harking back to the old health service. He ran rings round you.

'Anyway, you've got it wrong. The media may like the story for 24 hours. The general public don't care and they won't do anything about it. They don't want to hang on to a lot of elderly relations for ever and ever. Most of them aren't insured, can't afford to pay for treatment. Too many of us have bailed them out in our time – look what happened with your father - and all that's happened is that we've lost out. It's not as if many old people have any better quality of life; only the very rich 80 plus people. Just think of the hordes who sat for years in expensive nursing homes, suffering from Alzheimer's disease, Parkinson's disease or whatever, and not knowing what time of day it was. Maybe not treating certain life threatening diseases is a better and kinder solution.'

I said: 'You and Hitler would have had a lot to talk about.'

She shot me a look of pure loathing. Sipping her drink, she said: 'I was talking to Paul ...' Paul was the lecturer, the current lover. Was she still hoping to make me jealous? She can't resist letting me know. I shut my ears to what Paul had opinionated, humming to myself. I do not want to know what that pontificating supercilious bearded university bastard thinks.

When she shut up we sat there sipping our drinks in silence. I think we were both rather shocked by the length of the conversation.

She said, unexpectedly: 'I still think you're wrong about all this but maybe you were right to take a stand. I've never liked Hislop, anyway. Too smooth. He was gynae, wasn't he? Explains the bow tie. And the bedside manner.'

I laughed. It was an old joke. Gynaes wore bow ties or they ran the risk of ruining good ties while examining women's fannies.

I said: 'Margaret ...' I wanted to say. Can't we get on better. I don't mind about your lover ... lovers. I just want some companionship ...but the words wouldn't come.

She finished her drink and left the room, briskly. How have we got to this? We were so in love when we married, she had wanted me as much as I wanted her.

She was a theatre nurse, a bit stiff and starchy when I first met her. It is still part of her attraction, that rather prim demeanour. I'd got her to unbend in one of the private patient's rooms one night. The patient had been under heavy sedation but we made so much noise we'd woken him up and he'd surprised us by saying: 'Stop that fucking row.' Right on two counts.

She was not satisfied with nursing. She wanted more, even though her profession had won the right to do far more of what had previously been considered the doctor's responsibility and remit. Nurses still get very uptight by the fact that the general public on the whole still think of doctors as the elite profession.

Margaret had gone in for history and now archaeology in a big way. She'd determined on a university degree which she got last year and is following it with a PhD. A perpetual student supported by my earnings. What else is she going to do? The family I had always thought we would have together simply never happened after the baby died within hours of being born.

And then there are the lecturers, the randy buggers, imparting knowledge and imparting their seed whenever they can. And I've been busy ... getting on to more committees at regional, then national, level, appearing on television ... she's seen my success as competition and it certainly spurred her on to get a 2:1.

At some indeterminable point our marriage ended in all but name. I can't remember if there was an exact moment. Was that when I met Emma? The trouble is I still, still do, fancy Margaret. Sometimes she makes my balls ache with longing. She knows she does.

Today she surprised me with her criticism but at least it wasn't the awful neutrality.

Later after my bath, I found her in her bedroom, sitting at the mirror, applying make-up in that intense, scrutinising way she has.

'Maybe we should have a holiday ...?' Once I had said to her when our relationship was still capable of being at a low ebb ...perhaps we should try for another child. Her rage then had been frightening.

Now she just closed the discussion down: 'I've got other plans this summer.' I went into my room and lay on the bed, exhausted by the day's events. I heard her car start up and whine slowly up the cart-track to the road at the top.

I could not sleep. The adrenalin was pumping. Perhaps Margaret was right. Maybe the general public did not care too much about targets being set or treatment being denied. The young and middle-aged were getting better treatment than ever before and helped in every way possible to reproduce.

There was nearly full employment and controlled immigration ensured there were plenty of people to do the dirty jobs.

What the government did not want was an increase in the elderly unfit. Margaret had put her finger on it. Society had already lived through the consequences of that and had not liked it. Too many pockets and expectations had been hit. Public opinion had swung firmly against the concept of keeping people alive just for the sake of it; nobody cared about ethics ...had they ever?

At last I dropped off to sleep.

Maeve's diary

Fay died at 3am. Rory arrived at six. I stayed with her in the room for those three hours but I am no nearer coming to terms with her death. I did not expect it to hit me so hard.

CHAPTER 6

James Fields, via voice.

At the beginning of August, 2020, I was seconded to work on a joint project based at the Department of Health. I know, even without looking it up, that I started on the 3rd. Richmond House was uncomfortable and noisy with workmen, updating the building and using what should be the quietest month when a lot of people were on holiday. I was shown to a room on the fifth floor and introduced to my opposite number. Being bald, and early bald at that, I resent men with superfluous hair.

My very first impression was that Mac was mostly hair. He had thick, very dark curly hair which reached half way down his back and was scraped back into a pony tail. Despite the hairstyle, he had a suave elegance that is hard to describe. The sort of chap that comes across in 1930's novels as the epitome of sophistication? He seemed to have very long legs and a lean lanky body. He made me aware that I was beer-bellied, short and very, very bald. The expression on his face was hard to read. Resentment?

The woman who introduced us said: 'This is Ed Fish but he's always called Mac.'

'Are you a Scot?'

Mac looked at me hard. He spoke with an upper class home-counties accent. It instantly put me on my guard.

'What makes you think that?'

The woman laughed. She said: 'When he started here there was a really old guy still working, way past retirement. He nicknamed him MacFisheries. The Mac stuck.' She left us.

Mac said: 'I don't know why they feel it necessary to bring you over here. I've got a team together and we've made a lot of progress.'

It was an inauspicious start. It got better when we discovered a mutual interest in horse racing. Somehow it figured that Mac would know about racing, would feel at home on a course. It fitted his style. Most days we placed a bet or two. We got a system going that began to produce some cash. Despite his original boast, we were making slow progress on the project because the statisticians lower down, cogs in the wheel, were behind schedule. We had time on our hands.

One day we skived off to Kempton Park. It was at the beginning of September which was hot and sunny. The backsides of the horses shone glossily as they were paraded in advance of their races around the cinder track. How do they do that diamond pattern thing? Their corn fed shit smelled pungently sweet. We leaned happily against the rails, drank beer and studied form. Mac had high hopes for a horse he had been following. It came in fifth but Mac was sure the next time out it would win. I had a winner in the sixth and afterwards we went back to a pub on the river near Kew Bridge to celebrate.

We were still drinking and talking at 10.30. It felt like the beginning of a friendship. He was amusing and interested in a wide range of subjects. I've got a few men friends, but nobody terribly close. Mac was fun to be with and his sense of humour meshed with mine despite the age gap.

We began talking more openly than we had allowed ourselves to do in office hours ... about ourselves and about the work we were engaged in. Departmental gossip had made us aware that there was something being worked on and evaluated that spread across all departments and that what we were doing was part of a much larger project. Our bosses had not seen fit, or maybe had been forbidden, to explain what the overall picture was.

Mac said: 'Remember all that hoo-ha in the summer about targets for deaths, non-intervention in cancer and heart cases? That's just one piece of the jigsaw. What we're working on takes everything a step further. There's a new division at the Treasury called the Population Adjustment Programme. A mate of mine is working there. I can't get anything more out of him but I'm pretty sure that our project is the pilot for the whole country.'

We were working on a plan to relieve the problems of the poorest, the most deprived and depraved sections of the population in 'a northern city'. Our brief was to redesign the city in terms of planning, environment, health and education. The city was euphemistically called New Boscastle. God knows what idiot thought that would fool anyone. We called it Newcastle anyway. The old rules still applied; if you want to try out a pilot scheme go north.

We had already reached the conclusion that what we were being asked to design was ghettos. Ghettos for the rich, ghettos for the poor. All the problems in one containable area of a city, with all the facilities and services concentrated in a cost-effective way. Policing, health care and low grade schools attached to the ghettos for the poor because the government wanted an adequate supply of people fodder for the service industries. The rich could and would pay for themselves and continue to commandeer good jobs and high salaries. The planning was to be radically overhauled. Houses, roads, transport had to be as environmentally viable as they could possibly be. There was another element which was specifically aimed at nurturing families with children, of seeking out couples, married or not, who had the potential to have children. It was a sensitive issue.

This was the first time that Mac and I had faced up to the enormity of what we were being asked to do and how it related to a greater scheme of things. A lot of it was already in place. Transport had already been seen to. Population masses had become concentrated on the cities and the big towns and the one-car rule had cut savagely into the numbers living beyond a five mile radius of towns and cities. There were only a few exemptions; doctors, community nurses for instance.

My parents ... I grew up in Norfolk ... had long since moved from the village where I was born. They had to. The coastline that had been there when I was a child disappeared into the sea ten years ago. Now there were what people referred to as 'ghost villages', abandoned settlements for twenty miles inland all along the coast.

In the far west Cornwall was now a leisure playground with a population just sufficient to service its needs. Devon was following suit. The Dorset coastline was under severe threat. There were large areas of wind farms, generating energy. They took up vast tracts of land that had previously been farmed. Off-shore turbines dominated the coastline.

The whole of the East coast of England had flooding problems and any kind of development within a 50 mile boundary of the coast was prohibited. People were being re-housed in new towns on higher ground to replace all the vulnerable towns and villages along the river valleys that regularly flooded. These were falling into decay; uninsurable and inhabitable for the wet winter months.

The north ...well, the north was the north. The jobs were concentrated in the major cities. Only Newcastle, Manchester, Liverpool, Leeds and Sheffield had managed to retain any sort of credibility with major employers but they had plenty of other problems. The Newcastle ghetto we were working on would address some of these.

I said: 'Was this all sparked in the first place by global warming ...?' Mac snorted. 'Global excuse for railroading through policies,' he said.

We went on to a restaurant ... then a club ... It was four in the morning when I got back to Steph's flat. I tried to tiptoe in. Difficult when you're as drunk as I was. I stubbed my toe on a chair in the dark. Shit. I shouted it. She was awake, of course. She had reservations about Mac although she'd never met him. Grave reservations.

'If he wasn't so bloody clever and well-off, he'd probably be sleeping in a cardboard box and strumming a guitar at the bottom of the escalator. He obviously likes drawing attention to himself from what you say about him,' she said when I first told her about him. Irritatingly she then asked: 'Is he good-looking?'

'How the hell do I know? Why do you need to ask?' It irritates me this woman thing about what blokes look like.

Tonight Mac had got drunk very quickly. He was the kind of drunk who managed to retain some charm. He was both funny and very engaging to the gay waiter when we had our meal and I began to have a few doubts which he quickly dispelled. I was drunk enough myself to be amused rather than embarrassed.

I crawled in beside Steph, hoping she wasn't that wide awake but she said coldly: 'What the hell time is it?'

'Half past two.'

'Liar ... I was awake then wondering where you were. With Mac, I suppose? He's leading you astray.'

'Maybe that's what I need at my age. Maybe that's what I needed at his age.'

'Bollocks. Anyway, how old is he?'

'About 28, I think. He's on a fast track ... very bright bloke.'

'A bloody idiot.'

'I must get some sleep. Please make sure I wake up.' Steph turned and snuggled into me. It was all getting very serious ... I remember thinking that as I drifted off in her warm, pillowy embrace.

CHAPTER 7

Warne's manuscript

Margaret handed me the phone: 'It's that woman again.'

That woman was Maeve Dunlop. She contacted me a fortnight ago. This was the fifth call in three weeks. I was beginning to regret that I had been helpful when she first telephoned.

Her voice was soft, breathless. I imagined her small, maybe plump, faded blonde, china blue eyes. Margaret left the room impatiently. She wears her hair bobbed these days. It suits her. She was wearing shorts, going to play tennis, slender, long legs, slim neat figure. She has always conveyed this sense of being in complete control of herself. I've never known her lose control, even over the heartbreak of our baby. I tried to concentrate on what I was being told.

Maeve said: 'I did as you suggested. Got some statistics for the Bristol area and it looks like what we think is right ...'

I noted the 'we' with some irritation. 'How do you mean?'

She said: 'Well, comparing them with figures in 2005 the death rates for the 70 to 80 year olds have gone up by 20 per cent. That's a lot, isn't it? And the causes of death are principally cancer and heart. It all adds up to what you said on the television that day. Targets to be met ...treatment denied. That's what happened to Mum.'

I find it odd when women refer to their mothers as Mum or Mummy. I assumed Maeve was middle-aged.

I didn't want to get into this. Cancer, heart and stroke are always going to be the biggest killers. I had recovered completely and I was back at work, taking surgeries and seeing patients again.

I said: 'Look Miss Dunlop ...' 'Maeve' ... 'well, Maeve ... I explained before, I think, that doctors have to take into account the quality of life that a patient can expect with any long-term or terminal illness ... it may be that these people not only had specific things wrong with them but other things too ... things that would badly affect how they could live, how they would die ... then a doctor has to decide what is best, weigh up the pros and cons ...'

She said: 'So you've changed your mind? You doctors are all the same. Stick together. Defend each other. None of you ever gets it wrong, do you, and if you do you cover up for each other if you can. I've sat in enough meetings watching how you operate. It's like the mafia. How do you explain the percentage rise? We're only talking fifteen years ago. Why are so many more over 70's dying now than then? That's what I don't understand. Not unless it's organised. And that's what you said it was ...'

I wanted to put the phone down but my instinct told me not to.

I said: 'The targets that I was talking about were QALYs ... better assessments of people. In the past so many people were kept alive by methods, interventions that ... well, quite honestly ...'

She finished the sentence: 'They'd have been better off dead.'

'Yes.' I waited.

She said nothing for a while. Then she said: 'You're not going to stop me kicking up a fuss about this, you know. I'll start a campaign. I could get up a head of steam on this that would damage you, damage the government.'

I assumed she didn't mean me literally but me as in all doctors.

She was rushing on: 'We're back to doctors knowing best again, aren't we? I thought all that had been stopped when there was all that hoo-ha about informed consent years ago and every form got altered. Body parts, that was. Then there were guidelines so that patients or their relatives must be consulted about whether or not doctors should stop treatment. Now we're talking about people not being consulted at all and decisions about whether they live or die being taken entirely by the medical profession or by some sort of committee.

'What about denying stem cell treatment? You brought that up and I didn't believe for one moment that bit about research showing it wasn't effective after a certain age. I expect the insurance people are in it too. They can't afford old people. It didn't take you lot long to grab back your power, did it? And now the government's conniving ... why? I'll find out ... I'm not giving up easily.' She slammed the phone down.

Margaret came back into the room and stood aggressively near the door to the garden. 'Finished? Well, I've got something to say. We're putting this place on the market ... we agreed, didn't we, before you had the stroke.' She didn't wait for a reply but continued with the news that she had asked an estate agent out and that he'd be arriving within the hour.

I said: 'Fait accompli, then? And are we moving together into town or moving apart ...'

'What on earth do you mean?' She actually looked a bit flustered. She was not quite so sure about the boy-friend then, after all?

'I thought we'd agreed on one of those new places on the estate on Stoodleigh Hill ... they're still building them. The estate agent said something about a grant being available ... they're desperate to get everybody into towns, cities. It's environmental policy.'

'Well, how the devil are we going to sell this place, then, for what it's worth?'

'He'll explain it. Seems the government makes up the difference in some way ... or he may have an approved buyer.'

The agent turned up in a trendy-looking car which conformed to all the conservation standards but still managed to look sleeker and sexier than most other cars allowed on the road.

'Lovely place,' he said. He looked too young to have passed his driving test. 'Wonderful setting. But you're way off the beaten track out here, aren't you. You could face compulsory purchase ... that's the way things are going. What did you pay for it?'

I certainly wasn't going to tell him but Margaret jumped straight in.

'Well, you'll probably get your money back. In fact, you might do a bit better. The Countryside Agency is looking for a place like this for one of its Devon centres ... countryside pursuits headquarters - for the ramblers, bird watchers, all those sort of groups. It might not be quite big enough but they can always extend in an environmentally friendly way and the land would be good. They're keen on land. We might be able to do a deal, take into account what you're entitled to in way of grant for moving into the new house. Have you had a look at them? Beautifully done and they meet every single requirement that the planners and environmentalists want.'

'Little boxes,' I said. 'Rabbit hutches.'

Margaret shot me an angry look. The agent looked at me more carefully and noted me down as an awkward customer. 'No, doctor, you're wrong. They are surprisingly spacious once you get inside. Well designed. Lots of character.'

He shot a glance at Margaret which said you should have warned me, you'd better help. 'Not like this, of course, but just think of all the laws you're contravening here. You've been lucky to get away with it this far. You must know from your surgery building what the latest requirements are. I shouldn't think this place meets one of them.'

What a smart-arse. I picked up the paper. It had all been decided. I would not allow myself to get upset. Margaret took the agent out to show him the rest of the house. I could hear them muttering and mumbling in the distance and could imagine the agent exclaiming how quaint it was and emphasising the ecological damage we were doing to the world by living so far from the town.

Maeve the madwoman came back into my thoughts. I needed to do something about her before it got out of hand. I looked up Stephanie Meadows' direct line number at the Medical Association but it was her secretary who answered. She said she was in a meeting, and would then be in another meeting. She suggested that I phoned around 4.30 but could she take a message. I said it was too complicated. Perhaps Steph could phone me? She said that it might not be today and we agreed first thing in the morning, as soon as she got into the office, at probably around 8.

I thought about Maeve's mother. She probably could have had more treatment.

There might have been a remission after intervention on a grand and costly scale but non-intervention might have been kinder. Some patients voted themselves. I've had them. No more treatment, doctor. I've had enough. They wouldn't treat a dog this way. No, that was my father. He'd said that to me a week before he died. A lingering cancer that had followed Parkinson's disease and years of sitting in a nursing home waiting for it all to happen.

Maeve had described what had happened to her mother. I can't tell. Ten to one her doctors would have made the right decisions. She was probably too far gone to justify intervening and home nursing and an eased way out would have been by far the best option. She would have died with some dignity.

These days insurance means that most people are seen quickly and the waiting list to get on a waiting list to see an expert clinician is a thing of the past. That, of course, used to be another form of controlling the population. A patient could die on a waiting list and a lot of them did.

Those who can't afford insurance get the worst treatment. Maeve could have paid, though, couldn't she? She had told me that she was deputy director of social services for Bristol so she certainly could have forked out. It sounded like her mother might have been one of those bloody-minded principled sort who don't hold with any sort of private practice health. Maeve said she'd been a campaigner all her life, that she had been at Greenham Common. She sounded very proud of her.

When I started in practice, first as a trainee, then a locum chasing a partnership, the health service had been a nightmare. People whom I suspected had tumours were waiting nine months before they had an initial consultation.

Mrs Knott was by no means my only big mistake but she's the one I still feel worst about. She wasn't old, though I'd thought so at the time, early fifties. A couple of years older than I am now. Always in the surgery and seeing her name on my surgery list filled me with dread. I'd think of all sorts of things to delay me in pressing the buzzer when it was her turn but that didn't do me any good. She'd tell me that she'd seen my previous patient leave ten minutes ago.

She could be guaranteed to outlast her time slot, rabbiting away, bringing up one ailment after another besides the one she was supposed to have come about. My colleagues had their own Mrs Knotts and they fought their corner when it came to sharing them around. And those patients would wait, delay their appointment to make sure they saw their own doctor rather than go and see someone else. I could come back from a fortnight's holiday and she'd be there, somewhere in the waiting room that first morning back.

I should have taken the symptoms more seriously but I knew she was always taking patent medicine and complaining of constipation and unidentifiable pain, which seemed to shift around from visit to visit. It was several months before I'd decided to get her on the list for a barium enema and then there was a wait of another three months for an appointment.

It was far too late when the cancer was eventually found, high up where the large intestine joined the small. I was hauled over the coals by the senior partner in the practice but the worst thing was her immediate family. They were so nice. They told me: 'Nothing you could do, doctor. We know you did your best for her.' It was her cousin, a nurse, who kicked up the fuss.

There had been others, of course. Any doctor will tell you if they're honest about the avoidable deaths and narrow escapes. But Mrs Knott was my albatross.

The media made matters far worse for medics at the turn of the century, running one health scandal or scare story after another. It was always so negative. The media liked the scares and it kept the public on their toes. Doctors became public enemy numero uno and a number of them gave up at that time, claiming nervous breakdowns and early pensions. Mrs Knott's death had almost driven me out.

When I became a partner and had more clout I'd juggled the fast tracks, brought pressure to bear on consultant friends, had patients admitted to the emergency medical units at hospitals and done all I could to get the best for my patients. It was soul-destroying being thwarted again and again. One of my friends from university days had been struck off after drinking heavily, abusing drugs and making the wrong decision when he'd been called to an emergency at 4 in the morning. The child died. He was unlucky. Many more got away with it.

Other friends and colleagues put medicine on the back burner. They still practised but put their energies into other interests. They still do, some of them. I've got a partner who spends most of his time in his apple orchard; another has become a very good photographer.

I got interested in medical politics, thinking that I could make a difference. I got involved first of all when the government brought in the new Primary Care Trusts, trying to bury the old health authorities' debt burden. My partners hadn't objected, how could they? They were exhausted by years of almost constant NHS reform.

Then things began to change. The new doctors' contract in 2004 meant we weren't working nights or week-ends and we were earning a lot more money. The better-off patients had already started skipping the waiting lists and forking out for private consultations, operations, anything to get quickly what should have been standard health care. The GP referenderum, held after the government forced the out-of-hours work back on us and clawed back our payments, paved the way for private practice and the insurance based National Health Service that is now in place. The referendum choice was stark: private practice or a salaried service. 85% voted for private practice.

We voted and our practice went private, pushing the non-payers into travelling to Exeter or Taunton where the 'national' clinics operated. A coach picked them up at 8 in the morning and again at six in the evening. It was an exhausting job being ill and it was a poor service.

When the vote was taken nationally there were quite a few newly qualified doctors who took a moral stance and chose the salaried route. I should not think there are any now. The do-gooders soon decided they could square their consciences. I'm afraid I was one of them. I did not want to leave the practice or the area. The doctors who provide the national service now are the ethnic minorities, the immigrants, the very old and the disgraced who have wangled their way back on to the register.

I still feel uncomfortable about my decision but Margaret nagged and nagged. I thought if I did as she asked it might change things between us. How wrong I was.

Anyway I'm glad to be back at work. I like being a doctor and I don't think I'm a bad one. The prospect of the new box-like house, Margaret around but not as any sort of wife or companion and the fact that I'm still only 48 is another incentive for keeping me busy.

My partners are very glad to have me back; another pair of hands, another body on the rota.

Steph asked how I was when she phoned, prompt at 8. 'Much better. Your man Hislop wouldn't put one across me now,' I said. She giggled, rather guiltily.

I said: 'I'll come straight to the point. I think you may get a bit more trouble from that death targets thing. I've had a woman get in touch with me … rather mad, I think… a Mzzz Maeve Dunlop … no, Bristol. She's a big noise in social services so you may need to handle her with kid-gloves. She saw me on television and believes her mother was one of the cancer cases that got killed off to meet the targets. She may be right but I suspect that there was very little the doctors could have done. It sounded like a terminal case to me. Anyway, she's threatening a campaign, winding up public opinion, says she knows what she needs to do …'

Steph said: 'Thanks for the warning. I'll let the local doctors in Bristol know and our regional office. Sounds a bit as if you've changed your mind on the targets issue?'

'Not really,' I said. ' I just can't be bothered any more. I'm back at work. Oh and we're probably moving

... in about a month's time. I'll let you have the new address. The phone numbers and all the rest should be the same and you can always get me at the surgery. I'm fully fit if you need anybody for interviews.'

'Moving somewhere nice?'

'No, a bloody box on a politically-correct prize-winning 'conservation' estate. Big brother's got to me at last.'

CHAPTER 8

James Fields, via voice

I really don't know why I let Mac rent my house. I hadn't known him very long; maybe just over a month, but a day or two after that night out he asked me if I'd consider letting. I guess we'd done some male bonding at the racecourse. Steph was furious. I told her he owed the bookies some money and needed to cut back and that was partly true. He'd been renting an expensive flat in Chelsea and he knew I hardly ever went home to Putney. For an economist he was the most profligate man I'd ever met. He was on a good salary but he blew it on cars, meals, wine, women ... and he had an eighth share in a racehorse. I thought of it as one hind leg. I think he thought of it as the most vital bit, the nose. As I'd got to know him better I'd realised that the bets we had in the office were fleabites compared to the bets he put on for himself.

'Bit of an altercation with Herr Villum,' he told me. 'Got to stump up.' I knew William Hill wasn't the only account he'd got. 'You're never in the Putney flat, are you? I'll pay you rent.' On this, if nothing else, he was as good as his word.

I suspect ...why did I say that ... I know ... another reason why he wanted to rent the flat was because I had taken him back there one week-end soon after I'd met him when Steph was off at a conference and we'd bumped into the people from next door. I'd needed to pick up some papers and wanted him to see if they were what we needed.

The baby was now crawling. Fern looked absolutely stunning. I wish I'd had a mother like that. I could see Mac felt the same.

At his insistence we asked them in for a drink. The conversation was a bit stilted. Mac quite obviously rejected all his well-tested chat-up lines in the face of such a potentially attractive conquest. You could tell straight off that she had to be handled with style and delicacy. Then the little boy started to fuss and Johnnie said he'd take him home and give him some food.

That left the two of us with Fern. Instant attraction. Opposites. She was cool, blonde, thin, elegant and nearly as tall as Mac. It was like electricity crackling in the room and I should have known better than to let the flat to him. It was always going to be trouble and it was unfair to Johnnie.

Mac used to give me updates on his pursuit of her each morning. At first he got nowhere. He peered through the curtains out of the landing window which over-looked their garden. They had a patio and she was always lying out, keeping her sun tan topped up. September continued warm and sunny. Mac couldn't believe his luck. She must have been aware of him gawping through the curtains but she obviously didn't give a damn. Maybe she wanted him to have a good look but I don't think she was a tease. She was always topless, with the briefest of thongs, he said. I allowed myself to imagine it.

Johnnie was an account exec at one of the top ad agencies but she was the one with the balls. She told Mac they'd met when she was copywriting and that as soon as the baby was well enough she'd be going back to work.

'Bored housewife,' said Mac, grinning like a maniac. I asked him how the little boy was doing.

'She's a bit odd about that. Not a bit mumsy. I think it's doing quite well.'

'It does have a name. He's called William.'

He didn't tell me at the time that he'd fixed to take Fern racing with him but he went on interminably about it afterwards. 'The husband didn't mind a bit when I suggested it. Seemed only too pleased that Fern was going to be entertained. I took her to Plumpton on Monday. She looked absolutely beautiful. Stunning. I tell you ... heads turned.' So that was why he had taken the day off.

Mac, despite his straitened circumstances, had managed to hang on to his car. It was an open top BMW that only barely kept within the laws on engine size and emissions. He'd been stopped a few times and questioned but got away with it.

I could imagine him swerving in and out of traffic, cutting through the North Downs and sweeping noisily into the car park, with the elegant Fern at his side. She was the sort of girl who'd emerge from an open top with not a hair out of place on her sleek blonde head. Those long legs would swing effortlessly out of the low seat ... shit, I'm risking a severe telling-off if Steph ever catches sight of this.

'She knows some people who were at Oxford with me.'

I looked at him and he had the grace to blush. 'OK, I'm allowed to bullshit if it helps me get my leg-over.' He'd gone to the LSE, same as me which, of course, was much better anyway.

He had this habit of embroidering his conversation. If I'm honest he told lies, absolute whoppers. Most were so entertaining you didn't want to catch him out. It was obvious that there wasn't much truth; maybe just a kernel. He never did it with work. He applied very rigorous principles to his work but in his private life you had either to keep sifting for the truth or allow him to re-invent himself without question.

Every so often you caught him out but he always had a plausible excuse or blankly denied he'd ever said such a thing ... 'you must have misheard'. I'd now heard three different versions of his childhood and still didn't know which to believe. I didn't care much, accepted him for what he was. His embroidery really got up Steph's nose when I made the mistake of telling her about how I'd caught him out a few times.

That's why I didn't necessarily take the Fern thing that seriously. I couldn't imagine such a mercenary woman jeopardising her lifestyle on Mac. She'd told him, apparently, that they wouldn't be living much longer in Putney. Johnnie, the husband, was doing really well. She fancied Richmond. They might even start an agency of their own. The little boy would go to a good nursery school, then private education. She'd got it all mapped out and I thought that if Mac was telling the truth for once then she was simply having a fling.

I asked: 'What about the husband, the poor sod?'

Mac said that he honestly thought that Johnnie was willing to put up with anything so long as Fern was happy.

He said: 'She treats him like a dog. He seems to enjoy it. I can't understand blokes like that ... but he's besotted with the kid. He does most of the work when he's home. Mr Doggie Dogsbody.'

I said: 'She seems to have got you by the bollocks as well. It'll all end in tears.'

The days out at the week-ends became a regular occurrence – either racing, expensive restaurants or anything else which took Fern's fancy. They hired a boat and went up the river one week-end. She must have cost him a fortune because I'd bet a pound to a penny that she never pulled her wallet out of the old Gucci.

I just hope, as Mac constantly assured me it was, that the sex was out of this world. Apparently the rocking motion on the boat ...well, OK, I was jealous. I could feel the net tightening around me. Matrimony was in the air and though I wasn't totally averse to the idea I was frightened of making that commitment again. It hadn't worked out too well the first time but Steph wasn't Rosie ... nor Fern ... h'mm. Time to get back to work.

Via voice: I've got some notes that Steph has let me have about Maeve Dunlop and the campaign she started. I'm including them here.

Steph writes: I was contacted by the Bristol office. The woman, Maeve Dunlop, that Warne had told me about was causing trouble. A lot of trouble. She'd obviously got in touch with the Bristol Evening Post and the health correspondent had interviewed her. She'd got together a lot of facts, statistics, anecdotal evidence about the numbers of elderly people, those over 70, who had died in her health region. That's one which covers the whole of the South West. She'd done a good job analysing them. There was a definite trend in the last 5 years of the over-70s dying soon after they started drawing their pensions. There was evidence that fewer 75-year-olds in the lower socio-economic brackets were surviving until 80.

The paper had splashed the story on the front and given it a centre spread too. There were some big type bold screaming headlines on the piece – frightening stuff if you were coming up to retirement age. Maeve, staring out of the page, looked relatively harmless but there was a lot about her mother who had died, aged 75.

Feisty Fay. She'd been a protester from an early age. Camped at Greenham Common, done the rounds of road and airport protests. Picture of her in Trafalgar Square screaming for the allied bombing of the Afghanis to be stopped. A caption read: 'Fay campaigns from beyond the grave.' Emotive stuff.

Maeve's telephone number and e-mail address were given and it was obvious that this story wasn't going to lie down. She'd already set up a public meeting and the skeleton of a committee. One was a woman lawyer who I knew dealt with medical negligence cases. Tough cookie.

I advised the Bristol office to get a sensible doctor to go along to the meeting. They suggested a woman oncologist. I didn't know her but they said she was good. I told them not to let her get involved. Just observe. No need to stick her head above the parapet. Not yet, anyway. Then I thought of John Warne and phoned them back. They thought it was a good idea.

I finally got hold of him at the end of a morning surgery. I told him: 'Your mad Maeve is up to something. She's called a public meeting for the end of next week and got her story splashed all over the Bristol Evening Post.'

He cursed but volunteered to go. I gave him the name of the oncologist and wished him well. He said he'd report back.

🗆🗆🗆🗆🗆

Warne's manuscript

Maeve Dunlop's meeting was in a church hall on the Clifton side of Bristol. There were already people dotted about in the seats when I arrived, maybe thirty people in all. Nobody sat in the front three rows. I did a quick calculation ... maybe 12 rows of 15 seats. I was surprised that Maeve anticipated as many as 300. I remember wondering which one she was.

There were three women standing near the table at the front; a woman of medium height with severe glasses and close-cropped hair wearing a grey suit; another tall woman with long auburn hair in a smart black outfit and a small blonde woman, with round glasses and a round face.

I guessed she was the blonde so I was surprised when the meeting started to find it was the rather striking auburn-haired woman who introduced herself as Maeve Dunlop. The strict-looking woman she introduced as Janet something, a solicitor, and the other woman as a counsellor who had a lot of experience with bereaved people.

The doctor Steph had sent to the meeting had introduced herself and was sitting beside me. She murmured: 'We've got our hands full here. Maeve Dunlop's a hard nut I hear from colleagues who've come across her. Fights her corner.'

The room had filled up and five people even braved the very first row. I guess there were about 190 people but

I realised others were coming in after the meeting started. As always there were some unwilling to sit but were standing at the back, keeping their escape routes open.

Maeve spoke confidently. She said that although she was Deputy Director of Social Services for the area she was not acting in any official capacity. She was fulfilling the promise she had made to her dying mother. She outlined a plan of how she saw the meeting progressing. She would explain first why she had called it and would then ask for contributions from the floor. At the end of the meeting she hoped they could come to some joint decision as to how to proceed and campaign on the issue of death targets. The audience murmured approval.

She went into some detail of her mother's death from cancer, which had started in the bowel and spread to the liver and pancreas. She believed if it had been treated properly with an early exploratory colonoscopy and a surgical operation there was no need for it to have spread as it did. She gave a brief history of her mother. A campaigner at Greenham Common, she'd gone on to fight on the conservation front at every opportunity. She'd lived in a tree house in Devon for a while to try to stop a new road. She had stood against the Blair government for a Bristol seat as an independent labour candidate in the 2001 election, having become disenchanted with new Labour. She had lost her deposit. Later she had been a prominent peace-nik when the Middle East conflict blew up, first in Iraq and afterwards when it escalated to so many countries.

Just before her mother had died, Maeve told her audience, she had seen the news on television and had realised that she had probably been one of the government's targets. One of their QALYs.

Maeve said it bitterly. 'She didn't qualify. Not worth any extra years. She asked me to fight for her and for others and I promised. That's why I am here and why I hope we can campaign to get the government to change this obnoxious policy of non-intervention by doctors who like playing God.'

I could see that her eyes had filled with tears but she had been pretty impressive at keeping her emotions under control. I had expected a more hysterical performance. I saw the solicitor nodding her head approvingly and pointing to a piece of paper on the table in front of them. A prompt list?

Maeve opened the meeting to the floor. There was a silence for perhaps half a minute and then a short, thick-set fat man got up and started to talk about his wife. He was very emotional and went into great detail about how she had died from heart disease. It was fairly obvious that the wife would only have been middle aged and that it was unlikely she was one of the targets that the meeting was about. He held up a photo of an obese woman.

The solicitor stood up. She was obviously going to control this part of the meeting. She thanked the man, cutting him short. By then a forest of hands were going up to attract attention. She handled them diplomatically and gradually a fairer picture emerged of older people, relatives and friends and their deaths. The solicitor asked that the ages of the dead were given. A picture of people mostly in their early seventies began to emerge.

A black woman told a harrowing story of an elderly neighbour with no near relations who had been taken, she said forcibly, by social services to what she described as the workhouse.

Maeve intervened rapidly to explain what social services' role was in relation to the elderly. She impressed the policy of keeping people in their own homes as far as possible but of course there were cases ... there was a murmuring that indicated that many in the audience were not that impressed with her explanation. It was the nearest she came to losing control.

Many of the audience were incapable of giving factual information and emotional monologues had to be gently curtailed as others got impatient.

The solicitor said firmly after an hour: 'We have only got this hall until ten o'clock. I think we should now move forward to making some decision on what sort of campaign we run if that is what we agree. We should also elect a committee.'

I groaned and the oncologist looked at me, amused. 'Not another committee ...?'

An overwhelming show of hands confirmed that the meeting agreed with running a campaign to get the 'deaths targets policy abandoned'. Somebody suggested: 'Stop death by numbers'. The audience began to laugh, relieving the tension, but somebody got up and said: 'Good idea, why not?'

'A good emotive slogan,' I whispered and we both got up to leave as the proceedings towards electing a committee commenced.

Outside the hall, she said: 'Actually I know what we're talking about is non-intervention for elderly people where there isn't any other option but in a lot of ways I agree with this lot. It's yet more evidence of state control. Just look what they've done to this city; it's unrecognisable from even twenty years ago. OK, it's a safer place, a cleaner place, but there's an undercurrent of resentment that I think is going to boil over pretty soon. People are fed up with being ...'

'Homogenised?'

'I almost miss the 'Big Issue' beggars, the cardboard campers, the street musicians on the take with their greyhounds, even the drunks ... you're right, it's all too tidy. I think that lot in there are right to campaign about a policy which seems to be part of a larger policy. Get the old people tidied up and out of sight ...in their graves. I didn't know social services could do what they did to that woman's neighbour. Shove her in the workhouse ...oh, sorry, 'residential home for disadvantaged citizens'. I had more time for Maeve until she trotted out that piece of jargon.'

She asked me how I coped with elderly patients who had some life-threatening disease and I explained that I worked as I have always done, referring patients on to consultants if I thought it appropriate. 'But we have a private practice. I don't know what the safety net, the public doctors, are doing.

'I've been away from the surgery for a while since I had a stroke. I used to do far more geriatrics but now I'm concentrating on maternity and paediatrics. I do what there is of the ante and post natal cases... and children. It's so important to make sure as many as possible of the pregnancies come to term and that there is a viable child at the end of it all.'

I added: 'When I started in practice it was the long waiting lists which sorted out who lived and who died. Even younger people with diagnosed tumours were waiting weeks, even months for scans and further treatment. Heart by-pass patients were certainly dying before they ever got on an operating table.'

We said goodbye and I got in the car to head west. I had driven a couple of streets, en route to the motorway thinking about Maeve and her campaign. At least she had some fire in her and the guts to stand up and be prepared to make a fool of herself. Her mother must have been impressive, too. On impulse, I stopped the car and turned it around, heading back for the hall. It was nearly empty when I went in, only seven people gathered by the table at the front. Maeve and her two colleagues and four others. The committee?

They looked surprised as I walked towards them along the left hand side of the rows of chairs.

'Have you lost something?' the counsellor asked me.

'No ...no, I just wanted to have a word with Miss Dunlop if I could ... I don't want to interrupt. I'm John Warne ... we spoke ...'

Maeve looked at me, her dark eyes hard. 'The doctor ... what the hell are you doing here. You were here, in the meeting, I remember now...near the back, with a woman. Have you been sent to spy on us?'

It was too close to the mark and I was caught off-guard. 'No ... well ... observe, I suppose.'

'Well, you've observed and now you can bugger off. As you can see there was a lot of public support. You and the rest of your buddies, all you smug doctors aren't going to get off so easily now.'

The solicitor stepped forward. She said: 'I'm Janet Bartlett. Look, we've got to hand back the hall in a minute. We were going to the pub for a drink. Why don't you come with us.'

She turned to Maeve: 'He may be able to help, advise. You said he started off by going public against the government on this. He might know ways round the establishment ...?'

I was uncomfortable at being talked over by two women.

Maeve looked unconvinced and said ungraciously: 'Well, you'd better come along. We've got to get out of here anyway. The caretaker's getting pissed off.'

She was almost as tall as me and I felt disadvantaged. I struggled along behind her and the rest of them, along the wet pavement to the pub on the corner. I was still a bit slow and she turned, saw me struggling and waited momentarily for me to catch up.

'So have you changed your mind again?' she asked, over her shoulder. I said no, not necessarily. I tried to explain that in my experience some people, no matter how much treatment they had, were going to die. The public, fed by the media, seemed to think they had the right to eternal life. Medicine wasn't a pure science with a cause and effect. A lot of other factors came into it including an individual's attitude to their own disease. She strode ahead, not answering.

We reached the pub and the others were already sitting at a table. It was by now well after ten o'clock and there was plenty of room. It was a large pub with little character, clean and serviceable. Homogenised? There was a large notice warning that nobody under 18 would be served and the pub's staff would inspect identity cards of anyone they suspected of being under age and would report them to the police. Most cities were cracking down hard on pubs to cut down on drinking. I wondered whether the landlady in Exeter who had been on the train the night I had my stroke observed these kind of rules. I rather thought not.

I offered to pay for the round but the solicitor said they had already ordered a couple of bottles of wine. The black lady who had spoken eloquently about her neighbour was there. It was a good move to have her on side rather than off but I thought they might be taking a bit of a chance.

There were also two men whom I had not noticed in the audience and did not remember speaking. Then there were Maeve and her two friends and one other woman. I could not decide what ethnic minority she was, some kind of Asian. The black lady, Suzanne, was a nurse. The men, younger than me, did not say what they did. I think they resented me being there. Maybe they didn't like doctors, either.

The committee meeting, which had started in the hall, continued. I listened as they began to draw the threads together of a campaign. More meetings were proposed. More publicity. They needed to get this thing going nationwide. Meetings and publicity in other major cities. What about funds? One of the men asked that question. At last they began to think sensibly.

Maeve looked across at me. 'You'd better nail your colours to the mast. You're either for us or agin us.'

I knew I would be a feather in their cap if I joined. Why was I here in the pub with them, why had I turned back towards the hall when I was on my way home? I knew the answer; I'd known it ever since I'd sat in that committee meeting at the Medical Association's headquarters and had voted against the proposal. My hesitation following Maeve's phone calls had been a cop out for not getting involved. The government policy went against all my ethical beliefs. 'I'm with you,' I said.

□□□□□

Maeve's diary entry: November 12, 2020

The meeting went better than I could ever wish. There were so many people and it's going to make a big splash in the media tomorrow. I've had so many phone calls since I got home and the regional television news programmes are going to interview me in the morning. The interviews are all lined up, one after the other. It's going to make the national news. I am nervous but Janet and the others thought I did really well at the meeting. Even Suzanne seems to have been won round.

I spotted John Warne right at the beginning of the meeting before I began to speak. He's so familiar from all his television interviews. I've seen him often over the years and of course back in the summer when Fay made me promise. I decided right away that I would give him a really hard time if I got the chance. I was quite disappointed when I noticed him leave with that woman before the meeting finished. When he came back I was really on a high and felt I could be as bitchy as I liked. Fay would have been proud of me. The meeting went so well. Janet was dubious to begin with about the idea of a meeting but even she reckons that we have done well. The committee could prove a bit of a nightmare but now that we've got John co-opted on to it I think it will be OK. Very OK! By the time we finished at the pub I could see he was interested. I was still playing it very cool but I said that I would get in contact about the date of the next meeting. I really am exhausted tonight but I know I shan't sleep. The adrenalin is very high. The best thing is I am keeping my promise to Fay. We will get things done. I am really glad **he** has joined us!

CHAPTER 9

James Fields, via voice

I can't remember quite when Mac and I invented *Political Suicide*. I think it must have been early on, probably at about the same time that we worked out our betting system. I know we had a lot of time on our hands then.

We got this idea for a power struggle board game based on our intimate knowledge of the way the civil service worked with its political masters. Moves depended on the choice of a number of options on any one drawn card and sometimes the best choice was to do nothing. We'd made it very complicated. We still weren't entirely satisfied with it and kept it set up in the office and tinkered with it during lulls, rarer as the deadline approached, or when we were trying to think through legitimate work problems.

Just before Christmas, 2020, it seemed that *Political Suicide* was becoming a reality. The secretary of health started it. He became mixed up in an insurance scam and the tabloid press hounded him until he made a very public trip through the door at No 10 and came back out a backbench MP. A junior minister went at the same time. She said she wanted to spend more time with her family and would be giving up her seat at the next election.

We were hard at work finalising the Newcastle pilot. The deadline was the second week in the new year; it had been put back twice. We were called into a number of high level meetings which the new health minister chaired. He was a chap called David Nell. We called him Death Knell and on more than one occasion Mac spelled his name with a K in papers. He had a cadaverous face and a slow measured way of speaking which I think he thought gave him gravitas. So far as we and the other senior civil servants were concerned it slowed up meetings and irritated us all. Maybe he was having trouble grasping his brief.

Mac and I were going to have to give the presentation of the pilot to the secretaries of state of all the departments involved. Ministers and high ranking civil servants would also be present. Mac was going to be front man. He was good at putting across statistics and had a flair for presenting them in ways that even the dullest junior minister could understand. I was going to do the nitty gritty and organise the background with the technicians. Get all the techie stuff sorted and visually have charge of the presentation and be on hand for the awkward questions. I'm better than Mac at that who gets up people's noses.

Mac was pretty pissed off when he was told to get himself smartened up by the permanent secretary. He was in the wrong, of course, because Mac was smart and had style and wore clothes that probably cost more and were better cut than any of the rest of us, politicians, top civil servants, the lot. The pony tail and earring were singled out. In the end he conceded the earring.

It meant Christmas was a bit of a nightmare. I kept having to go into the office over the holiday period. Steph did too because Warne's ... or rather this woman Maeve Dunlop's lobby group ... started making headlines. They knew what they were about. News slowed down over the Christmas period so the media was more than grateful for a good running story.

Christmas Day itself was a nightmare for different reasons. We spent it with Steph's people who lived in Surrey, not far from Guildford. I'd burned my boats by this time. Proposed ... or agreed we should get married.

There's a bit of a blur in my mind over the exact words but I obviously did the right thing. Engagement ring, celebration, all the kind of stuff that despite all the advances and battles won on sexual equality is what girls still demand. We were officially engaged and the wedding was set for June. White one, bridesmaids, wedding gift list ... all the trimmings.

I'd only met the future in-laws once and that was in Fulham when we went out for a meal just after we'd got engaged. They hadn't seemed too bad. I'd quite liked the dad. More dubious about the mother-in-law who seemed a bit ... couldn't quite put my finger on it. Self centred? Possessive? Fussy? A bitch of the first order?

I could see as soon as we got in the door on Christmas eve how the land lay. House-proud wasn't in it. The high priestess of quality control. I doubt that she ever picked up a duster herself. She was bossing everyone around. Immediately asked me to take my shoes off and put on a pair of those travel slippers over my socks, the sort you get on long haul flights. She'd obviously saved them up.

I looked down at Steph's dad's feet. He'd got slippers on. Steph's brother-in-law who I hadn't met had obviously been trained. He'd got rather sophisticated leather slippers. Steph's sister had those bloody daft slippers that are enormous and furry. She'd got a pink rabbit on each foot, with floppy ears. Maybe she was protesting. The mother had gold coloured soft shoes on her neat little feet, bit reminiscent of a belly dancer, but that's where the resemblance started and finished.

Steph muttered: 'Should have warned you.' I noticed she changed into a pair of soft shoes as soon as we crossed the threshold.

It got worse. Neighbours came in for drinks and they brought indoor shoes which they changed into in the lobby outside the front door, hopping around and clutching each other for support, while being harangued to hurry up by their hostess who wanted to shut the front door and 'stop the draughts coming in'. One old boy went red in the face as he teetered on an obviously gippy hip. Heart attack? It would have livened things up considerably.

I guess the level of conversation hasn't changed for half a century in that neck of the woods. They've had the same topics, generation after generation, for ever. Holiday one upmanship, bargain purchases, favourite supermarket chains, the stock-market and the interest rate, the government, television soaps and reality shows. And, of course, the immigration policy. And the immigrants themselves. Cue racist jokes.

They were all anti-government given that the Labour party was so strongly back in power. They resented being marshalled in ways that had long since been proved to be the only effective solution for saving the country, the economy and the population. In my ignorance of this cross-section of society I'd have thought that they, of all people, would have been giving their support to a lot of the policies. After all, their middle-class descendants were going to be the chief beneficiaries and God, how we needed the immigrants to do the dirty work in society.

But it was moan and gripe all evening until it became evident that the whole party was expected to put on its outdoor shoes, coats, get into a procession of cars and drive to midnight mass at the church we had passed less than half a mile away.

I got Steph on her own: 'I'm not into this. You know I'm not. You're not going, are you?'

Steph hesitated then said that she was. She always did go to midnight mass. I didn't have to come. She'd love it if I did but ... well, I bloody well didn't. And that really was the declaration of war between me and her mum. Snidey remarks right through Christmas Day and a hard peck on the cheek when eventually we escaped on Boxing Day. Christ. All the bounce seemed to have gone out of Steph once she was back under the family roof.

Fortunately once we got home we were both back into hard work which didn't give us the option of having a major bust-up. The 'stop death by numbers' lot were on the rampage and Steph was up to her eyes, conniving with government to get the heat taken out of it. Warne's lot kept coming up with case history after case history of over-70s failing to get the treatment they needed and dying prematurely. All the cases seemed credible. Somebody had been very cute. The media loved it ... and him. He was on telly a lot. A sensitive good-looking man, warm family doctor oozed out of his common sense performance. The occasional inspired flash of snappy sound-bite brilliance in his remarks guaranteed headlines. He just made any opposing spokesman, government or medic, look devious. He even made Hislop lose his cool in one memorable head-on debate.

The whole thing didn't help us much. People were beginning to get the jitters about launching a radical scheme which smacked of heavy-handed government control and interference. The health department's senior press officer was fully involved with us by this time. He was a bluff, down-to-earth sort of guy. They'd have done much better to field him against Warne. He had a habit of appearing in our office early in the mornings and was full of terrible stories which he was trying to cover up or the truth behind what we had just read in the papers.

Bill Hancock had his head screwed on and even managed to out-manoeuvre the notorious Emma Moorhouse from Lifestyle. He got the date altered for the internal government presentation and kept it low key. It was the same day as the major debate in the House on the country's chemical weapon stockpiles which were causing great public concern despite the continuing threat from the Middle East.

Two days before the launch our pilot project leaked. I've never seen a witch hunt like the one that followed. Mac and I were grilled hour after hour. Anybody who had anything to do with any of the planning or the presentation was given an equally hard time. Suspicions centred on the junior minister who had resigned at the same time as the previous health minister. She had been around at the time the inter-departmental exercise had been started. We had plenty of new material for *Political Suicide* but we were far too worried about our jobs to incorporate it.

The media had got a lot of detail. Some aspects of the pilot scheme had already begun in Newcastle. People had been re-housed. A few of them were quite prepared to say that they had been forced to move. A heavily built Geordie mother, with a string of fostered handicapped children behind her, called it blackmail.

'They said I'd lose my benefit if I didn't move where they wanted me to,' she said, straight to camera. Drug addicts, in a building specially designed for them to live in with built-in re-hab care, were filmed sitting on a communal green, while the recreational space for a day care nursery for special needs children appeared to be right next door. It wasn't, but the camera team were clever.

The 'Stop Death by Numbers' lot cashed in. A press release said that it was another example of government engineering only this time it was the most disadvantaged in society who were being targeted.

I don't know if it was Maeve Dunlop or Warne who first used the word ghetto. The tabloids took that one up. Good headline word. Social affairs programmes made comparisons to Germany under Hitler. Life was hell for Mac and me. Our hard work was about to be thrown out and we were desperate not to be made the scapegoats.

□□□□□

Warne's manuscript

We had just watched a television programme, using a courtroom format, to assess the ethics of government intervention in manipulating the population and its environment.

Margaret said sarcastically: 'What a star you are.'

I had acted as prosecutor, arguing that ethically and morally it was wrong. I was allowed to bring in others to give evidence and I had made use of the recent publicity over the Newcastle pilot and of course, used the death by numbers evidence. Maeve Dunlop had been a witness. I had also contacted a number of protest groups, including the remnants of the Countryside Alliance, a spent force since the wide scale demise of agriculture in the country. A man who had once been a household name ... and face ... came on to say his piece.

The points I made showed how successive governments since the millennium had intervened to alter the nature of both city and countryside and the way people lived. I think my coup de grace had been that government was now intervening to control the population itself and how it lived ... and died. I introduced the idea that cloning might be next on the agenda. There had been more and more in the medical press about scientific breakthroughs in cloning. I admit I really only did it to back my case. The jury had come down strongly on my ... our ...side.

When the phone rang Margaret said: 'That'll be the girl friend. Please answer it here. I'm going to bed.' She went out of the room and I could see she made a great effort not to slam the door. She had always made such a thing about there being room for other relationships in our marriage but I was very aware by now of her jealousy.

I was increasingly being recognised in public and she did not like my being a celebrity. People came up to me in the street, in shops, in restaurants and told me to keep up the good work. A few even asked for my autograph which I would not give. I hate that sort of thing. Twice Margaret has been with me and I saw her lips purse with annoyance but she could not bring herself to mention it afterwards.

Maeve was another matter. The campaign meetings had escalated. We were seeing a lot of each other, usually in the company of others. I found her very attractive. At the same time Margaret's lecherous lecturer had turned his attentions to a young student in his department. Rejected and unhappy, she was spending more time at home. We even occasionally spent time watching television together, having meals together.

I picked up the phone as Margaret slammed the door. Maeve said: 'I thought that was great. You did so well.'

'You did well too.' There was a pause.

I said, scrambling for a safer footing: 'The Newcastle scandal couldn't have come at a better time for us. It's made people focus on what is happening in this country. I think the programme tonight may wake people up a bit more. A lot of the changes have been low-key; insidious interference. Now they can see that Big Brother really has taken over.'

Maeve said: 'Did you mean that ... about cloning? I was worried you'd gone too far.'

I admitted that I had flown a kite. 'But it is a logical step, isn't it?'

She said: 'That guy from the Countryside Alliance was good, wasn't he? I thought they were right over the top at the time but now, when he explained what's happened to the land and the farmers, you realise they should have made much more noise.'

'No, it's a big step forward. I'll be interested to see what reaction comes into the office tomorrow.'

The most recent development was that we had a headquarters, based in Bristol, co-ordinating the campaign. It was in an empty flat, over a parade of shops, and had been loaned by the butcher in the shop below, a man whose mother had died of cancer at the age of 73.

There was talk of employing a professional fund-raiser. The committee had been surprised that the appeal for funds had had such a good response. People who believed their relatives had died because of non-intervention had been prepared to give something in their memory – quite big donations. It had been merely a suggestion in the campaign literature but had proved to be a money spinner. A part-time press officer had been appointed and the committee was considering whether this might become a full time post.

'Are you at home?' I asked in another awkward silence. She said she was. I'd been there a few times when the committee first started meeting and I could imagine her in her sitting-room, a cool room with a number of good prints on the wall and some rather fussy china objects on shelves and side tables. They didn't seem to fit with her free-wheeling liberal background, certainly not the sort of upbringing she had had. She spoke of her mother often and I wondered about the relationship. She had obviously been dominated by Fay.

When I put the phone down I went into the kitchen. Margaret was still there making herself a hot drink. She poured whisky liberally into it.

'Proud of you, was she?'

I said, more acidly than I intended: 'Makes a change to have somebody who is.' Margaret turned away but I could see that she flushed. She said: 'Well, goodnight then. See you in the morning.'

Later that night I heard her get up and move around the house. The floorboards squeaked and despite constant telephone calls and an equal number of promises from the nationwide firm who had built the estate I could not get them repaired or replaced. From the low murmuring it sounded as if she had switched the television back on. I turned over and was drifting back into sleep when I heard her shouting. I was dopey and unprepared for what I found.

She was holding the phone, tears streaming down her face and shouting ... 'you bitch, you bitch, how dare you fuck my husband ...how dare you break up our marriage...I'll drag you both through the courts then where will your precious campaign ... your goodie-goodie save the oldies, hearts on your sleeves, bloody stupid ...' she started coughing and snot was running down her face. I made a grab for the phone but she held tight and it developed into a wrestling match.

I heard Maeve's voice: 'What are you talking about ...I'm putting the phone down ...what's going on.'

I finally wrestled the phone away and said: 'Don't worry Maeve. Just a matrimonial. I'll ring you tomorrow.'

Margaret was lying now on the carpet, face down, shaking. Hysterics? I thought about slapping her across the face but could not do it. I've never hit her, never in all the years. I got down awkwardly beside her, stroking her shoulder.

I said: 'Come on, don't cry.' She'd shown so little emotion throughout our marriage. I had never seen her so upset, even when her latest romance ended. Angry, cross, bad-tempered, but not weeping uncontrollably as she was now. Then I remembered that she had cried once. It was immediately after we lost the baby.

She turned over and sat up, wiping her nose with her sleeve. Her neat features were blotched, her eyes puffy. I stroked her hair and it still felt soft. She said: 'How stupid. What a fool I've been.' The admission was so unlike her.

There was a long silence. I said: 'Do you want a cup of tea ... or something stronger?' She got up and turned to help me to my feet. 'Tea, please.'

She was like a little girl, entirely biddable. I took her arm and led her into the kitchen. It was clinical, tidy, full of work surfaces and cupboards and labour saving machines. A load of washing was whirring in the utility room. I wished we were back in the farmhouse with the sofa to sink into. She sat down at the table. While my back was turned, making the tea, she said: 'I suppose you want a divorce.'

I was astonished. All the times that she had been unfaithful the question had never, ever been raised.

I said: 'Nothing has happened. Why would I want a divorce?' I remember thinking I must be very careful.

She said: 'You're obviously in love with her. I could see the way you looked at her in that programme. And she at you. It was humiliating. I could see straight away. I should think everybody who watched it would have realised immediately. I've never seen her on television before, you've grabbed all the interviews. I heard her voice on radio interviews a few times. I didn't realise she was so ...handsome.' It was a strange old-fashioned description, the kind people used about those full-bosomed Edwardian ladies, but spot on in Maeve's case. She was handsome.

Margaret said: 'From how she's always sounded on the phone and in interviews I thought small, mousy, oldish. But she isn't, is she? No wonder you've fallen for her.' Then more to herself she said: 'I didn't know I could be jealous of you.' She didn't sound angry now, just puzzled.

I gave her the tea. She sipped it slowly. I waited until she had finished and then followed her up the stairs. She turned into her bedroom and shut the door. I waited outside for a while but it was quiet.

Chapter 10

Steph insisted on making a voice contribution here. She says its chronological but I think it's self explanatory why she wants to stick her oar in. She listened to my description about that first Christmas. She is not pleased.

Steph via voice.

It was a nightmare preparing for our wedding. June 16 was the big day. James was really, really bolshie... yes you were ... go on leave me alone to do this ... the whole bloody time. Come on, I've not interfered with your history of events before - only when you asked me.

He hates my mum and I know he thinks he's got good reasons but she can be kind and although she's fussy that's just her. My sister, Dad and I got used to that ages ago and know how to handle her when she gets in one of those moods. James just gets it all wrong and they were at each other's throats the whole of that time.

But the nightmare wasn't just about organising the wedding. It was because of what was happening at work for us both. First of all the 'Stop death by numbers' campaign got really out of hand. Hislop seemed to think it was all my fault. Am I being paranoiac? Probably.

Then it just seemed as if the tap was turned on. Stories leaking all the time about the massive government population project that was supposed to be top secret and which the treasury were masterminding and which James is involved in.

Of course, all sorts of horrors came creeping out of the woodwork and a number of the doctors, prominent members of the Medical Associations, were involved. They'd been consultants on some of the pilots. So I was involved. Involved is definitely not the right word.

I was up to my neck in it. For starters there was the whole issue of the healthy baby programme. It had been going on for ages, of course, and people know about it, that's what gets me, but it all got dragged out and presented again in a totally anti way which was really shitty. Like a factory process with carefully selected couples, married or not.

Then there was the ghetto stuff that James and Mac were involved with. All the planning stuff came out at the same time. The public just believed all the scare stories. They certainly believed that the government was now about to force people to relocate to cities or sizeable towns, not just encourage them as they have been doing with good relocation deals.

It was a can of worms. For weeks it was like ... well, the media were springing some new alarming surprise on the public every single day. Screaming headlines. The Sun and Mail were the worst. Pressure groups were multiplying by the minute.

We all knew that England had to change and to change radically but in our heart of hearts we didn't really believe any of it would happen, certainly not in our lifetimes, certainly not disturbing our comfortable lifestyle patterns.

Scotland had already forged ahead in certain respects. A lot of their environmental economic strategy had been worked through and put in place. People were accepting it. The Welsh assembly was about to vote to rejoin England. They'd found it hard going economically, and wanted England to pick up the bills again but the headlines were scaring the voters.

For years government had been shelving decisions, either because they weren't certain that their party would get back in at the next election and didn't want to be unpopular or because they couldn't really believe what the economists, the environmentalists, the medics and the scientists had been warning about for such a long time. Now that they were pushing through the projects, the policies, necessary strategies, they were being attacked on all sides.

So the whole of that spring I remember being rushed off my feet, helping to make policy on the hoof, defending doctors who opened their mouths too soon, too often and without engaging their brains. I was digging people out of bigger and bigger holes.

At the same time I was getting aggro from Mum about the wedding plans and James about the futility and hypocrisy of his being involved in a church ceremony. I know he's been married before and going in for the full monty wedding was rancid but Mum was really looking forward to it ... and actually so was I.

My sister just went off and got married on a desert island or something so we all felt we'd been done out of her big day. And dad, being dad, had taken out some insurance ... annuity, don't know, years ago ... to pay for both our weddings so he was itching to get the money out and blow it on a big white wedding splurge and knees up. Mum's plans were really costly and so, so elegant and tasteful. Actually, I think James might have met her half way if they had only been a bit more kitsch.

Anyway, I was really busy at work and with the wedding. It took God knows how many Saturdays for us to decide on a wedding dress that flattered my fuller shape, as one bridal adviser kindly put it. My sister and Mum came round with me. Then there were all the other details, shoes, flowers, food, invitations, who to invite. I'm sure half of it was unnecessary but Mum insisted on the whole caboodle. What the bridesmaids should wear, the little page boy's outfit – my parents' neighbour's son was going to be that. He was very cute. Just three. We got him a little sailor's outfit. We didn't have anybody in our family, not with a little kid, that would fit the bill. It's so sad. People make such a fuss of the little ones that do make it ... particularly if there is nothing wrong with them.

James thought I didn't know what he was up to while I was working so hard. He and Mac were spending more and more time together on Saturdays. Mostly they went racing. At first I didn't mind. It kept him and my mother apart. Then I overheard a conversation on the phone and you could tell straight away that James was trying to shut Mac up and was answering in that non-committal way that people do when they're trying to cover something up.

Yes, no, no, no, yes ...stupid bugger. We had a mega row afterwards and I got it out of him. Apparently this Fern girl was going off to the races with them. I was bloody furious. I thoroughly disapprove of that woman, leaving her husband to look after the little boy all the time and screwing Mac. OK, he is very good-looking but his personality, his lies. I just cannot stand him. Anyway I know it was then that I said, quite categorically, that I didn't want Mac at the wedding and when James told me he'd already invited him and wanted him to be best man I blew my top. I managed to get agreement on his not being best man and I know, damn well, that I also said that if, if, if he came then he was not to bring Fern. On no account - she was never invited.

I saw them the minute Dad and I turned down the aisle. It just spoiled the whole day. I know this doesn't sound like it has much bearing on James putting together this report but actually it does. Because it was that day ... our wedding day ... that Mac met John Warne.

I'd invited him and his wife to the wedding. With my MA hat on I know I shouldn't because he'd been causing me endless grief but as someone I'd liked and worked with over the years, I wanted to send him an invite. I still felt guilty about dropping him in it over that interview with Hislop.

There was a lot of pressure from Mum to invite doctor contacts from the MA. Kudos. Impressing the rellies and the neighbours. She liked the idea of John Warne, too, but for different reasons. He was well known from his telly appearances. God knows why people are still so impressed with doctors but they are. And any kind of telly pundit ... well! Certainly in our neck of the Surrey suburbs it means a lot.

In Victorian times doctors were looked down on as tradesmen by the higher echelons of society. They didn't come in the front door. And surgery developed from butchery and Mum certainly didn't want any butchers at the do. Anyway, I'd invited John Warne and he accepted but made some excuse about his wife.

I saw Mac first. His hair was hanging loose and curly down his back, that bloody earring and a sharp checked jacket which he probably wears to go racing. He looked more like a rat-catcher. That she-devil was by his side. She, of course, looked a dream. Cool, elegant, in ivory ... probably chosen specifically to steal my thunder ... and with every man in the place having a good gawp at her. I think they must have come into church just ahead of us. I'd really struggled to lose weight for the big day but I can remember feeling the size of an elephant against that competition. Small, dumpy ... my eyes filled with tears. Beyond her I spotted Warne. He winked at me and smiled. He's a kind man. I struggled to smile back and then we were into the march up the aisle and I kept on smiling ...fixedly.

I could see James looking relieved as I walked towards him. He thought he'd got away with it but as I drew level I hissed: 'What the fuck's going on. I said she wasn't to come.'

The vicar stepped forward and we were off into the ceremony. I didn't get another chance until we were being driven away – horse and carriage – up the road to the reception which was being held in a Victorian gothic 'castle', now a high class hotel, about half a mile from the church. Let's just say it was a humdinger of a row. Even the horse farting in our faces for half the journey didn't raise a giggle. Just the right start to marriage and a reception which was being attended by over 140 people.

We managed to keep the peace while we stood in line with the parents, mine and his, to receive the guests but there were a lot of muttered asides whenever there was a lull. His mother made matters worse by asking who the beautiful blonde was, obviously a friend of her son's as she'd been on that side of the church.

I was pleased to see James flush red in the face and having to explain Fern and Mac. Served him bloody well right. They were just behind the deputy secretary and his wife, the Judkins, who Warne had joined. I suppose he knew them, well, knew Henry anyway.

Hislop, of course, hadn't deemed my wedding smart enough or important enough to accept but to give old Henry his due he had thanked me quite genuinely for asking him and his wife and had turned up. A good Catholic, of course, believing in the sanctity of marriage. They had a large family, probably around the same ages as James and me, some older, some a bit younger. Mrs J was a real pill and had an opinion on everything and a homily to answer even the most innocuous remark. I think she was a big noise in prison reform, the Tory party and flower arranging.

Warne shook James's hand as he came alongside and told him he was lucky to have me; 'if he'd been a young man' etcetera etcetera. He gave me a double dip kiss and we bumped noses as I wasn't expecting the second. We're strictly one cheek kissers in our family. I was embarrassed to hear mum buttering up Warne. She'd more or less ignored Judkins and his wife which wouldn't go down too well. Mrs J certainly thinks she runs the country and what she doesn't run, Henry does. Must irk her that he's Hislop's deputy.

I think Mac and Fern were going to sidle past me while all this was going on, Mac had been yakking to James, but I was buggered if I was going to let that happen. But it was Mum who stepped forward. I suppose I must have moaned on about Mac to her at some time and told her about Fern and him. Anyway she really got the bit between her teeth.

'No, I'm not shaking your hand, young man. You were told not to bring ...' she indicated Fern, who actually went a bit pink. 'And you, young lady, should be home with your husband and little boy. You're so lucky to have him, don't you know that?' Mum was red in the face, which clashed with the lavender coloured outfit.

Mac bawled out: 'We were both invited by James. Nothing to do with you, you old boot.' He steered Fern off, out of range, and through the French windows, out onto the terrace. I know I told James that if he laughed I'd kill him. Dad took Mum off to the ladies to get her to calm down and James' parents looked on and said nothing. I hate to say it, James, but they are a couple of dormice. You say so yourself. They presumably thought this was the way the smart Surrey set behaves.

To cut it short, that's when Warne and Mac met up. They sat near each other at the meal and I'm certain that they began to plot things together then. James probably knows more about what was motivating Mac ... all I know was that the bastard ruined our wedding day. And then there was that ridiculous extravagance with the champagne ... it was just so ... so ... it still makes me furious.

James via voice

It's quite useful that Warne's also included an account of our wedding. He left a big gap in his manuscript about all the campaigning he was doing that spring but the wedding day was significant for him, too. I'd like to think his version is more accurate than Steph's.

⬜⬜⬜⬜⬜

Warne's manuscript

I accepted the invitation to Stephanie Meadows' wedding. I've always had a soft spot for her and it was kind of her to ask Margaret and me. Margaret refused to come; she was depressed and I could not find a way of shaking her out of it. I did not want her to start on the anti-depressant medication route but I was worried about her. It was so unusual for her to behave in this way. I couldn't believe this was just about Maeve because since that night she had not mentioned her. She had a friend staying with her for the week-end, a friend that she had kept from her nursing days, and I felt free to be away overnight but I was not happy about her.

I found myself in the reception line behind Henry Judkins, the deputy secretary of the MA, and his wife, a heavily-built, over-bearing lady, with a flowing floral dress and a big hat. By the time I reached the happy couple I knew all there was to know about Judkins' children, their amazing achievements, the obvious genius of the only grandson, now aged 18 months, and Mrs Judkins' opinion on the government, the health service, law, order and prison reform.

She was on the board of governors of a category B prison, served as a JP and generally 'did good' in her community. Judkins shuffled slowly along beside her, his face averted.

I thought at first he was embarrassed by his wife but I suddenly realised he did not want to speak to me. I was being given the cold shoulder but his wife had not yet got the message.

I was at medical school with Judkins but we were never friends even though, at that time, I was still a practising Catholic which was a link. There weren't many of us.

Judkins was a cold fish. He did general practice for a short time but soon gave it up and joined the staff of the MA, BMA as it then was. He had obviously hoped to reach the top but Hislop is too young to leave dead men's shoes behind and Judkins will be too old to apply for the top post when it does become vacant, unless Hislop gets run over by a bus.

I said, in an effort to stop Mrs Judkins' flow: 'Lovely girl, Steph. She looks great today. I've always been very fond of her.'

Judkins reacted unexpectedly: 'Bit too pushy for my liking. Hislop's let her get above herself; given her department too much power. But then he likes his high public profile. Sets great store by public relations. We could do with a change. Maybe she and what's he called …the groom …James … if they have a family … that could shake things up.'

He looked at me: 'You've been creating a song and dance, lately, yourself. Never off the television, are you? You should know better than to rock the boat. You've let down your colleagues.' So that was it. I was about to retaliate but a flunkey was busy asking names and pinning labels on us.

I kissed Steph when I reached her and shook James's hand. 'Lucky man.' Steph blushed.

Mrs Judkins was ahead, having her hand clasped firmly by Steph's mother who, in one fluid action, moved her smartly on to her husband. Judkins got the same treatment. I almost got by before she said: 'I've seen you so much on television; I think you're quite right to speak out. Someone's got to save us oldies.' She obviously wanted an instant contradiction but I can't do that sort of thing. I don't have that sort of small talk. She gushed on for longer than she should have while the queue behind me waited impatiently.

I went on into the reception. I knew one or two of the other MA people but they made it fairly obvious beyond the desultory greeting that they didn't want to talk to me. I wished that Margaret had come. I went and sat on a window seat and looked around the room. The girl who had turned so many heads in church and her partner, a good-looking dark-haired boy, were now speaking to the groom.

Suddenly Steph's mother's voice was heard loud above the babble. 'No, I'm not going to shake your hand. You were told ...' the room went silent. The young man shouted: 'Fern and I were invited by James. Nothing to do with you, you old boot.'

He took the girl's arm and steered her through the French windows onto the terrace. The babble in the room slowly picked up again to its previous pitch, with only a few sidelong glances at the couple.

I watched them outside on the terrace for a moment and then got up and followed them into the garden. My thinking was that we could all be pariahs together. He struck me as a bit of a maverick, cocky and self-assured. Maybe too much of him would be a bad thing but by that time anyone would have been preferable to my splendid isolation.

They were standing on their own, the girl still icy cool, sipping her champagne. I said: 'I'm John Warne, a doctor pal of Steph's.'

The boy introduced himself as Mac and the girl as Fern. No surnames.

'Pretty name,' I said.

Fern said: 'Aren't you the one ... I know, I remember. The doctor who's leading that campaign, Stop Death by Numbers. It was my baby they used as an example of saving the lives of little children right at the beginning ...'

Mac said: 'Your campaign hasn't helped James and me one bit. We're in danger of losing our high-flying civil service careers.' He said it with a certain amount of animosity.

'How come?'

Mac explained briefly. I was interested, said: 'So they are back-pedalling? We thought they might. What are you doing now?'

'More number crunching but not on anything nearly as contentious or interesting.' He stopped, evidently not prepared to say any more but then muttered: 'You may be getting to them, you know. A few other things have been pulled out of the overall plan, my friends at the Treasury tell me.'

A flunkey approached to marshal us into the room for the wedding breakfast and I didn't have a chance then to ask anything else.

There was a kerfuffle over a seat and table place for Fern but she stood elegantly waiting for a couple of minutes before sinking into the seat that had been set for Mac. I was two places up on the opposite side of a long table. My heart sank as I saw that I had Mrs Judkins on my right hand side. She was in a quandary. Mac was persona non grata and he was directly opposite. Her husband had obviously told her about me so that cut off any conversation in that direction which left her to talk to her own husband for the duration of the meal.

Mac said loudly as everybody sat down: 'Anybody here interested in racing? I want to know what won the 2.30 at Lingfield. I had a horse running and I didn't bring my mobile in from the car.' He certainly had self-confidence.

The other guests on our table looked sideways at him, embarrassed, waiting for someone else to make a move or for general conversation to begin. Only one, a jolly faced man with a high complexion said anything. He called from further down the table: 'What's it called?'

Mac said: 'Civil Disobedience.' He added: 'By Mandarin out of It's a Riot.'

'Clever name,' I said.

Fern said: 'Not Mac's idea, uncivil servant though he is. It was the breeder's, wasn't it?'

Mac looked slightly crest-fallen. 'Yes.'

The red faced man with a spectacular beer belly welling over his trouser line, called: 'I've got an up and down cross double at that meeting. We'll check later but let's get on with the grub first.'

I asked more about Mac's horse and his interest in racing. He said he'd had a schoolmaster who had got him keen on racing and then he'd been encouraged by a lecturer of his when he was at the LSE. At first he'd like the mathematics of betting but now he really liked being involved with owning a horse. He qualified it. Part of a horse. I asked: 'Which bit.'

'The nose, I've decided. I like to think our horse might win by my nose.'

The topic kept us occupied until after the main course – a chicken dish that tasted of nothing in particular. Fern sat passively, toying with her food, until Mrs Judkins, curiosity getting the better of her, asked where she lived.

Fern said: 'Putney. Next door to Mac, actually.'

'Oh, not together then?'

'No,' said Fern. 'We're next door neighbours. I live with my husband and little son and Mac rents a house that James ... the bridegroom ... owns.'

'And couldn't your husband and little boy come?'

Fern leaned towards her confidentially: 'Actually, they weren't invited. Neither was I officially. But you see, Mac's my bit on the side so he was coming and thought he'd bring me along. It gives us time for a bit of sex. I find a threesome makes my marriage work better. Have you ever tried it?'

Mac and I stopped talking. He grinned broadly and I'm afraid I laughed out loud. Mrs Judkins was red in the face. Embarrassment? Rage? She choked on the remains of her chicken and I thumped her on the back.

Judkins said, through gritted teeth: 'Leave her alone.' Mac started laughing, then choking, too.

'An epidemic,' I said to nobody in particular. The other diners at the table stopped talking to try to find out what was going on. Those nearest who had overheard something began whispering.

The man who had expressed interest in horse racing got up from his place and came down the line of chairs.

He said to Mac: 'If you've finished choking on that dreadful chicken come out to the car park. We'll try and get some results.'

I said to Fern: 'My wife had the same idea as you. About triangles, I mean. I can't say I was happy about it but we are still together. I'm not sure what that proves.'

Fern took a sip of wine and looked at me and smiled. I could see she did not give a damn what anybody thought.

She said: 'My mother was the same. She went off with one of them when I was 19. I think there were others. Probably still are. She's a complete cow. Must be in my genes.' She had a rather low, throaty voice.

Mac and the man came back. Mac was clearly exultant. 'The little bugger won,' he said. 'We should have been there.' He stopped a waiter. 'Champagne,' he said. 'All round. Not the crap imitation stuff we had before. The real McCoy.' There were 140 other guests. Fern tried to stop him but he wouldn't hear of it. 'I had a grand on at ten to one.'

I was amazed and could only wonder at what civil servants earn nowadays.

I wanted to talk to him before I left. I had a long journey back to Devon. I needed to get back into London to catch the train and had planned to leave after the meal. I leaned across the table to ask him if I could have a quiet word with him as I had to go.

'Better do it now,' said Mac 'I can feel an under-the-table episode coming on. Be warned, my girl. You may have to carry me up to bed.'

Fern smiled, cat-like. 'I shall leave you where you fall,' she said.

The desserts and Mac's champagne arrived at the same time. He got up and said loudly: 'Enjoy it and our very good health to the bride and groom.' He included Fern in the toast by gesturing at her. People looked puzzled, one or two cheered. The Judkins sat stony faced, not touching their glasses.

Fern leaned forward: 'It's OK. Infidelity isn't catching and certainly not from a glass of champagne.'

Mac got up, taking his glass, and I followed him out onto the terrace.

Much later on when I was on the train I turned over in my mind what he had told me about the Newcastle pilot. It was at Paddington, waiting for the high speed connection that I decided finally that I would break my journey at Bristol. I wanted Maeve to know what I had learned.

□□□□□

Maeve's diary

Diary entry: June 17.

****!!!! Definitely an eight of ten, maybe a 9. He stayed the whole night and it was wonderful. He is like a little boy at times, needing so much love, affection and cuddles. It was only at lunch-time when we went out to the pub by the river that he had a bit of a guilt-trip. He says it's his Catholic past. I bit my tongue. I cannot stop thinking about him. I was so surprised when he rang from the train and said he was definitely coming. I really thought he would call it off. Back to business: he thinks the government is going to drop the non-intervention policies and he believes they are going to do something else about the population crisis. It is something to do with ensuring the birth rate goes up and encouraging immigrant women who were not affected by the contamination to have more children. He met a man at the wedding who works for the Ministry of Health and he is going to let John have more details. I hope it means that we can continue working together ... as well as everything else. I **really enjoy** our working relationship!

CHAPTER 11

Via Voice

It is pretty obvious what Warne and Maeve got up to that night. Fortunately they spare us the details.

I didn't see much of Mac after our wedding. Steph saw to that. She can deny it if she likes but she kept a tight rein and there were no more outings to the races. Fern's name was strictly verboten. In any case I had returned to my own department, Lifestyle. They wanted me back after the fiasco of the Newcastle pilot and I was given another project, not nearly as interesting ... or important. Mac remained at Health.

I guess it must have been a couple of months, late August, before we went out for a drink. I think he texted me and we fixed to meet at a pub down by the river, the big one just over Putney bridge. Star and Garters? I know I was a bit frayed. Steph had just missed a period and we thought she might be pregnant.

I should have been overjoyed. After all, we're the lucky ones but I'm afraid my immediate reaction was that it would mean moving house as her flat wouldn't be big enough and there was no way she was going to live in my house next door to Fern. It came as a shock. I didn't feel ready for fatherhood. Does anyone? And it's such a high risk.

When I got there Mac wasn't anywhere to be seen. I thought at first he'd stood me up and I was pissed off. I got a beer and went and sat at a table by the river wall. One of the bar tenders was collecting glasses and he came over to my table, although there were no empties on it.

He said: 'Are you waiting for Mac?' I said I was. He said: 'He wants you to meet him up the street at Il Positano ... it's an Italian restaurant on the right hand side. Something cropped up.'

I found the restaurant and Mac was sitting at a table in the gloom at the back. It seemed a pity on such a sunny evening. He looked rough. He'd lost weight and had a rash on his neck. His hair looked squalid, still scraped back in the pony tail, and the earring was in place. He had a bottle of wine on the table, of which he had already drunk half.

He told me at once that he and Fern had split up a few weeks before. She'd finally got Johnnie to agree to move house. 'Something much bigger, better and grander in Richmond. That probably applies to a new boy friend, too.' He said it bitterly.

She'd gone back to work. He was obviously taking it badly and it didn't help when I tried to point out that he should view the whole episode as one of life's better experiences.

I said unfeelingly: 'It was never going to last. Ms Mercenary.' Poor sap told me that I'd got it all wrong. It wasn't Fern who had broken it off, it was him.

I'm afraid part of my reaction to news of the dumping was tempered by the thought that maybe Steph and I could now go back and live in my house. The drawback was I'd have to give Mac notice which would be difficult when the poor bloke was so obviously struggling.

But it wasn't that he wanted to talk about. He was nervous, kept looking past me at the people walking up and down the street.

I laughingly said: 'Are you afraid you're being followed? I should think that was far more likely when you were screwing Fern. No embittered husband in the background now, is there?'

'Why, why do you say that? Why do you think I'm being followed?' He spoke vehemently.

I hadn't laid down the groundwork for a long night out and said I needed to phone Steph but he wouldn't let me use my mobile. Kept saying it was better that I didn't. He was really twitchy.

There were two other couples in and they were already half way through their meals. He kept saying how quiet it was, that it wasn't what he'd planned.

We ordered another bottle of red. I said, hoping to jolly him up: 'OK, let's have it. What's eating you? Is it just about Fern?'

He was silent for maybe as much as a minute. It seemed a long pause. He said: 'I've let someone have some information ... classified. It's high risk stuff. Dynamite. I think they might be on to me.'

I didn't need to ask who. MI5 had been very busy throughout Whitehall since the Newcastle fiasco and the other leaks.

Every single bit of paper, every policy, was graded for different levels of security. Even low grade papers carried weasel words or phrases that identified them. Enormous lengths were being taken to ensure that information wasn't leaked. The result of the official investigation into Newcastle kept being delayed. The government did not want the publicity. There had been other considerations which I have still not got to the bottom of.

Mac and I had already blotted our copybooks in terms of security. We'd been officially cleared but it was entered in our files and mud sticks. I couldn't believe Mac would compromise himself so soon. By having this conversation he was compromising me. I felt a hot flush of apprehension spread up my spine to the base of my head.

We earned high salaries with benefits of all kinds and were pretty well protected but we had to behave ourselves. There were enough regulations in place to get rid of us instantly if we didn't.

He said that he had stumbled upon something while working on statistics for the healthy baby programme. I said I certainly didn't want to know. He said that he was thinking of 'dropping out' for a while. 'They owe me some sick leave. And I've got holiday. I thought I might go abroad for a week or two. Then if the story blows I'm officially out of the way.'

'What do you think the person you gave the info to will do with it?'

'I think he will give it to the media.'

He paused, then said quietly: 'It might bring the government down. It's part of a highly secret project. Far more hush-hush than the Population Adjustment Programme. A lot of the schemes to do with that have been reached by what they like to call public consultation. They've been well publicised. The reasons have been debated, voted on, accepted. None of this stuff has ever been part of the democratic process. The theories, yes. Endless ethical debates. All coming to the same conclusion. It cannot and must not happen. But it is happening. It has been happening and for far longer than anyone could have imagined. There was a loophole in the law which they didn't properly close.'

'Could they trace the leak back to you?'

'That's what I'm not sure about. I copied some info onto a disk and took it home. I know, I know. I just wanted to look at it. I did it late one evening and a security guard questioned why I was still in the office. That will be down in the book. I don't know if someone checked back on the computer whether they could find any sort of record. I guess they could find out when the material was accessed, tie up the dates. It was fringe to what I was working on.'

The couple nearest to us got up to go. I spoke softly. 'Why the hell did you give it to ...whoever.' I had absolutely no idea who it was.

Mac said: 'I was pissed off. To tell you the truth I've been looking to get out. The Newcastle flop really got to me. I know, you know, it's done our careers no good even though it was nothing to do with us. Moment of madness ... and something else. I'm really worried about what is going on. Somebody's got to put a stop to it. I tell you ...'

I said quickly, no don't , I don't want to know.

He looked at me. 'I need a go-between. The bloke needs some positive proof before he can use it. I've told him I'll get it. I think I can get hold of some names, some addresses. I can leave it up to him ... his group ... to verify the ... I'm sure I'm being watched. I daren't get in touch again because it will almost certainly be traced back. At the moment I don't think I'm suspected of anything because nothing's happened.

'It's only when the media gets hold of it that the witch-hunt will start but I've got to cover my tracks. You see, you actually know the bloke I've given the info to ... that doctor ... Warne ... he was at your wedding. We got talking about the other stuff ... Newcastle and the immigrant women. About why the population programme is such a big thing ... he told me more about the background to the 'stop deaths' campaign. I like him. He's a good man. He said he'd been chairman of a medical ethics committee once. You don't come across many of his sort ... decent ... people with principles. When I came across this stuff ... well, he seemed the obvious one ... and it's got to come out. It must be stopped. It's already gone too far.'

I had never imagined that Mac could be so passionate about anything. Or that he could do such a stupid thing. He was under strain. He was obviously really upset about Fern. He didn't look well. If I was a psychiatrist I'd say he was showing all the signs of manic depression.

I was angry that he was daring to ask me to get involved. I told him again that I didn't want anything to do with what he was doing, what he was planning and said I had to go. He actually held on to my arm.

I didn't want a scene. I tried to change the subject. I told him about Steph's pregnancy. He looked at me strangely. 'Sure it's yours?' I got really angry then. 'What the hell ...'

'Keep your hair on. No, sorry.' It was the first time he'd smiled. He almost laughed and then to my horror started gabbling away. 'That's what it's about. Don't you see. It's cloning. They've been doing it. Oh, not in any sanctioned government programme to do with cells to help cure diseases. Therapeutic cloning. That's been going on for ages. No – real cloned humans. It's the only way, they think, of keeping any kind of balance in the population. The contamination wiped out so many people's chances. And they need the managerial, professional, brainier classes; it's like Nazi Germany but they think they can justify this because of the low birth rate. There are so many infertile people, men and women. So many men and women whose reproductive organs have been damaged.

'You're one of the few ... so far ... but then, sorry, but it's early days. And Fern and Johnnie ... Fern.'

He banged his fist down on the table. 'I don't want to think about what they've done. And that little kid of their's. It's not as if he's really right. He may not be able to contribute later on. May not reproduce. But that's what they want. It's sick, sick.

'That's what started me off. I came across all these categories of childless people. People in their teens, twenties and thirties. Then there are the people who might be able to have kids but don't want to and the gay population which has more than doubled since the start of this century with people far less afraid to own up to their sexuality and refusing to compromise. Then I came across this section of statistics that seemed to indicate that there were clusters around the country where the figures for live births, viable babies were way above the national average. I couldn't work it out at first.'

All the time I was trying to stop him. I didn't want to hear. But his words kept tumbling out. More people were coming into the restaurant now, clattering about, hanging up coats, seating themselves. He kept talking. It seemed to go back years. Back to when there was this loophole in the law and some doctor had started experimenting, seeing if he could help childless couples. That had been stopped in a notorious court case, stopped again in an appeal to the House of Lords, although nobody was quite sure if he hadn't succeeded in cloning a baby which came to term before the law cracked down.

In 2002 permission had been given so that the foetal route could be used to develop therapeutic cloning. Very strict controls had been put in place and nothing had changed on that score. Officially.

Now Mac said he had evidence that the government had secretly sanctioned a privately funded trial programme for cloned humans within the last four years. He told me that there were special maternity homes, baby care units, special nurseries, special pre-school facilities set up to look after the cloned kids and that immigrants had been used. He wasn't yet sure if some of the children had stayed with the families of the genetic parent or given to approved families for adoption. He was sure others with cash and influence had gone in for cloning their own child. He started to say something about Fern but stopped. He said it was the addresses of the special maternity homes that he wanted to get for Warne.

I said, appalled: 'The children will all look the same.'

Mac said: 'Don't be daft. That's science fiction. They'll be cloning from cells from one of the genetic parents. Nobody will be able to tell. It's a bit like they used to do when people donated sperm and family planning doctors deliberately didn't keep records of the donors. It was disgusting. A lot of people grew up not knowing, or ever being able to find out, who their fathers were or what genes they had inherited. It's odds on that there will be cases where a donor-created child will have married their half brother or sister unwittingly. The donors, who fathered any number of children, would have been from within quite a small area. Medical schools. Friends of the medic who ran the clinics. That sort of thing. People have tried to find out ...' he broke off abruptly.

Cloning does scare me but I couldn't work out why Mac was so perturbed, seemed to care so much. He was the last person whom I would have termed ethical. He had never struck me as having much of a social conscience . He was really churned up about this.

I don't know much about his background because he'd told me so many different things ... maybe there was some religion in there somewhere. Roman Catholic? It was possible. Pro-Life? But logically that lot ought to be in favour if the human race is in danger of dying out.

Did I care about human cloning? Yes, I did. Unethical. Big brother. Realms of science fiction. Would Steph care? Yes. Straw poll ... I looked round the restaurant. Mostly thirty somethings. Maybe not if they really wanted a family and couldn't have one. Steph and I were lucky. I didn't want to get involved. I didn't want to be part of the battle to get it stopped. I certainly did not want to lose my job.

I told him that I wouldn't be his go-between. At last he seemed to accept my refusal. We ate and drank and parted, me paying the bill. He was strapped for cash because of a horse, couple of horses, that had let him down badly. What was new?

I worried all the way home; not just about what he had told me but also about what Steph would say when I got in. I didn't want a cross-examination, with the emphasis on the cross. I was lucky; she had had a late night, too, and arrived after me, full of apologies. She'd got trapped into going out to dinner with the inner circle of the consultants' committee – the politicians who really stitched things up behind the scenes.

The next I heard was that Mac was off sick. I'd needed to get in touch professionally. I then tried to phone him at home, my house, but I could get no answer. This must have been the middle of September.

Chapter 12

Warne's manuscript

I phoned Maeve to tell her that I wouldn't be able to see her. It was a difficult call. She was very indignant. She said: 'What do you mean? I thought it was all settled. It's just hysterics on her part.'

I said: 'No, she's in hospital. Psychiatrist says it could be for a while. I can't leave her. She tried to commit suicide, not very efficiently.'

I know I sounded helpless and hopeless. I'd finally told Margaret that I was leaving her and that I wanted a divorce. She'd started to scream but the scream didn't come properly and she lost her breath and fell heavily taking me down with her.

Maeve said: 'It's blackmail. You know it is. Women ... wives ... do it all the time. So do men ... people who want their own way, want to be in control. I expect I could do it if I tried but I never have. I'd find it demeaning. But I'm not going to argue with you. If you think you must stay until she's got over this hysteria, well, you do that. But she'll be just the same at the end of it all.'

I said, hoping for some sympathy: 'I hurt my leg. She fell on it. It's bloody painful.'

Maeve laughed. 'You shouldn't have been so gallant. But you are, aren't you? A gallant knight. Principles. All that sort of thing. Ethical, stoical but not very brave.' She changed the subject and talked about a response the campaign office had received from a government minister. It was in a written answer to a parliamentary question that we had got a sympathetic MP to ask. It at last gave the comparison figures, year by year since the turn of the century.

There had been a 25 per cent increase in the number of deaths among the 70 year olds and over in the twenty years but the statistics also showed that there had been a percentage increase in the numbers of men and women who had reached that age. The proportion of elderly in the population was now greater than at any other time. One in five people was over 70. It did not mention targets or non-intervention. It was simply statistics.

I said: 'It doesn't alter the fact that the principle of having targets is wrong. Does it give the definition of elderly?'

'Anybody over pension age. 70. But that's what's so wrong. Seventy year olds aren't old any more. They have to work until that age to pay for their pensions and their health insurance. This country would grind to a halt if it didn't have 'the senior workforce'. There certainly aren't enough youngsters to take on all the work. And there won't be. Maybe we should get the births figures for the last twenty years?'

I hesitated. What Mac had told me only a few days before had come as a shock. We met at Heathrow, terminal 2, where Mac seemed to think we would be safe. He had been twitchy, speaking rapidly, anxious to pass on the information. I asked him for proof and he promised it. I haven't seen it yet.

I know that medically cloned humans have been possible for a long time and I've read a great many scientific papers on the subject over the years. I always thought that governments world-wide would stick to the 2005 agreement, though I'm aware that the cult Clonaid are insisting that cloned children are still alive, in their teens in the USA.

It is possible that this is also true in Britain despite it being unlawful. Couples are so desperate for children. An Italian doctor made a song and dance about a baby he said he had cloned which was born in 2003 and then he said it had died.

I said, tentatively: 'We could widen our remit. We could turn ourselves into more of a lobby group on the wider issues of population.'

Maeve said: 'We aren't getting as many donations now and the butcher downstairs at headquarters keeps asking how long we'll need the office. It seems he wants to sell up and there is a property development company interested in that whole parade of shops. Good job we decided against the professional fund-raiser and didn't make the press officer full time. She wants to cut down her hours anyway. She's got another part time job with one of the really well-heeled animal charities. A damn donkey sanctuary.'

I said: 'We'll have to talk to the committee. See if they are interested in taking a wider look at how rapidly things are changing in this country, particularly in the balance of the population. I had a chat not long ago with a very clever guy, statistician, at the department of health. He filled me in on a lot of things that are going on.'

Maeve said that I had told her. I had forgotten that. Of course, our first night that we'd spent together after the wedding.

I said: 'Look, Maeve, I'm really sorry about all this but honestly, I can't leave Margaret in this state. It will all come out all right. I promise. I'll see you on Thursday night?'

Thursday was the next committee meeting. It was going to be a full agenda with a lot of decisions to be made.

She said coldly: 'See you then. Don't worry. I'm sure things will turn out OK.'

'Love you lots,' I said, sounding ridiculous. Why wasn't she angrier? I deserved it.

I tried Mac's home telephone number without success, only the anonymous answer phone. I didn't leave a message and then I tried the mobile but it was switched off. Finally I phoned the health department.

Mr Fish wasn't in today, I was told and when I pressed further the woman who had answered started asking who I was, what it was that I wanted to know, could she help. I fobbed her off.

I went to see Margaret in the hospital. I felt so guilty. It was so out of character for her to behave in this way. She had always been so in control and this cloying dependence unnerved me.

The drugs they had given her had made her face puffy. She was sitting out on the verandah of the mental health unit at the hospital in Taunton and had obviously made some attempt at putting on make-up. Her lipstick was smudged. She was normally so precise, so organised. She put up her cheek to be kissed and asked me if I'd eaten that day. I sensed danger and tried to make small talk but I found it difficult. Suddenly she took the initiative and told me about people who were in the unit. She talked as if nothing had occurred between us, as if we had always talked in this chatty, familiar married-people kind of way.

I said, plucking up courage: 'I haven't changed my mind about our getting a divorce, you know, when you're back on your feet. The doctors think you'll be over this soon. You're a very strong woman, you know.'

Her reply astounded me. She smiled : 'Don't be bloody daft, darling. We can't split up. Not now. I'm going to have a baby.'

I looked at her aghast. She continued to prattle on: 'It's not unheard of at my age, not these days. I'm only 47. I'm going to go to a fertility clinic. A nurse here says that there is no reason why I can't have a baby at my age. I asked Dr Tanner. He thinks it's a good idea. You don't have to pay anything these days for fertility treatment.'

She was looking at me brightly, expecting an answer.

Psychiatry was never one of my special interests but now I wished I'd paid more attention to my student lectures.

'Delighted? I knew you would be. I just want to make sure that you'll tell that woman, that Dunlop woman, that you're going to be a dad. You'll have responsibilities. You can't continue on that committee any longer.'

She smiled at me. 'I'm sure she'll be very disappointed because you must have been a tower of strength this last year but she'll get over it. What a good job you didn't get involved with her. Sexually, I mean. I'm sure that's what she was hoping for.'

So the affair with Maeve had been buried somewhere deep in her psyche. I had to see her psychiatrist. She was obviously in a really bad way.

Margaret said: 'I'll get the nurses to tell Dr Tanner you're here, if you like. I'm sure he'll want to talk to you about how we arrange everything. He'll have to refer me on to the fertility clinic.'

Everything she said sounded so false, so unlike her. The words she was choosing, the coyness, the flirtatiousness. It had to be at least 20 years since I'd received the treatment.

A nurse came onto the verandah. She said: 'I've been looking all over for you, Mrs Warne. It's time for your medication.'

She said hello to me, in an off-hand way, no warmth and said: 'She's doing fine. Coming on well.'

I wanted to shout at her. This isn't fine. I asked to see the medication but it was a drug I would need to look up.

Margaret told the nurse that I wanted to see Dr Tanner.

'I'll see if I can find him. He may have gone off duty.'

I said: 'I'll come with you.' The thought of listening to any more of Margaret's bizarre plans unnerved me. I was already walking away when she got up and followed me. 'Aren't you going to kiss me goodbye? These men ...' The nurse looked embarrassed as I pecked at her cheek.

Walking down the corridor with the nurse I said: 'She seems to be in a bad way. She keeps babbling on about making arrangements to have a baby.'

'Yes, she said that to me. Funny, isn't it?'

'It's no laughing matter. I must see her doctor. I've never seen her like this before, she's normally so self restrained, so in control.'

The psychiatrist was in his room. I introduced myself again although I had met Tanner briefly when Margaret was admitted. He was a young man to be in charge of the unit - maybe I was getting old. He was very short and I must have been a good six inches taller. He answered my first question aggressively. It set the tone for the rest of the conversation in which I found myself being pushed into the role of the errant husband responsible for Margaret's present condition.

In desperation I asked: 'But what about her wanting to have a baby. Thinking she can have one. She's ...' I just stopped myself from saying 'completely off her rocker', aware that Tanner would find the phrase more evidence of my insensitivity.

Tanner looked at me: 'She's clearly very much in love with you and has been badly hurt. She is doing anything and everything she can to win you back. Of course, the baby is just an obsession but at the moment I'm prepared to let her indulge this fantasy. She's only 47. Women of her age are having children. With help, of course. It's quite possible.'

I said: 'Margaret didn't want children. Not after the baby died. Afterwards we stopped trying.'

He said: 'Others have used different fertility methods to achieve their families. You must know that. She seems to feel she is unloved, unattractive and clearly is missing the sexual side of your marriage which she tells me ceased when you began an affair?'

My anger and exasperation boiled over at this latest piece of fiction. I said: 'I think there's some things you should get straight.'

Tanner cut in. 'I'm running late for a meeting. Nothing is ever black and white and it is obvious to me that your wife's condition is not recent. She lacks self-worth, self-value and is possibly very jealous of your success as a doctor, a medical politician and something of a media celebrity. She's felt left out and now it has all come to a head. She was obviously drinking too much but we're doing very well on that front. She's making desperate attempts to win you back. Look, I'm sorry but I must go. Make an appointment with my secretary and we'll discuss this further.'

I wanted to kick the self-satisfied little prat up the backside as he turned to gather up papers from his desk and swiftly left the room.

Driving home my mind was in turmoil. I didn't know she had a drink problem. I tried to visualise the number of bottles collected every Tuesday in the green box at the end of our drive. More than usual? I didn't think I'd seen her drunk but then she was usually in bed and recently it had been her own. I'd been coming back late from Bristol and would not have known if she had drunk herself to sleep.

I found I had driven the motorway on automatic pilot and suddenly found myself passing the speed limit signs into town and driving far faster than I should. I braked apprehensively and glanced in my mirror. There were no police cars.

At home I went straight for the whisky bottle. There wasn't much left and I found another in the kitchen cupboard. I was not on duty until the morning and I felt it was a night I needed to make the strongest possible attempt to get drunk. I had drunk half the bottle when I heard a tapping sound at the French windows leading out on to the small patch of garden. It was so slight that at first I thought it was a branch but it persisted. I went to see what it was and was startled by a face looking in at me.

Mac pushed his face right up at the glass. He looked rough.

'Quick, shut all the curtains,' he said when I let him in. He stood to one side of a dresser we had in the dining room end, so that he could not be seen through any of the windows. 'They may have followed me.'

I did as I was asked. It looked like I'd got another lunatic on my hands. I poured him half a glass of neat Scotch. The boy was obviously unwell. He had lost more weight and all the bounce had gone out of him. He kept saying he must not stay long, that he'd got the proof I needed. 'It must be stopped. You must get it stopped.'

I told him to hang on. I needed time to look at what Mac had brought but he was fidgeting. I said that he had better leave it with me.

Mac showed me a list of addresses where he said the children were born and where the special baby units and nurseries had been built; they all seemed to be immigration centres.

'They are not manufactured in a laboratory, then?' I didn't mean to be flippant.

He said: 'I'm sure they could grow a laboratory full but it seems they used immigrant women who need the cash. The cells were implanted in embryo form and carried through a full term pregnancy. At first the women kept the children. Later they carried the cloned cell of a family which wanted to adopt. They were well looked after, produced the babies who went for adoption with the genetic family and the women then returned to their own families who were given good class accommodation in large cities, mostly in the north.

'You know that Newcastle pilot that almost got James and me the sack? One of the elements in that was to provide housing for immigrants. I told you, didn't I? I've gone back over some of the stuff we were evaluating then. That doesn't give us any more proof. Really, it boils down to going and having a look at these immigration centres. Even just one of them. I can't go. I'm being watched. I've seen them following me around but I've given them the slip. I don't think they know I know you.

'I thought you might have a pal with all your connections with the Medical Associations. I thought there might be someone, I don't know, research guy, paediatrician ... you know better than I do. You mentioned someone who'd written a research paper that made you suspect there might have been a human clone. Someone, somewhere must know something.'

I said: 'You'd better leave it with me. There is no way I can go public on what you've got so far.' I added: 'You look ill. Have you seen a doctor?'

'I'm seeing one now.' Mac laughed feebly but insisted he was all right. He added: 'But if anything happens to me you must get in touch with James Fields. I've told him some of this. He knows I've told you. He doesn't want to get involved but I think he will if it's really needed. Wife hates me, of course. The wedding ...they're expecting their first child. I think they'll kick me out of the house in Putney.'

I wondered then why Mac was so keen for the information to get out into the public domain. What was his agenda? I've been around politics, medical politics, not to know when someone has their own agenda.

The phone rang. It was the hospital telling me that Margaret had discharged herself.

Tanner came on. He sounded belligerent. He had been going to suggest discharging her in a couple of days, anyway, and it was nothing to worry about. Please would I let them know that she had returned home safely. 'If not ...' he hesitated.

I asked acidly: 'Police?'

Tanner blustered. Surely not necessary. He was sure she would come home perfectly OK. One of the nurses had said she had ordered a taxi. She had taken her medication with her. I must make sure that she kept taking it. He'd see her as an out-patient in a week's time.

Mac took fright. 'I've got to get out. I mustn't be found here. You haven't seen me, do you hear?'

I told him to calm down but he was gone, out the way he had come in and I heard a car start up further down the road, wheels spinning in a fast start.

He had left the print-outs with the information, statistics and addresses and the disk and I locked them into the wall safe. I looked at the glasses on the table and took them out to the kitchen and swilled them under the tap. I put the glasses away and replaced the whisky bottle in the dining room.

I heard a car and opened the front door. Margaret was getting out of a taxi. She shouted at me: 'You'll have to pay. I haven't any money.' She had her dressing gown on, over a nightdress, slippers on her feet.

She said: 'I've decided to come home to start having the baby.' The taxi driver looked embarrassed. 'She's been on about that ever since she got in ... she doesn't look ... well, sorry, mate, but ...'

I said: 'It's OK. I'll take care of her.' I paid the man much more than he asked for.

□□□□□

Via Voice

That's about as far as Warne's material goes. I'm not sure how he was planning to publish it when he'd got all the later events in place. He kept switching styles so maybe he was trying out a kind of faction. All the information that I've got shows it's a fairly accurate account of what went on.

I've got to get on with the official report. Although they've put the deadline back yet again ... February 1 next year ... there is still a lot to do. A great deal happened, of course, which is not appropriate to deal with in this way.

PART 2

CHAPTER 1

The idea came from Jawad Mahmood. They called him 'brains' just like they had when the three of them were at school and the others caught the habit. Certainly two of the others were as intelligent but their fanaticism marred their ability to think laterally as Jawad did.

The rest of them had been brain-washed, fanatical with one-track minds. Kill the infidels, kill the infidels. Jawad in his heart tried hard not to find this annoying and prayed that he could share their uncomplicated commitment. He shared all their ideals but he knew, deep inside himself, that it would be a long slow process and even then there would always be people of other faiths or worse, no faith at all, in the world. He was unable to subscribe whole-heartedly to the concept that Islam would conquer and rule the whole world within the short time span that al-Qaeda had decreed.

Jawad used the name Khalid to outsiders. There was a white girl, Karen, who had shown interest in him and he had taken her back to the barely furnished house in Staines that they were living in, They had all had sex with her on the stained mattress with the leaking stuffing in the back bedroom. She seemed to find it exhilarating that they were Muslims and that they treated her roughly and called her pig and infidel. Later he was told to stop her coming round. He roughed her up and left her badly beaten in a multi-storey car park. He told her if she squealed to anyone they would all come looking for her and she knew the score, knew what that meant. One of her mates had died in a park nearby after she said she'd go to the police when the sex had turned really nasty.

He had called himself by yet another name when he was with the girl. Not Khalid. Naseem. He rather liked the challenge of remembering who he was, sometimes from hour to hour. It was a good exercise. Sometimes he chanted under his breath. I am Khalid, a militant terrorist. I will conquer the infidel.

They moved after that. He and his sister rented an end-of-terrace house on a small estate at Hemel Hempstead and pretended they were a married couple. N had said find somewhere that looks like you are rich people. He did not mean stinking, gold jewellery, Mercedes rich. He meant reasonably affluent. Middle-class and professional were not concepts N really understood. He understood money, though. Jawad's sister went to work in a travel agents in the town. The others came and went. They told the neighbours that they were family. Jawad or Khalid and Sula got quite friendly with the neighbours in a sort of 'putting out the dustbins' 'taking in flower deliveries' kind of way.

Jawad had got a degree, 2.1, in bio-chemistry at Sheffield, pleasing his parents who ran a street corner post office and shop in the city. They attended the degree ceremony. That was in 2003. He had already joined the Islamic militant group by then although his parents had no knowledge of it. They were pleased he spent what they thought were holidays in Pakistan and had tried to fix him up with a wife over there but he had refused to meet the girl or her family. He needed to be single, not have the expense or worry of a wife, of kids.

By 2005 he had been to Pakistan eight times, taking different routes; ferry or train and then plane from a variety of European airports. He had worked hard to save money, taking any job he could get. There had been money too to help him from the Imam at the Mosque. It came from al-Qaeda, he was told. In Pakistan he had crossed the border into Afghanistan and had been trained extensively how to use explosives.

During the daytime when Sula was working members of the cell met up and generally messed about, in Hemel, Luton and Watford. They hung around at places like the Laser Quaser centre. They spent a lot of time there practising target shooting and fooling about, talking to Muslim youngsters and they tried to convert them to militant Islam, sometimes with a modicum of success. The manager, another Pakistani, knew what they were up to but did not want to antagonise them. They helped out when he was short-staffed. They were all good with kids, white, black, Asian, whatever. Jawad, who was very good-looking, had quite a fan club of teenage girls.

The trial in 2006 of the seven warriors from Surrey and Sussex was a watershed. The cell was excited, exulted at the publicity. Once in the trial it had been mentioned that the targets considered by the group included public utilities. Jawad was already thinking along those lines. When he had been doing his degree he had come across what had happened to the water supply at a place in Cornwall, not far from where his family had once had a holiday when he was about 9 years old.

The place was Camelford and he collected as much information as he could about the effects the contamination was supposed to have had on the population. The long-term effects. He knew originally the official inquiries had denied any long-term effect on the residents who had used the water from the holding tank where 20 tons of aluminium sulphate were mistakenly dumped. Then a woman died with 20 times the normal level of aluminium in her brain 16 years after the incident and another woman, in her 90s, died in 2007 again with high levels. The investigations were re-opened. At the time his tutor was doing research on 'gender bending' hormones in the water environment. The Camelford contamination had nothing to do with this but it turned up when Jawad was helping him with his research.

He began to kick the idea around in his head. He thought it through thoroughly, doing careful research and then he contacted N. He was high up in the chain of command, one of the men who could make things happen, based in Pakistan. There was a lot in the papers about the problems the country faced with having an ageing population, about there not being enough young people.

Jawad told N: 'We should think even longer term about what damage we could do to this country, to the economy, by reducing their population, interfering with their ability to reproduce. The disbelievers must be dealt with long-term.'

N took it from there. Terrorists world-wide, many working independently with no links to al-Qaeda, had decided soft targets would cause more long-lasting damage. Computers, banking, that sort of thing. But the damage to the economy long-term by altering the fertility of young people ... nobody had had that idea until Jawad thought of it.

The stock-piling of the estrogen and chemical plasticisers, chemical insecticides and herbicides, was done on the continent. Jawad never knew exactly where. He assumed Belgium or France but it could have been further afield, maybe in one of the countries that had been within the Eastern bloc. It was the mix and quantity that proved most hard to get hold of. A lot of palms in countries all over the world were greased. A number of Indian drug companies co-operated with generic estrogen products, not knowing what the ultimate destination was. The money was good and they asked no questions.

The world's leaders, particularly the US government, had completely underestimated how much funding was available to al-Qaeda. The drugs and other chemicals were gradually moved into England, through the

Channel tunnel. Lorry load after lorry load over two years. All the papers were in order. The drugs were stockpiled in large warehouses on industrial estates, mostly in the north, belonging to sympathisers. There were some rich individuals involved who offered practical help but wanted no involvement and did not want to know any details.

It was not Jawad who had the idea about an attack on a reservoir. That came from higher up and the idea was never going to achieve what they wanted though the organizers didn't know it then.

Jawad was asked about a possible target. With the Olympics in the offing he recommended the King George V reservoir on the Hertfordshire/Essex border, up the Lea Valley.

However, his main task was trying to get the chemicals into the drinking water supplies in people's homes. Another cell, based in Leeds, masterminded the delivery system. Another cell did the requisitioning and training of drivers. Yet another cell bought in and garaged the quantity of delivery tankers required. A company was set up, complete with branding and the tankers acquired their new livery. This was envisaged as a long, on-going operation.

A few trial runs were made in late 2006 to see if the system worked. Chemicals were dumped into rivers and lakes. The next step was to see if they could be introduced into water pipes leading to people's houses.

All through the autumn and winter of 2007 and into 2008 Jawad and Omar and sometimes Abdul went off in the camper-van they had bought and parked some way from the house. They went on recces all around England, Scotland and Wales. They'd already narrowed down some targets from the Water Board web-sites. The customer service information was excellent. By the spring of 2008 they had a long list of possible locations.

Abdul, not his real name, got caught on the M1 for speeding at 100 mph in a car that his brother had 'borrowed' from an uncle. The police gave him a good going over, asking a lot of questions just for the sake of it, roughing him up a little but not enough to cause themselves any trouble. They were stupid, Abdul told the others. They missed out on everything they should have asked. Nevertheless N ordered that he be banned from the cell and told not to return to the house. He protested but he went.

Once Jawad caught sight of him in the road late at night and caught up with him and beat him up to make him understand that he could no longer be any part of the operation. Jawad threatened to kill him and his wife and child if he came near them again and told him not to even think of betraying them.

Jawad's sister said, quite early on: 'But it's going to affect our people too. Our men won't be able to father children if it works.' Jawad told her it would not, could not, be widespread throughout the country. It had to be targeted, mostly in the smaller cities and larger towns. 'We can pick places where not many of our people live, only the ones who have sold out to the filthy western civilisation,' he said. 'We can do other things, too, to discourage our people from drinking their dirty water.'

Jawad contacted N and from the beginning of 2008 a campaign began on web-sites, in Mosques, in Islamic newspapers, by word of mouth. The government was putting chemicals into the water, chemicals that went against Allah. There was urine too, infidel urine, recycled. Dogs, pigs, unbelievers had contaminated the supplies. Muslims should not drink the tap water. They should drink bottled water from reputable suppliers. A company was set up to sell purified water in large containers and the Muslim community began to buy it.

The training of the MH-47EChinook pilot, hand-picked from the growing army of volunteers who knew that the attack on the King George V reservoir would be a suicide mission, was carried out in Afghanistan. The organizers thought that by setting the target date for the operation at the start of Ramadan when people would be fasting then fewer people would be affected in the North London area.

The plans for the attack gathered pace. More and more threads came together but the individual cells working on the project were kept apart. They were only cogs in a much greater wheel being operated by N and the hierarchy.

Jawad thought they were ready to go in late 2008 but there had been too much activity, too many trials. Surveillance had stepped up. The orders came. Next year. 2009. Surveillance throughout the world had become much more successful. People were prepared to talk if guaranteed immunity, new lives, cash, and there were a number of traitors who were giving away vital information.

That winter Jawad went back to work, finding a job in the hospital as a lab technician. He struggled to keep his spirits up; he had been so excited by the thought of the operation going into full production. The cell kept in close contact, keeping the brotherhood alive. Everything was in place. All the work had been done.

All through the summer of 2009 the UK's Muslim leaders, appalled by a campaign of suicide bombers on buses and trains in Paris, Berlin and Toronto, maiming and killing hundreds, sought high-level talks with government and were included in statements that went out condemning the atrocities.

'They are in the pockets of these dogs,' said Jawad.

The early summer was wet, which was unusual. Even the south east of the country had more water in reserve than for any of the other years in the new century. Restrictions were not lifted, though, so fearful were the water companies of a return to the dry conditions.

By July the weather had turned into a heat wave for the whole country except the north of Scotland. It continued on through August, just as the start of

Ramadan was being determined and the wise men were looking out for a sickle moon. It was scheduled on or either side of August 21.

Jawad was asked if the heat might lower the water levels of the King George V reservoir in the Lea Valley too much. There needed to be enough depth to make a recovery of the Chinook difficult and time consuming. There had to be a time delay while the rescuers worked to release those they thought trapped. In the meantime the chemicals would be leaching out. Only the estrogen-like pesticides were to be used, plus ricin. The timed underwater explosives would hasten their passage. Then it would take time for analysis before the authorities were sure what they were dealing with. They would think it was just the one isolated attack.

In the meantime the undetectable infiltration into the water pipes of areas within main conurbations through the rest of the country would be well underway. They were to start in earnest at the beginning of July.

The middle of Ramadan, which was the August Bank Holiday week-end, was judged to be best for the kamikaze Chinook attack. The weather that week reached the 80s. All the usual headlines and speculation were running about global warming. People had had seven weeks of hot weather. Even the nights remained unusually hot and humid and Jawad could see that people would leave the cities for the long week-end to find some relief from the heat and that was not what they wanted. There were a number of coded messages sent back and forth but it was too late to stop the machinery. Too many parts of the jigsaw were in place.

Then late on the Thursday night the weather broke. Torrential storms swept up through the country from the South West. Jawad and the others took it as a sign from Allah. Allah had given his blessing.

Jawad and Sula packed up their belongings and moved out of the house.

'Going somewhere nice,' the neighbour asked.

'Lucky my wife works for a travel agents.' Jawad winked at them. 'Oh yes, send you a postcard when we get to Lanzarote.'

He started the camper van and eased it out of the parking space in front of the house. Sula waved energetically, even kissed her fingers to the two little boys who were staring out of the downstairs lounge window. They waved back.

CHAPTER 2

The helicopter came in low over the reservoir, then pulled up sharply and flew east. The security guard was alerted by the dog barking long before he could see it. He watched idly. It was one of the big troop and machine carrying sort. He wasn't particularly interested in aircraft and did not know what it was. Chinook, maybe? There was something that had happened with that kind of helicopter not so long ago. Some government scandal. Too many ordered, money wasted? They were big. He looked at it closely as it swooped away westwards.

The day had been wet but now the clouds had broken and the sun was coming through. The clouds had a pinkish tinge. Red sky at night ... maybe a better day tomorrow. His family were spending the day at Legoland, birthday treat for the wife's niece. July and August had been dry and at times exceptionally hot but at last the weather had broken. They had planned to go to the beach for the party but the weather change had altered that.

He convinced himself he was glad he had had the excuse of work not to go with them; the children would be little bastards, quarrelsome. The little 'un was getting over a tummy upset and was whingeing. The oldest, the eight-year-old, had become stroppy, difficult, treating him as if he was an idiot. He couldn't lay a hand on him, the wife saw to that. He wasn't his. One she'd had before he knew her. He'd had a row with the wife about whether she should take the children and go with her sister and her family. He didn't see why they should have a good time while he was working.

They should be heading home now although they would probably have stopped at a McDonalds. Once the wife was off with that sister ... all hours. Bloody cow, that sister of hers.

He turned to look at the west. The dying embers of the sunset reflected pinkly in the calm water. He could see the black shapes of the wildfowl on the far bank, swans in serene silhouette. The reservoir was low, not as low as at the worst time the previous summer. It would be dark in another half hour. He had the next day off so it looked like they might all get another day out. He didn't fancy the sea. Maybe Epping Forest? Not far to go.

The dog suddenly started barking wildly. He shouted at it to shut up but behind him, out of nowhere, the throbbing judder of the helicopter's propellers were loud, really loud. He turned to look and at that moment the helicopter crashed into the middle of the reservoir. It halted briefly, momentarily on the surface, then sank head first almost immediately, just the propellers carving and slashing the water. The waves created so suddenly were sucked into the vortex. There were ripples and then the water was as undisturbed as it had been a minute before ... two minutes ... more, less? He could not tell. He felt both sick and elated at the tragedy. He ran back to the hut and dialled the emergency number. It took a long time waiting for the emergency services to arrive, then they all swarmed at once. Fire, police, ambulance. It took much longer before they got the diving team together.

When the divers got down to the wreck they saw the exploded containers and the crater in the reservoir bottom. There had been massive chemical leakage. Suddenly the disaster turned into a terrorist attack. Thames Water put the reservoir off-line immediately and switched to other reservoirs to make up the water supply to the treatment works. All the forces concentrated on this small part of Essex. The close proximity of the Olympic Games arenas focused more attention and top level secret service officials were called in.

The chemicals were tested. Estrogen-like pesticides and some ricin. N and the organisers had not anticipated that so many disaster plans had been rehearsed, that such quick action could be taken. Nevertheless the attack caused widespread panic and consternation in North London. The media helped to fan the flames. There were a lot of 'what if's'. A lot of scare headlines with stories which weren't substantiated but who read those?

The Prime Minister was on a visit to the USA where there were high-level discussions on the Iran nuclear threat. There was now distinct probability of a nuclear bomb being used in the middle East. His deputy, not long in post, stepped in.

Plans had been made for terrorist attacks on reservoirs and the water authority reacted well. The deputy prime minister was presented with cohesive emergency measures and the security heads, the emergency services and the scientists gave good advice.

The Prime Minister returned two days later to find the country far from pacified but the battle in the media was being won. There was some rioting in the streets of Essex towns and North London suburbs aimed at the Asian community. The helicopter's route had been determined, the stockpiled chemicals sourced back to a warehouse near Luton. MI5 soon knew most of what had happened concerning the helicopter. They still knew nothing of the other contamination seeping down water pipes to people's homes.

A number of old people in Walthamstow died from conditions their relatives said were unexpected and there was anxiety that perhaps Thames Water was not telling the whole truth. Could poisonous chemicals have flowed from the reservoir through the treatment plant and out through the taps? The experts all knew that this was impossible but to allay public fears the autopsies were hurried through and the results showed that the deaths had had nothing to do with any contamination of the water supply.

The significance of the possible long-term affect on people's health was mentioned from the first day by the medical columnists ordered by their news desks to look for a link. The government scientists and medics spoke with one voice to rubbish their scare stories. A united front was held and although the helicopter crash had shown how vulnerable Britain still was to unexpected attacks there was a sense of pride, generally, that the terrorists this time had got their information badly wrong. Beyond the inconvenience and the quite considerable cost nobody had been hurt.

It took weeks before Thames Water finally brought the reservoir back into use. The cost of the attack was, in fact, greater than it had previously been calculated and in this, at least, the terrorists had caused damage. Within three months, however, things returned to normal and the reservoir was put back on line.

But in Plymouth, Exeter, Bristol, Worcester, Bournemouth, Chester, Cardiff, York, Norwich, Bath, Lancaster, Richmond, Eastbourne, St Albans, Guildford and parts of leafy, suburban South London there were areas where Jawad's cell had done its work well and where a high level of estrogen had flowed. The infiltration into water pipes had continued over a number of months, the deliveries being done in a regular way by the now familiar tankers which gradually used up all the stock-piled chemicals. By April 2010 the deliveries ceased.

It took another two years before there was any suspicion or alarm raised and it was triggered by something quite different.

At the end of 2009 there was a nation-wide epidemic of mumps: the result of the refusal by parents to have the triple vaccine for their children following fears over the Mumps, Measles and Rubella vaccination in the years following the millennium finally came to fruition.

The medical profession feared a substantial increase in male infertility and the epidemiologists set to work. By then government was already concerned that the number of elderly was outstripping the birthrate. At first it was just suspicions that there were other agents beyond the mumps epidemic involved. Careful research was done and in a high sample of men it was found that their fertility had been compromised by estrogen. It was so bizarre a finding that Muslim extremists were not the main suspects. Given the scientific connections it was thought that it was probably one of the Animal Rights groups which had instigated the attacks.

Painstakingly the Counter-Terrorism Science and Technology Centre put together the evidence. The key experts, brought together only in 2006 to co-ordinate Britain's scientific response to terrorist attacks, predicted the long-term effect on the nation's fertility from both the mumps epidemic and the sabotage on the water supply.

It was never found out who leaked the findings to the Guardian. The story broke on February 12, 2012.

Jawad was never caught. He and Sula had gone to Pakistan to live by that time and Sula married there. The operation began to unravel and in late 2013 there was a trial of 20 people. The operation from start to finish had employed more than 300. The company that ran the tankers had become a business in its own right. It held office parties over the years, almost forgetting the real purpose of the business it was in. Some employees never knew.

Abdul was a key witness for the prosecution at the trial. It was said in court that he had gone to the Crown Prosecution Service with information.

Jawad told Sula that they had achieved their objective. He said discovering the long-term effects would be equally disruptive to the government and to the population. They will have to put resources into things they have not planned. The economy will be disrupted. He said the operation had been a success.

Jawad said: 'As for Abdul. I should have slit his throat that night I caught him in the road.'

The Sun was the first to coin the splash front page headline 'gender bender'. The scale of Jawad's operation was gradually pieced together and the areas affected determined. Health checks were carried out on all age groups, but the major concern was for those in the age range 18 to 40, the pubescent boys and the younger children. Results of a study in 2013, at the time of the trial, showed that 1 in every 100 young males between the ages of 13 and 19 was to some degree infertile and that 1 in 10,000 of those in the 20 to 45 age group had impaired fertility. What the analysis could not say was how much was due to mumps and, where applicable, how much to the tap water.

Four years later the infertility figures were far, far worse but by then Iran had unleashed its two bombs; in the spring and summer of 2013. The radio-active fall-out affected so many - men, women and children throughout Europe, the middle East and the former Russian states and the caesium stayed on and on in the ground and water supplies. The combination of all three factors hammered death-nails into population viability – particularly in England, Scotland and Wales.

The radiation fall-out was undoubtedly the component that really reduced the viability of the population all over Europe.

Fern was 18 when the news was first revealed by the Guardian but by then she already knew of her own infertility.

Mac's father told him that he might be infertile. Mac was 19, rebellious and difficult. He did not like his father who was dying of cancer. It did not help that his father, during the course of the next weeks and months and the medical tests, kept reminding him how he too had had to come to terms with knowing that he could not father children.

Mac already knew that his mother had undergone artificial insemination by donor (AID) to conceive him - his parents had introduced that information as gently as they could when he was twelve but he had received the news badly and declared his intention of finding his 'real' father as soon as he was old enough. He did not come within the younger age category who had been given legal backing to do this but nevertheless he felt that he had the right. His relationship with his nominal father had suffered.

James Fields missed out on the mumps epidemic and the estrogen attack because he was on a two-year secondment to Brussels at the time and had had, in any case, his MMR vaccinations. Stephanie Meadows had also been out of the country for a considerable part of the same time. She had spent a 'gap-year' after getting her degree and spent nine months travelling and working in Fiji, New Zealand and Australia. Both were back in the country by the time the radiation fall-out was swept westwards on prevailing winds but they had shown no symptoms of being affected.

John and Margaret Warne were in Devon. Margaret had long ago decided not to attempt to have any more children. She saw to it that they never needed any form of contraception. She told her girl friends: 'I call it abstinence.' Behind her back they laughed and pitied her husband.

Maeve already had problems with fertility although at the time she did not realise the cause. She had contracted chlamydia when she was at university. It was only in her mid-thirties when she was attempting to have a baby, unknown to her long term partner who wanted neither marriage nor family responsibilities, that a gynaecologist broke the news to her that her tubes were irreparably damaged.

Chapter 3

Edward Fish came home from school and flung his bag down on the kitchen table. His mother, a nervous woman in her late fifties, who had watched him come up the drive and heard him open the front door, decided to stay in the conservatory. They had recently built it onto the house they had bought six years earlier.

The house was in a quiet, tree-lined street, in what the estate agents described as an exclusive area of St Albans. They had managed to buy it just before prices rose way beyond their reach. They'd moved to that area in order to get Ed into a good secondary school but a year later that became unnecessary because he won a place at the private St Albans school for boys, near the Abbey.

She was glad they had made the move. It was a house built in the thirties, a bit careworn but with plenty of room, too much really with only the one boy, and a long garden that she was always meaning to do more with. If only the house could have the peace it deserved but there was constant turmoil. This latest thing had made matters even worse between Ed and his father. She heard Ed slamming doors, the fridge opening and shutting. Her stomach twisted, anticipating yet another scene.

She went back into the sitting room, glancing at that first proper portrait of them all on the shelf by the fireplace. The dark haired baby, eyes remarkably alert, in her arms. She looked so thin. Jim, bald and pot-bellied, was leaning over looking down at the baby with an expression of such love and care. The birth had been difficult. He'd been so big for her. 8lbs 9 ozs. One neighbour had looked in the pram and said: 'Big just like his dad, then.' She had not answered.

How thin she looked. Scraggy. Exhausted with trying to breast feed and failing. She was nearly 42 when that picture was taken. Elderly primogeniture. Now she was 57 and Jim nearing retirement. They had been wrong, she could see that now. Too old to cope with a lad like Ed. It had been all right when he was tiny but even then he had been a handful. Spoilt, her mother and sister had kept saying.

He had been difficult with other children, hitting out, biting. Even when he was very tiny and she had taken him to the little music group he had not behaved as the other children did. Later, when he could talk, he'd gone on about the mean pigs. He meant the other children at his play school. She didn't know where he had heard that phrase. 'I don't like them,' he said, very clearly to her, in front of the other mothers. He was only 3.

There were a number of photos of Ed as a baby, then a toddler beginning to lose the baby look, photos turning him into the beginnings of a small boy. A school photo of him, aged around 5 - lively face, pixie like, dark curls and smiling for once. The photographer must have been good at his job.

They started going regularly to services at the Abbey when he was about three. Jim said it was sensible if they were to have any chance of getting him into the Abbey primary school. It wasn't as if they had never been to church or didn't come from Church of England families. Both had been confirmed. Now they were strong members of the church. The Alpha course had revitalised their faith. She remembered the thrill they had felt when they heard he had been accepted at the school.

The teachers were the old-fashioned sort and he seemed to respond reasonably well to the discipline after the first two traumatic terms. There had been a veiled suggestion at the first parents' evening that if he didn't conform they had better start thinking of placing him somewhere else. Somehow they had managed to get him to understand that he must behave better at school.

He made a friend who came from a big family. That had helped. It was at home that he bossed them about. Even at five he manipulated them, playing one off against the other. And he told lies. At first she'd pretended he had a vivid imagination and that there was some excuse. Later she remonstrated and quoted the scriptures to him. Jim tried to deal with it a different way, painstakingly proving the impossibility of the lie. Both ways ended in rows and the boy being sent to his room.

Ed was particularly good at maths and science. Unsurprisingly, given the primary school, his background and his ability, he won a scholarship to St Alban's school for boys.

He settled in well and they thought the time was right when he was 12. They'd been advised to tell him sooner but each time they had made up their minds to do so something would happen; the inquest on yet another lie, a surly mood, a prolonged silence. There had been a lot of publicity about children's right to know when the law was changed. They read how badly some children had reacted when they found out much later in life.

'It's like adoption,' said a friend who was a social worker. 'Better to break it gently now. After all, it's not as if he wasn't wanted nor that you really are his proper mum.'

They finally managed one Sunday morning at breakfast. She'd left it to Jim to do most of the talking. He hadn't done it well, fumbling for the right words. Ed grew redder and redder in the face. He started to shout, angrily, tears running down his face. He said they had tricked him.

She said: 'But I'm your real mother and Dad's always wanted you, wanted you as his son. You couldn't be dearer to him than if ...' but he didn't let her finish. 'I'm not his real son. Whose son am I?' On hearing that they did not know, knew only a few details, he ran out of the room and up the stairs. They could hear him sobbing in his room and he refused to go to church with them. Recently that had been the norm, Ed picking a row just before they were ready to go but this was different.

From then on the tension mounted. Even Jim, calm, peaceable Jim, shouted back. Jim and Ed started fighting, Ed hit hard, hitting Jim in the stomach. Jim cuffed him over the head but now Ed was as tall. Once he pushed Jim hard back against the stair rails and hurt his back.

Jim didn't try to fight him now but often Ed would flick a wet towel at him as he passed him on the landing on the way back to his room. 'I'm turning the other cheek,' Jim would say. She wanted to tell him, he thinks you're a wimp, he thinks less of you for making stupid jokes.

On the good days they would get through without the doors slamming, Ed going out for a couple of hours without telling them where he was going, demanding money from her and losing his temper and saying dreadful things if she refused. How did he know such words?

What would it be like today? She plucked up courage and went into the kitchen. He was sitting at the table with a mountain of food on a plate, some of which was to have been their evening meal. She said, brightly, more brightly than she had intended: 'Good day?'

He didn't answer. She went to make a cup of tea and when her back was turned he said: 'I want all the information you have got about him. I want to see it. You must have got more than you told me. It's just not possible that you don't know who he was, what he did.'

She didn't answer at once. He shouted: 'If I'd been born now I'd have the right to know. It's important. How do you know what might be in store for me. I want to know who my father was ... is. Whose genes have I got? What illnesses may I inherit? How the hell do you know he didn't have AIDS?'

The question stung the reply from her. 'No, no, there are checks for all that sort of thing. Only healthy people …' She turned to look at him and he met her gaze, eyes full of hatred.

'All right. I'll show you the papers again. There really isn't very much. You saw it all when you were 12.' He followed her upstairs to her bedroom where she kept the locked box. Their wedding certificate, all their birth certificates, the passports. She lifted them out carefully. He spotted the birth certificates. What does it say on mine then?

She showed him. Jim's name was on it. 'That's fucking untrue, for a start. He's not my father.' He said it angrily, spitting out the words. She said: 'It was all right to put that. Legally you are our child, Dad's and mine.'

She dug out the papers. White, dark brown hair, brown eyes, 6 foot tall.

'Is that all?'

'All I was allowed to know. I asked for dark brown hair and brown eyes to be like Dad.'

Ed looked mutinous. She said: 'Jim … Dad … is your father. He is. He's done everything for you. We both have.'

'Well, what clinic did you go too? You can tell me that at least.'

She told him the name of the clinic in North London.

He said: 'I shall find out. I shall. When I'm 18 I'll register with UK Donorlink. I've found out all about that. They can trace donors through the clinic that was used. Tie up the dates. Use DNA. And the minute I'm old enough I'm leaving this house.'

CHAPTER 4

Fern had had non-Hodgkins lymphoma when she was 9 and the chemotherapy had both cured her and rendered her infertile. She had not been told at the time but her mother chose to tell her when the question of infertility hit the papers at the time of the mumps epidemic. She thought it would lessen the blow by telling her then when infertility was headline news. She had never been a sensitive mother and in her manner of telling Fern she made an enemy of her daughter for life.

Fern had disliked her mother for as long as she could remember. She was an ambitious woman and made sure that the family's lifestyle reflected the high earnings of her husband who worked in the city. They moved often, always to better houses and superior neighbourhoods. The phrase 'don't let me down' was a constant on her lips. Fern was the eldest child and bore the brunt. She could remember on more than one occasion being smacked before they went out, having done nothing to warrant it. She assumed it was punishment in advance, just in case she had any ideas of being naughty. She was aware of the quite different feelings her mother had for her younger brother, Nick, who was indulged, feted and petted.

During her illness there had been some sort of truce although she had sent her mother out of the hospital ward in a rage on many occasions while she sobbed into her pillow, hoping the nurses would ask her what the matter was. She wanted somebody to say that her illness was her mother's fault but nobody ever said it.

From the age of 12 onwards Fern reacted to nearly everything her mother said or did with rages or sulks. When her mother suffered pre-menstrual tension they resorted to physical violence. She once went to school with a deep scratch down her arm from the manicured, blood-red nails.

The teacher asked her how she had got it. I had a fight with my mother, she had said, looking him straight in the eye. He raised an eyebrow. Dread to think how your mother looks, then. It wasn't the response she had expected. I hate her, she said and turned and walked away, swinging her hips ever so slightly.

The shock of her mother telling her that she was infertile and the way in which she was told widened the gulf between them. Her mother had said that she was lucky, lucky not to have to put up with 'all that mess of childbirth and small babies'.

By the time she was 17 she was 5 foot 9, elegant, blonde and thin and the subject of envy and mean gossip. She did not care. She said she was going to be a model and she got some work, through the mother of a friend of hers. While she was still doing her A levels she began to appear in mail-order catalogues. Her mother privately boasted of her success to her friends but teased Fern unkindly about the magazines she was appearing in. Why not Vogue, why not Tatler?

Eventually she grew bored by the long hours and dictatorial direction, the photographers who pawed her. 'You're touching me inappropriately,' she said. 'I can report you to the police. Get you put on the sex offenders' register.' She decided, that after all, she would work hard for her A levels and go to university and she did well.

She had the almost compulsory gap-year, spending some time in Costa Rica teaching in a school and getting a great deal of attention, some of it acceptable, from the men she came across. When she returned home she found that her mother had run off to live in France with a man she had been having an affair with for years, a wealthy lawyer. She hadn't known for sure about the affair but she and her brother had suspected it, keeping silent for their father's sake. They found out that their father had known for a long time.

He said: 'I never thought she'd go. I've let her do everything she wanted.' He was depressed for months and then two years later died of cancer. By that time Fern was in her second year, reading English at Magdalene College, Cambridge. Her mother and her partner came to the funeral, causing more anguish by their presence. Fern's anger spilled over at the tea party in a local hotel after the burial service. It was a sad, ill-attended affair and only the relatives and a few close friends witnessed the bitter scene. Her father had been ill for too long for work colleagues to feel they needed to make the effort.

There was some money for Fern and her brother, left in trust, but the bulk of their father's fortune went to his wife whom he had never divorced. He had not re-made his will and this neglect deepened Fern's loathing of her mother.

Despite the anguish over her father, she was disciplined enough to set her feelings aside and got a 2:1. She got a graduate placement at one of the top ad agencies and that was where she met Johnnie as part of the crowd she at first went round with.

He was on his way to being a top account handler and asked her to marry him just as she was getting over a two-year-long affair with a married man, one of the agency's top clients. The man had died suddenly of a heart attack. He had been very rich and as his mistress she had got used to all the good things that his money and status could provide. Her grief at losing him was genuine; he had been a kindly and amusing lover and she had revelled in the treats he had showered on her. There was a big gap in her life.

She had, inevitably, become distanced from the lower ranks in the agency and although many, both inside and outside the agency, said her advancement to a top position as a creative writer owed everything to her ability between the sheets and the fact that she had mixed socially with top management and directors from the agency and a number of other companies, she did have talent and warranted the position she had been promoted to.

Johnnie seemed like a good bet and he was good-looking in a sandy-haired, blue-eyed, freckled English way. He was easy-going and got on well with people and he handled his portfolio of accounts well. People were talking about him moving up through the ranks to one of the top positions in the agency. He talked about starting on his own but would be open to being dissuaded if she felt it was not the right move. She felt she would always be able to direct the course their lives took.

She regarded the small house in Putney that they bought when they married as a temporary stepping-stone to much better things. She would not allow her mother to attend the wedding even though her in-laws urged her to 'bury the hatchet'. I will if she turns up, Fern warned them. They let it alone.

Johnnie started talking about having a family the minute they were engaged. She said she was sure it was unlikely and eventually, just before the wedding, she told him that she was infertile. She asked him if he knew if he was OK and he said that he was, he had been checked out thoroughly. To her surprise he wasn't angry or upset at her revelation. He said it didn't make any difference. There were other ways, nowadays. So many had the same problem. She had seen some scientific papers which suggested a number of solutions for infertility while researching on an account she was writing a commercial for. Human cloning was now viable, it said, but was outside the law 'at present'.

Johnnie said that he handled an account for one of the big drugs companies and there were all sorts of experiments going on. The idea of a child appealed to her. Just one would do. It would spite her mother, show her that she had been wrong. She remembered so clearly the way her mother had told her about her infertility.

'Lots of people will be like you,' her mother had added after the remarks about the mess of childbirth. 'Children ... don't mean you and Nick, of course, darling, but well ....can be a bloody nuisance. Such a tie. If I had my time over again ... I envy you. Footloose and fancy free. You'll just have to tell whoever you marry, if you do marry, that it's their fault. Probably will be, anyway. Don't let on. There aren't going to be that many young men capable of fatherhood, after this.' It was typical of her mother to suggest cheating.

Having a child, by whatever means, would be a kick in the teeth for her mother. When Johnnie introduced her to Dr Radetski who explained how it all worked she said she would try. He said that it had to be kept quiet although the treatment was going to be openly offered soon. The law would have to change. There was no other option for government. He would put her on his trial list which was being properly researched and tested and it just meant coming to the clinic one day with Johnnie. Just a scrape. Nothing at all. Yes, it could be a boy or a girl, depending who gave the skin cell. Which did they want? Fern did not hesitate. A boy. She wasn't going to mirror the relationship she had had with her own mother.

The implant in her womb worked, the baby took hold but she had never expected to feel so ill. When the baby came prematurely, 10 weeks before it was due, she wanted it to die. It was months before she could begin to think of the baby as William. The television appearance helped. So many people had seen it and congratulated her on her beautiful baby son. They could not see the operation scars on his thin little body. They had not seen the needles going into those tiny veins, the cry that was more like a kitten than a baby.

The first time she met Mac when they went next door for a drink she knew she would have an affair with him. She had never felt such a sexual attraction for anybody in the way she had when she first met him and shook his hand. He looked down at her in that slightly supercilious manner and she was lost. The middle-aged lover had pursued her for weeks before she agreed to go out with him. He had been reasonably good-looking but had the beginnings of a paunch which she teased him about. She wondered afterwards if the fitness regime he embarked on to lose weight had actually signed his death warrant.

When Mac moved in she watched him unload his car and make the necessary trips back and forth into the house next door from her bedroom window. Once he looked up and waved. The pony-tail and earring intrigued her and he had on a collarless silk white shirt and jeans so tight they seemed welded to his skin. His dark sulky good looks, his thinness, elegance and sophistication, were just as she remembered them from that brief meeting.

She had just begun to re-awake after having the baby. She was in no mood for Johnnie's mechanical unimaginative approach to love-making which he had adopted once the initial thrill of courtship had worn off. She wanted romance and the lusting for Mac began to fill nearly every waking moment.

She began to sun-bathe on the patio in the long Indian summer that stretched well into October. She knew he was looking from the landing-window and once she turned deliberately on to her side, facing him.

The following evening he came to the door. Johnnie answered it and she heard him ask if they would like to come in for a drink.

'We can't leave William,' she heard Johnnie saying. 'We've put him into bed for the night and we can't leave him in the house alone. I don't think the baby monitor would reach next door. It might ...but well, he's very precious and we've had a lot of worries ...it's very kind of you. Why don't you come here?' Fern was irritated. Typical of Johnnie not to ask what she thought.

Mac said: 'I've got a decent bottle of red. I'll go and get it if you're sure ... what about your wife ... Fern, isn't it? She might have other plans ...'

She came into the hall-way. 'Hello,' she said, as coolly as she could.

Johnnie said: 'Mac wanted us to go in for a drink but obviously we can't. He's going to bring a bottle in here if that's all right. Could we make the meal stretch to three?'

She said: 'We can if you don't pig it like you usually do.'

She couldn't remember afterwards when they had got on to the subject of racing, maybe on the second bottle which Johnnie produced. Mac talked about the horse he owned. At that point he said nothing about the syndicate. She learned later that he only had an eighth share.

He said it was entered in a hurdle race at Plumpton and that he was going down to watch it run in a couple of weeks time. She said she knew nothing about racing but had always wanted to go. Cheltenham always seemed fun. She'd been invited a couple of times by clients but hadn't been able to go. Too much work. She pulled a face ... and now with the baby ...

Johnnie said she ought to go, maybe Mac would take her sometime? He'd look after William, maybe take him to see his grandparents who had been agitating for some time that a visit was long overdue.

Mac looked at her. 'Want to come?' He smiled slightly and added: 'Why not the Plumpton meeting when my horse is running. It's a pretty course under the South Downs. Only thing is it's a Monday. I've arranged a day off. How about it, Johnnie?'

Later, in bed, she asked Johnnie: 'You don't mind? I'd love a day out. On my own.'

'Poor sweetness, you've had a rough time with the baby. We didn't expect it to be as difficult, did we? You deserve a day out. I can fix that Monday, I'm sure. I'll take William down on the Sunday, if you like. Stay overnight. Give you a break. It's kind of Mac, he's good fun, isn't he?' Why did everything Johnnie say annoy her, sending shivers of irritation through her shoulder blades?

She turned away: 'Did you believe all that stuff he was telling us? All that about his father having been an SAS officer and killed on a secret mission during the Afghan war? And his mother being high up in MI5. He made it sound so exciting, his childhood. All the holidays with the grandmother in the house in Northumberland because the parents were away. Which Oxford college did he say he was at?'

'Magdalen.'

'Who do we know who was there? Caroline? Tim?'

'Why?'

'I don't know. I want to check him out. He's like a child seeking attention. I think he tells lies. It's not playing political games like we all do at work. It's something else with him.'

Johnnie said: 'You're so cynical.' He said it with affection and she flinched as he reached under the bed clothes to stroke her leg.

She was far more excited than she wanted Johnnie to see as the day approached. On the Sunday she waved him and William off first thing in the morning for their trip to Winchester. She wondered about inviting Mac in for a drink at lunchtime. She fantasised about the sex that would follow. They would make love all afternoon. Then she heard him drive off in his car.

He did not come back until after she had gone to bed, having spent a day unsure of what to do with her unexpected freedom and a considerable time examining her wardrobe. In the end she took herself off to Sloane Street to buy a new and very expensive jacket. She had already asked a girl friend what she should wear to a race-meeting at Plumpton.

'Cool, smart. Don't try and do the country thing. You'll get laughed at by the real McCoy. He probably likes stable girls, too. Tight jeans. You've got the legs and figure for it. That should knock him dead.'

She settled for the jacket, silk shirt and expensive jeans and was pleased at the way Mac looked at her when she went out to the car.

The weather had broken at the week-end but on the Monday the sun shone and although it was autumnally sharp it turned out to be a golden day and by late morning it was warm. They were already on their way by then, the car open-topped The autumn leaves after the long dry spell were stunning and Mac turned off the main road, headed for Ditchling then stopped at the Half Moon pub not far from the racecourse for a drink.

She asked for white wine, dry, and watched him as he went to the bar to get the drinks. The conversation in the car had been stilted, the wind whipping their words away so that in the end they had driven in silence.

When he brought the drinks he said: 'We must get to know each other better. I think I've been doing all the talking ... I was so nervous that night ... you look so cool and collected. I've never met anyone like you. You've got to tell me all about yourself.' From someone else she would have thought it a limited chat-up line.

'No,' she said. 'I want to hear about your job first, then I'll tell you a bit about myself.'

'Did I tell you I worked at the Department of Health? I'm an economist. James and I are working together on a big population project. He's come over from Lifestyle to give us a hand though quite honestly there was no need for it. Nice bloke. Haven't met his girlfriend, Steph. Do you know her?'

Fern shook her head. 'What sort of population project?'

'Not enough people in the future to keep the country going. You've done your best with William but we're going to need a lot more Willies ...' he stopped, raising one eyebrow. She looked at him then began laughing herself.

'I didn't think you ever laughed,' said Mac. 'I don't think I've ever seen you laugh. Giggled once or twice but not what you could call a laugh. You look ...'

'I look what?' she said, recovering herself.

'Unfrozen,' he said, unexpectedly. He reached for her hand across the table. 'Do you want to?'

'Yes.'

'Now?'

She looked at him, hoping to conceal her excitement. He got up and spoke to the man behind the bar who fetched a woman from the kitchen area. Fern watched while Mac spoke to her, moving away from the bar area. She fiddled with her bag. The bar had filled up with other race-goers. Mac came back. 'They have an annexe they use for b and b's. We can have a room there. They didn't seem too phased. Probably get asked all the time by randy race-goers.'

She followed him out of the pub and across a courtyard. The south Downs were whale-like lumps of sunlit green from the window of the room that Mac unlocked. She drew the curtains, raising her arms provocatively to do so and he put his arms around her, sliding them up to hold her breasts.

'What about the race your horse is running in?'

He said: 'Bugger the horse.' She did not know until later that the horse was in the 5.20 and they still got there just in time, while the horses were parading in the paddock.

Each time she tried to get out of bed he pulled her back. Just one more time, just one more time. 'I can't get enough of you.' His energy was flattering. They even slept briefly, her wrapped safely in his arms, his legs twined round hers.

She had never known such ecstasy in love-making before, never felt complete abandonment, detached from her brain, she had never allowed herself to be that generous. Mac's hair lay loose on the pillow, then dropped round her face, then tickled her belly. He was gentle then strong, then gentle again, stroking her, kissing her mouth, her breasts, her belly, her cunt then all the way back again, slowly unfreezing her, releasing her from herself. She was no longer in control. It was something she had never allowed herself to be.

They finally got dressed. He showered but she did not want to. She wanted to smell his love on her. She told him so and for once he was at a loss for words. They got back in the car. At the racecourse they were waved through to the car park. They were just in time for Mac to put some money on with the bookies. She didn't know until afterwards that he had backed another horse which came in second. His own, Civil Disobedience, was pulled up at the jump before the last and she wondered at the time why he wasn't more upset.

Afterwards he introduced her to his trainer, Jack Bamfield, and to one of the other owners, a scholarly, thin faced older man, whom Mac seemed to know very well. 'This is Dick,' he said. 'Taught me all I know.' The man was barely courteous to Fern and paid little attention to her once they were in the bar. He talked racing exclusively to Mac. She was annoyed and Mac, sensing it, said that they must be getting back.

His trainer said: 'Did you just come to see the horse run? I looked for you earlier. I'd got a tip for the second.'

She saw him wink at Mac. 'Kept busy at work?' The man wasn't asking, just looking at her. She pretended not to notice.

'Sorry about that,' said Mac later. 'You'll have to get used to that kind of conversation if you come racing with me. It's very sexual, racing. Horse flesh and flesh in general. Seems to go hand in glove. He's been having it off with his stable-girls all his married life with the full knowledge of his wife. It's droit de seigneur once a new girl starts work. He expects it; they expect it. They'd probably be miffed and wonder what was wrong with them if he didn't try it on. And the ugly ones are really grateful.' She swiped at him with the race card.

On the way back to Putney he told her that the other owner she had met had been a lecturer of his at the LSE and had introduced him to racing.

'I thought you went to Oxford?' she said.

'Went to the LSE afterwards,' he said, smoothly, 'to do a Masters.' She still wasn't sure. She tried again. 'When were you at Oxford? I had a friend who was at Magdalen. Tim, Tim Broadhurst.'

Mac said: 'What year?' and when she told him, he said: 'I'd have left by then.'

'How about the girl I work with, Claire Skinner?'

He said it lightly, but it was the first time she recognised that he had a temper, that perhaps his anger could be dangerous. What did it matter? She didn't want awkward questions either. Their ill-fated relationship, intense, sexually exciting, began and continued with deception on both sides for as long as it lasted.

CHAPTER 5

Mac never thought of them as lies. He knew that what he said often got him into trouble. He could remember, as early as his third birthday, when he told a roomful of children at his party that his mum and dad had bought him a pony. He said it in front of his mother and father, aunt and grandmother.

'Want a ride,' one of the little girls said.

'No,' said Edward. 'No, you can't. My pony doesn't like little girls. He only lets me ride him.'

'EDWARD,' said his father.

'He's got such an imagination,' his mother said to his aunt who was scowling at him. She said to the children: 'Shall we play pin the tail on the donkey?'

After that he was more careful. He kept his stories for the children at school, though once, in his final year at primary school, one of the children told the teacher that Edward had been on holiday to the Antarctic with his father who was a scientist, part of a team examining the hole in the ozone layer.

'I thought your father worked in the city,' she said, confronting him.

'He does now,' said Edward. 'This was quite a long time ago. When I was small. And I didn't say he was a scientist. It was about lending money on a scheme scientists are working on.' The teacher gave him an uncertain look.

In his first year at St Albans school for boys he was a victim of bullying. He was different, quirky. Fair game for bullies. It was then that his stories got bolder. He thought of them as stories. If he could keep the bullies interested enough they stopped hurting him. He became clever at gauging just what would intrigue his contemporaries. How he could make them laugh. After his parents broke the news about his father, his real father, he began to invent him. He told whoever was listening, always in a one-to-one situation, that he had been adopted. Then he invented why and it was always because his real mother had died at birth and his real father, because of his occupation, could not look after him.

At various times his real father had been a member of the SAS, an expert on nuclear weapons who worked in America, a surgeon who worked in a leper colony in India and a conservationist trying to preserve the rain forests in South American countries. Usually he said Brazil but sometimes he changed it for Colombia. He told his listener in strictest confidence and boys not being the gossips girls are he was not betrayed until his third year.

By that time his guile carried a certain cachet. Others wished they were as quick-witted as he and liked the way he could dupe teachers. He was regarded as a character and gathered some lively minded friends who encouraged him to go to further extremes with his outrageous inventions.

He was in his first year of A levels when he began to get interested in racing. The betting side of it appealed to his mathematical brain and a maths teacher at the school, who found him studying the racing pages of the Times one day in the library, began to talk to him. He was a keen race-goer and he asked Edward if he wanted to go to one of the spring meetings at Newmarket the following week-end. He said his wife would be going too. Edward didn't bother to tell his parents where he was going but they found out afterwards and were very angry. He repaid them with a massive bout of sulking which lasted weeks.

It was after his father, or Jim as he had steadfastly called him since he had found out that he wasn't, died that he got seriously interested in racing. He now had some money - too early, too soon, he'll squander it, his aunt told his mother. Jim had left his estate in trust to Edward after his wife's death but there was a straight bequest of £40,000. It was the lecturer, Dick Rawnsley, who first suggested that they bought into a syndicate to own a horse.

The first horse they bought was a raw-boned Irish bred chaser, that only really went well in the mud. It won a selling chase and the syndicate decided to get rid of it. Civil Disobedience came up at the Ascot sales when it was a yearling and after a lot of e-mailing back and forth the eight partners decided to buy it. The hammer finally went down at £10,000.

Nothing happened for a year or two. The trainer decided the colt should be gelded, turned out, allowed to grow on. It was too big for the flat and looked like it would make a chaser.

Bamfield had a yard at Newbury and Mac, who had by now joined the Ministry of Health as an economist and acquired his nickname, went down often with Dick to see the horse and when it was judged ready to race they went and watched it on the early morning exercise gallops. The first race it ran in was a hurdle, jumping too big, at Devon and Exeter in the spring of 2018. The jockey pulled it up after a mile but it was all according to the trainer's plan. He'd enter the horse in a chase after a few more outings over hurdles.

By the time Mac started taking Fern racing Civil Disobedience had been placed a couple of times and was showing the promise of a good career. Mac had long since used up his inheritance and was relying on his salary to pay his racing debts and the syndicate expenses which were heavy. It was OK for Dick, he thought, who had made money on the stock exchange and had never married, never even had any sort of partner that he knew of. A lonely, solitary, man. He wondered about Dick sometimes. Internet porn? A bit of cottaging. Something. At least the obsession with racing and horses helped to help keep him out of jail.

Mac had begun to bet heavily, losing more often than he won, and was relieved when James agreed to let him rent the house in Putney.

He liked James but he thought of him as one of life's losers. The fiasco over the Newcastle project and the horrendous plans for the suburban wedding to Steph confirmed it. He blamed James, unfairly he knew, for the fact that he was working on other projects and he had, to all effects, been demoted. He thought James could have made more of a stand; he was the lead player in the project. He'd had a go at his superiors but it hadn't done any good. At present he had work through the Treasury on the birth rate aspect of the population studies.

It was a way of getting back at James, inviting him to come racing that spring. Steph would find out. It was inevitable and then James would have to face the music. Mac smiled. He sent him an e-mail. How about Kempton on Saturday? Meet you in the car park about 12.30? The answer came back quickly. James wasn't finding work that stimulating over at Lifestyle. Yes, good idea. See you there. It was late April and the wedding plans were escalating.

He told Fern who had snatched an hour and was lying naked on his bed. They could hear Johnnie out in the garden with the kid, with William.

'He must know,' he said. It wasn't a question. Fern said: 'Of course he does. I told him.'

'Isn't he worried you might get pregnant? You have before. Why not with me?'

She turned away from him, on her side: 'I imagine you can't?'

'No, I'm fine. My parents were great worriers but they had the sense to have me vaccinated. So the mumps didn't get me. We weren't in a water contamination area – anyway, I hate the stuff. Always have. Then when the bombs went up I was away, staying with my grandmother up on the Scottish borders and the drift didn't get that far up. I always went there for my summer holidays.'

'So you don't fire blanks then?'

He was trapped into another half-lie. 'No.' He had never been certain. St Albans had been one of the cities. It was certainly possible for her, though. She'd proved that with William. He had wondered why it hadn't happened already because he took no precautions and he was pretty certain she didn't either. Perhaps he was affected. He changed the subject.

'Want to go to James' wedding? I've got an invitation ... or am getting one. I think he quite wanted me to be best man but Mrs 'I'm wearing the trousers in this marriage' vetoed that. Anyway I'll ask him at Kempton on Saturday.'

Fern shot back over to stare at him. 'You've asked James on our day out? Without asking me? What a bastard you are.'

'Sshh, Johnnie will hear,' he said and at that moment they could hear William's high pitched voice shouting insistently 'Mummy.'

'I don't see why it will make much difference to us. He won't hang round our necks and anyway I've got to see Mike about the horse. There's a syndicate meeting I'm going to be involved in. It may take a while. James can look after you. He needs a treat and his tongue was hanging out that day we met for the first time.'

'Thanks a million.' She got out of bed. 'I've got to go. See you Saturday.' She gave no indication whether or not she was going in answer to William's continued shouting.

Mac thought about her as he heard her shut his front door then moments later open her's. Nobody, nothing, had prepared him for Fern. She was so heart whole, so pitilessly neutral, so distant in all her relationships, save for the one they had in bed. He had never come across anybody who hated their mother as she did. He'd hated Jim, but then he wasn't his father. And his mother … no, he didn't hate her. He still kept in touch and visited her from time to time where she was living with her sister down in Bournemouth. If there was a race meeting somewhere not too far away. Wincanton, Taunton, Exeter even.

He visualised taking Fern with him to meet his mother. What would that be like? He smiled as he thought of his mother doing everything to break the ice. Some ice. And when she found out that Fern was married and had a kid. What then? That would bring on a mega Alpha spasm.

CHAPTER 6

James looked at Fern. Mac had just left them and they were leaning against the paddock rails, watching the horses parading round for the fourth race. The trainers and owners were beginning to congregate in the centre, waiting for the jockeys to show up.

'How's ...' he struggled.

'William? Or Johnnie? Or how is it fucking Mac,' she said. She gave him a thin smile.

'William.'

'Well, beginning to say what sounds a bit like Mummy, not walking, behind his peer group but catching up. He should make it. How are the wedding plans?'

James mumbled something. 'Sorry, can't hear,' she said.

'I said as well as can be expected. My future mother-in-law is a complete nightmare. I thought her sort only happened in old comedy films. Or jokes. I've got the prototype. She's organising everything down to the loo paper in the bogs, I should think. Colour co-ordinated. Steph and I are her ultimate chance to shine in the Surrey set. Steph's not a bit like that, you'd like her.' As soon as he said it he knew Fern wouldn't.

'Get out of it, then,' said Fern. She looked at the race-card. 'What do you fancy in this one.'

'Mac reckons the big bay over there, Rouge et Noir. It was fifth last time out. Usually a good sign.'

'And your opinion? You don't have to do everything he says. He's big-headed enough. Have you really invited us to your wedding?'

James looked awkward. 'Well ... er ... yes. I sent Mac an invitation.'

'Not Mac and me?'

'Well, of course. Of course you can come.' He looked flustered now.

Fern grinned. 'Well, I just might do that. You don't like me very much, do you, James? As opposed to getting in my knickers. Don't trust me. Well, you're quite right. I am very untrustworthy. But Mac ... you like him. And yet he's blaming you for what's happened to his career. Did you know that?'

James shook his head. The jockeys were being legged up, their silks shiny in the sun, the horses dancing about, bucking, kicking out, impatient to get on with the race. As they left the paddock Fern said: 'We'd better make a move for the stands. Mac will find us.'

They walked past the bookies, now offering 5 to 1 on Rugget Noyr. 'Stendhal would not be flattered,' said James. He added: 'There was nothing I could have done. It was political. Taken out of our hands. Mac knows that, surely.'

'He's a spoiled child. At least I've never been that,' said Fern. 'Not nearly enough spoiling for me. If things don't go his way then he wants to find a scapegoat. You're it at the moment. Don't worry, he'll get over it. It's one of his less endearing features. That and telling whoppers.'

At that moment Mac caught up with them. 'We might buy another horse,' he said.

'What with?'

'Oh, I'll find a way. Anyway this horse might win. That would give me the stake I need.'

'Rugget Noyr?'

Mac looked at James who said: 'That's what the bookies are calling him.'

Mac laughed.

James said: 'I hear you blame me for the Newcastle fiasco. Bit unfair, isn't it?'

Mac slapped him on the back. 'I did. Don't worry, I'm over it now. I can see it was the politics of the thing that went haywire. And that bloody campaign 'Death by Numbers'. The PM got jumpy. Can't say I blame her. Now let's watch the race.'

It was exciting from start to the close finish and Rouge et Noir won by a short head. Mac was leaping up and down, hoarse with shouting. He grabbed Fern's hand and they flew down the steps of the stand. James caught up with them at the winner's enclosure.

Afterwards Fern said: 'I felt like Alice being flown over those patchwork fields by the Red Queen. My feet never touched the steps.'

It was the first time James had seen her so animated. Her cheeks were pink and her breath was ... he thought of the obvious phrase and giggled. Very unsophisticated. Not her at all.

She asked immediately. 'What are you laughing at?'

'Nothing.' Steph would have laughed at the coarseness of 'short pants', but not Fern. He felt a twinge of guilt for being here with Fern and Mac when Steph thought he had gone to look at what they needed to add to the wedding list. The acceptances were 140 and growing. Fern and Mac. Two more. How was he going to introduce that subject. Oh shit.

Mac ordered champagne, on the strength of his win. They missed the next race, and the last race. By the time they got to the car park Mac was incapable of driving. James said: 'Give me the keys. I'd better get you both home to Putney.' Fern sat beside him. Every time he changed gear he shot a look at those long legs. Mac was snoring in the cramped back seat.

He said: 'What about Johnnie if you come to our wedding?'

'He won't give a damn,' she drawled. 'Cold feet? Don't worry, I won't upstage the bride ... if I come. It would give us a good excuse for a week-end away. I'd like that.'

But of course, she did upstage the bride.

CHAPTER 7

Mac looked Warne in the eye. They were about the same height. 'You almost lost James and myself our jobs, certainly you've held our careers back. Did you know that?' It was the second time he had said it. The thrill of having had such a big win made him feel drunk, though he wasn't ... yet. They had walked out into the garden and Warne indicated they should walk away from the terrace and out of view of the room where the rest of the wedding guests were eating their desserts.

Warne said: 'I get the feeling they are running scared, as I said before. Do you know what the current position is?'

'You can't ask me things like that,' said Mac. 'You must know that I'm governed by the official secrets act.'

'Sorry. I suppose I am too. I used to be on the committee that ordered the targets for non-interference. I had to sign it then. I've never 'unsigned' it. I don't know if you can.'

'Search me,' said Mac. He could not see much point to the conversation and wanted to watch how his champagne went down, particularly with the bride's mother. He hoped she would choke on it. His wedding gift to James.

Warne said: 'I wondered if there was anything else that came up from the Newcastle project. I saw something, a bit of research in the British Medical Journal the other day, it was by a paediatrician who was at university with me ... something about babies born to immigrants and specific maternity facilities at one of the immigration centres. The article was about survival rates and the ratio of handicapped children to the norm for the rest of the country. They've got a lot of migrant workers there, haven't they?'

Mac looked at him. 'I'm working on child population strategies at the moment. There was a bit of it in the Newcastle pilot but I've got access to different statistics in the project I'm working on now. There do seem to be certain places, pockets in the country, if you like, where a higher proportion of children are being born. Higher levels of babies without defects. I couldn't say whether it matches immigrant populations or not. I could do some cross-checking, I expect. Why are you so interested in this?'

Warne said: 'I had a thought the other day. If the government is trying to keep the survival rate of older people down, then they might well be trying to push the birth-rate up as fast as they can. Well, not just the birth-rate but normal, full-term babies being born without any medical problems. They could do that. There are ways.'

Mac flushed slightly. 'A number of ways, I suppose. Artificial insemination, donor eggs, all carefully selected. Surrogacies, maybe using women who aren't affected.'

'What about cloning?'

'It's illegal.' Mac looked at him more keenly. 'Is that what you are thinking?'

'Possibly.'

'I can't believe they'd do it. Not government backed, anyway. It would bring them down. People wouldn't stand for it. I haven't got many morals but anything like that, mucking about, somebody could just get a bit of skin, a hair, their own, anybody's, and put a cell in a Petri dish. What about the kid? How's that going to feel? It's disgusting. Anyway, there has never been anything remotely suggesting that it's been possible to bring a human baby to term. Only animals. Only spare parts from human embryonic stem cells. Kidneys, bladders, that sort of thing. Spare part tissue for medical therapies, therapeutic treatments.'

Warne looked at him, surprised at his vehemence. He said: 'There have been rumours. More than rumours, in fact. I'm sure that reproductive human cloning has been achieved, maybe not in this country but elsewhere in the world. I've followed this for years in medical and scientific journals. It was thought that the children would not be viable. I'm sure that at first that was the case but eventually the science improves, the outcomes improve. The situation here is getting desperate. We all know that.

'I'd be interested if you do find out anything. I'd like our campaign group to look at the wider population issues. We're in grave danger. This country, I mean. Well, more than just this country. This isn't an isolated problem. Governments will go for anything which in their view helps us, the human race, to survive. It's not just here that the birth rate is disastrous or that there are far too many old people and not enough young people to support them.

'We've had to deal with the fall-out from the contamination, mostly from the radiation. Other countries have had their own disasters, including the radiation fall-out throughout Europe and the middle East. Famine, AIDS. Look at what's left of Africa, of the Far East. Whole continents unsustainable beyond 2050. Look at the earlier disastrous one-male-child only policies of China, the wide-scale abortion of female foetuses in India. If we are to survive governments will get desperate and many of them will turn to cloning. I think this government in particular would be prepared to contemplate it and I don't want to see it introduced. I find the idea abhorrent and, more than that, scientifically unsafe. I think there are still ways of increasing fertility and viable babies despite all the problems.'

He watched Mac while he was talking. For once Mac's laid-back sophistication was shattered and he said, probably louder than he realised: 'Cloning ... I agree with you. Couldn't agree more that it's just so disgusting. Children shouldn't be put through that sort of thing. They should have two parents and know who those parents are.' He grasped Warne's hand and shook it. 'Look, I'll help if I can. See what I can find. It's risky but I feel really strongly about this.'

Warne waited a minute until Mac got his composure back and then they walked back into the wedding breakfast together. Fern watched them coming back to their seats, Warne limping slightly. He was definitely fanciable, she thought, and rather charming and for an older man, not at all bad-looking. Much the same sort as Mac, come to think of it. Dark, tall, lean with expressive rather aesthetic faces. No pony tail, no earring on Warne though. Not the sort. Not as overt as Mac at drawing attention to himself but there must be something. He'd become quite a media star when he was involved in that campaign. He obviously liked the limelight.

As soon as they reached their seats the speeches began.

Warne muttered: 'I've got to catch a train. I'm going to dash off when this one finishes.' He turned to Fern. 'I've enjoyed today. Take care of him, won't you?' He nodded towards Mac who was already ordering another bottle of champagne. 'It looks like it might be a long night. And look after that little boy too. You've done well to get him through the first months and I'm sure he'll go from strength to strength now.'

Fern hadn't realised she had said so much to him about William. Unlike her. He was probably a great family doctor.

She said: 'What about you? More media appearances lined up?'

'No, it all seems to have died down at the moment. I've hopes they are going to acknowledge publicly that they have stopped the targeting . Who knows? I expect if there is an announcement you might see me on the box again. Or on other issues to do with population. The media seems to have got me down as a man who is always good for a quote - you know the sort. Rent-a-mouth.' He said it in a self-satisfied way.

Unexpectedly Fern leaned forward and kissed him goodbye. Warne stumbled as he got up from his chair. The Judkins turned away.

He saw the look on their faces and said: 'Goodbye, Henry. So good to see you again after all these years. I had a stroke, OK, I'm not in the slightest bit drunk.' But he was a little and the adrenalin from his conversation with Mac had exacerbated it. The possibility of another campaign, another public fight with him on the side of the angels. It was appealing. Wait until he told Maeve.

CHAPTER 8

The rest of that summer was very hot, punctuated by violent storms. In the middle of one of them, late in July, Mac and Fern drove down to Brighton. Mac had booked them in to the Grand. Johnnie took William to see his parents and set off just ahead of them.

'They must wonder what the hell you're up to,' Mac said when she got in the car.

'They think I'm very busy on an idea for a client. I need a lot of peace and quiet when I'm creating,' she said. She had gone back to work four weeks previously.

The sky was blue black by the time they drove across the Sussex weald and later they had to pull up in a lay-by on the A23 because the rain was so heavy the windscreen washers could not handle it. By the time they drove into the hotel's car park the sun was shining again. They booked in, then immediately went out, walking first along the promenade then pottering through the Lanes. Fern delved into antique shops, Mac waiting impatiently outside. He disliked the crowded interiors, dark and dusty, and he wasn't used to high-maintenance women.

Once back in the room there was still the urgency of new lovers. Nothing had altered in the course of the affair and Fern was amazed that she had not tired of Mac. He could be gentle, playing her like a violin but at times he was rough, almost as if he hated her. She liked that even more, fighting back, scratching, digging her nails in, raking them across his smooth chest and his back until he pinned her down and pushed himself inside her harshly. Turning her over, throwing her across the bed and kneeling, forcing himself into her from behind. She found the humiliation a turn-on. Then she turned, lacerating him, pulling his hair, biting hard into the fleshy part of his upper arm until he shouted with pain.

He ordered a meal and wine in their room and she went to have a bath. The suite of rooms were the most expensive the hotel had and there was a balcony to sit on. When she came out, wrapped in a towel, he was sitting there.

He said, looking at her in the virginal white hotel bathrobe: 'Do you know ... I wish we could have a kid together. I'd like to be a Dad.'

'What's brought this on.' She was genuinely astonished. He had never ever mentioned anything like that.

'I've been doing a lot of work about infertility ... there's a big study going on. I've got to produce the statistics. It's for the Lifestyle and Health departments but it's Treasury-led. The lack of babies, lack of potential wage-earners, professional people, entrepreneurs, hard workers, is causing major head-aches.'

He rarely talked about his work and, self-absorbed, she had never shown any interest.

She sat down at the table on the balcony beside him. There was a warm wind coming off the sea. 'So you think you and I could produce a baby? We haven't done so yet. And we won't. I was badly affected. I had to have chemotherapy when I was a kid.' The words were out before she could stop them. She looked out across the sea, gathering her thoughts, aware that she was going to have to do a lot of explaining.

'What about William?' He leant forward and took her chin and turned her head to face him. She looked him straight in the eye.

'Special arrangement. Johnnie knew someone. Through one of the drug company accounts. Someone very special. Haven't you wondered why William and Johnnie are so alike?'

She said it almost carelessly. 'We're not the only ones. Others are doing it. And we're being encouraged. They want our sort of people to have more children, more children like William. Like you just said.'

She hadn't reckoned on his response. All of a sudden he had withdrawn from her. She'd lost him. She could see it. Physically, mentally. And he was angry, so angry.

'How could you? How could you? You mean cloning, don't you. You do, don't you?'

She looked at him, unsure how to handle his rage. She said: 'But you, of all people, working for the health department, must know what the score is. There has to be an increase in the birth rate. We just won't survive. There has to be ...' she still could not bring herself to say the word. She never had. It sounded cold, futuristic. It wasn't what William was, is. In Mac's mouth the word had sounded so ugly.

'It's disgusting. What will William think when he grows up, when you tell him. It's just the worst thing for a kid. It's humiliating, soul-destroying. God, I don't want anything more to do with you.'

He got up from the balcony, knocking over the wine glasses which splintered into pieces on the floor.

'It's no different ...' she said. 'No different from all the other methods used for infertility. The donor sperm, the donor eggs, the surrogacy ...that's been going on for years.'

He had gone into the room and was flinging his things back into his travel bag. 'All of it. It's all disgusting. Kids not knowing who their real parents are. What do you think it does to them. And cloning. A cell off anyone, maybe a parent, maybe not. Any old egg. How the hell are they going to cope with that.'

Suddenly she understood. How stupid she had been. She said: 'You're one, aren't you? You're one. What are you? A surrogate baby. Donor sperm. What?'

He paused in his packing. The look he gave her was one of pure hatred. 'Yes. AID. I'm one of the ones who cannot find their real father. There are no records. I was too early. Now you can find out; it's legal. Records are kept. Fathers know they might be contacted. I've tried over and over again through the Donorlink register. Nothing. They can't find anybody who matches me, my DNA. Nobody. I'm the kid who never had a dad.'

Fern said: 'You might not like him. I hate my mother. I wish I wasn't related to her.'

'It's completely different, you bloody cow.' He zipped up the bag. Then he looked at her again. Fern thought if I was a different kind of woman I would cry, try and get round him that way.

He said: 'I'll give you a lift home but that's it. I can't get my head round what you and Johnnie have done. I never will.'

They drove in silence. Finally, passing the Gatwick turning, he said: 'Why did you do it? You've never given me the slightest impression that you are that keen on babies, on children. I suppose it was one upmanship. The original Mrs Jones. And Johnnie ...'

'You thought better of him,' she said bitterly.

'I can see that he really loves that little boy. I can understand that. But for both of you, it's the greed, the only thing that matters is what you want, what your desires and aspirations are. It's the child as status symbol. The 'look what we've got that you can't have and sod the rest of you.' Sod the baby, come to that. Can't you understand any of this?' He was driving erratically, speeding up, slowing down. They passed a police car in a lay-by.

'For God's sake,' she said. 'You'll get pulled up for drunken driving, in a minute.'

'I'm not drunk,' he said.

Again there was silence. When he pulled up finally outside the house she started screaming at him, scratching the backs of his hands, digging her long, sharp nails in, fighting, pulling his hair, twisting her hands in it, anything to break the silence. He would not talk. He broke away, roughly, hitting out at her, opening the car door. He left her to pick up her bag which he flung out on to the pavement from the back seat. He walked into his house and slammed the door.

A neighbour across the road, clipping the hedge, stopped to watch. Fern picked up the bag, took out her keys and let herself in. In the hallway was a sock belonging to William. She picked it up, smelling the sweet dankness of his feet. She did love him, she did want him. How dare Mac think that William was just a status symbol. In her other hand she realised that she was still holding several strands of Mac's long dark hair and beneath her finger nails was his skin.

PART 3

CHAPTER 1

'So how are we going to play it?' The speaker was sitting in a room high up in a building with a panoramic view looking south over the Thames. It was late afternoon and still sunny. There had been an Indian summer for the last two weeks of September but now the mornings were sharper. He and two others, a man and a woman, stood looking out over the river, east towards the Eye, motionless while a health and safety inquiry continued over a recent accident with one of its capsules. A child had been killed and there was continuing media intensity.

'I'm not clear what exactly Lifestyle wants. I get a lot of mixed messages.' The woman was slim almost to the point of anorexia. 'In some ways I think they'd like it to get out into the public arena so that there can be adjustment, acceptance. At other times they can see quite clearly that it will almost certainly cause panic, revulsion because of the way the media will handle it. The secretary of state vacillates. His civil servants are fed up to the back teeth with him. At the moment it's all systems go on containing it … them.'

The third man snorted. 'I don't think any of us are naïve enough not to think that the media will tackle the whole thing head-on in the most counter-productive way.'

'It moved,' said the first speaker. 'Sorry … the Eye … no I'm listening. Must be tests.' He had an annoying habit of clinking small change in his pocket which irritated the woman more than the man. Not for the first time she resisted the urge to tell him to stop it.

He said: 'Helen, I think what we want is the usual ... You draw it up. Dave, you bring together the profiles. We'll meet up in the morning. That's already scheduled. I'm going over their heads. I've got a meeting with the PM at six. I need to get my skates on.'

He was a middle-aged man, not tall enough to compensate for his beer belly and Helen gave a catarrhal snort at the idea of him skating anywhere. Dave looked at her and raised an eyebrow. Their boss, Mike Gladwin, ignored both of them and left without saying anything else.

Alone in the room they immediately began to talk about him. Gladwin was having an affair with his secretary and they made an incongruous pair ... she being much taller. Dave had only recently caught up with the gossip which had been rife among the lower ranks for several weeks and Helen knew more details than he did.

Eventually Helen said: 'I'd better get my skates on too. At least I could stay on my feet. I'm actually quite a good skater. I think I got the short straw. You've done most of the work already, haven't you?' Dave nodded.

He went back to his office and typed in his password, then another more complicated security procedure. The files came up on screen. He hit the one which said Edward Fish. There were pictures inset in the profile.

A dark haired, dark eyed baby in the arms of a thin woman with fair hair sitting on a sofa. There was a balding man leaning over, looking down at the baby. Born April 3, 1993 at Hemel Hempstead hospital. Birth normal. Baby weighed 8lbs 9ozs. Father, Edward James Fish, mother's name Katharine Mary Fish. There were no other children. Dave looked at the couple again. Despite the thin prettiness of the woman she was not in the first flush of youth and there were lines around her eyes. She gave off, even in the photo, an aura of neuroses. She was 42 at the time of the photograph.

The only child of elderly parents, then. What was the medical term for her? Elderly primogeniture. There were a number of photos of Ed as a baby, then a toddler beginning to lose the baby look, photos turning him into the beginnings of a small boy. School photo aged around 5 - lively face, dark curls. They had got him into the Abbey primary school in St Albans where he did well. God-fearing lot or had they played the religious ticket to get the boy a place? He was particularly good at maths and science. Unsurprisingly, given the primary school, his background and his ability, he won a scholarship to St Albans School for boys.

The boy was bright, very intelligent, even though the competition was keen but he had not been popular at the outset. His personality hadn't endeared him to his peers or to the teaching staff. School reports mentioned consistently that he seemed to live in a world of make-believe and exaggeration, that he was a bit of a loner. One teacher, the sports master, had thought him rather effete. The team had gone to great lengths to find out more from Fish's teachers. Those who knew him best described him as a liar. Somebody mentioned that he was too sophisticated for his years.

Cocky bugger who thought too much of himself, his last head of year teacher had written in response to the team's inquiry. Told a lot of fibs. I sensed insecurity, he added, but there was a grudging respect for the boy's achievements. With justification, Dave thought. He had had excellent A level results and secured his place at the LSE to study economics without difficulty.

In the first year he had commuted from home. Insufficient funds to live in London and pay his fees or Mummy and Daddy not happy about their only little boy leaving home? At the start of the second year in 2013 he was sharing a flat in Hoxton with two fellow students, one male, one female whom he had been screwing, pre-flat sharing.

Dave, already familiar with the early stuff, concentrated on this part of the report. His team had determined that Ed Fish started gambling on a regular basis at about this time. He started in a small way in the local casino and got hooked. The team wasn't sure when he switched to horses big-time but he had been successful at first. Boasted about a formula. There was evidence of an addictive personality. Smoking, drinking. Not unusual student behaviour but maybe he had displayed rather more excesses than the norm?

The affair with the girl in the flat went sour and she moved out. He got a first class honours degree and was pictured with his mother and father. His mother, still painfully thin, was happily smiling but the father looked very ill. The early pictures had shown him as a large framed type. Now he was wasted, his face emaciated, completely bald. The shiny baldness of chemotherapy treatment.

Ed came into money at the age of 23 when his father, who had worked in the city for one of the leading insurance firms, died of bowel cancer. It seemed he had not trusted his wife sufficiently to leave her his considerable fortune outright and had put it in trust for Ed. £40,000 had been paid over straight away. Ed had bought a share of a racehorse with one of his tutors from the LSE and six others. It wasn't clear if he had known the other syndicate members previously or not. He splashed out on his first car, a second-hand BMW convertible which was just within the legal limits, emissions-wise. Bad Man's Wheels on purpose?

At around the same time he had secured a job at the Department of Health. By this time he had his own flat in South Kensington and, according to the next-door neighbour, an elderly Nigerian, a constant flow of long-legged, blonde girl friends.

The mother was still alive but had moved to Bournemouth after the father's death to live with a sister who was a Jehovah's Witness. Not much evidence of Ed visiting. Quarrels over money? Lifestyle? Religion?

The team had put together a very good record of his gambling. Debts and wins. William Hill had benefited considerably.

There were detailed entries over the Fern affair, with an exhaustive profile of her and her family. Including her medical records. Dave pondered over these, making notes. A child? How? Could be ... he made a note.

The links to James Fields and his wife came into this section and the work that Ed Fish and James had done on the Newcastle project. It was the first time he had been involved in an important project at such a high level. Nothing until the last few entries in any way indicated that he was a security risk. The tail had been put on him directly after he had taken the disk. The meeting with Fields in the Italian restaurant had been bugged. Not so lucky with the meeting with Warne at Heathrow but surveillance had been present.

The last entry caught Dave's attention. It had been added that day. Ed Fish's name was on the UK Donorlink register. Somebody had been doing some meticulous checking.

He went back to the menu and logged in on the James John Warne entry. Born at home, Rosemount, an old Edwardian semi-detached in Priory Road, Bristol, on December 5, 1971. Second child of a hospital doctor, later consultant in paediatrics, and the mother was a general practitioner. With working parents, the boy and his older sister were brought up largely by the paternal grandparents at their home less than a mile away. The mother's parents had lived in Waterford. Warne's parents had met at medical school in Nottingham. Roman Catholics both of them.

John Warne went to an RC primary school, then on to Downside as a boarder. There seemed never to have been a question but that he would study medicine. He got into St Mary's medical school in London. Met his wife Margaret Simpson, non Catholic, theatre nurse, when he came back to the west country to do general practice training at the Royal Devon and Exeter Hospital. He went back to Peru for six months where he had elected to spend some time when he was a student.

It seemed his faith lapsed at about this time; no reason was given. He kept his promises to Margaret, the nurse, and came home to marry her.

The wedding was in the Exeter register office on June 10, 1999. In a photograph of the two, Warne was making a statement in a white suit, very tanned, dark curly hair, an aesthetic rather elongated face. The bride was both elegant and beautiful, dressed in an unusually delicate pale mauve outfit - lavender? A very beautiful girl. Dark-haired, blue-eyed. A very good looking pair.

Warne was taken on at the health centre situated in the old woollen town which borders the Exe in the same year. Within two years he had become a partner. In 2002 they had had a child, which had only lived for a few hours. By 2004 he had begun to show his face in medical politics, locally at first. He got his first taste of media exposure in 2005 when he was interviewed on local television news. It was a time of struggle with the government and with the doctors' trade union over both the hospital consultants' contract and the general practitioners' which government had realised was far too generous. The doctors fell out with their own trade union.

Warne became the spokesman for doctors in the south west and got elected onto the new general practitioners' national committee where he eventually joined the top level negotiating team. In 2010 he was offered a staff post at what was still the British Medical Association in Tavistock Square but he turned it down.

He at first resisted the move by his partners for the practice to go private in 2011 but he had finally agreed and worked with them, from all accounts a good and well-respected doctor in his community. There was a question over one of his patient's deaths but the family had resolved the matter without going to court.

An affair with a fellow member of a national committee, a GP from Worcester, lasted for nearly 18 months. There had been a short affair following that with another doctor, a paediatrician at the William Ashford hospital in Kent. Both women were high-ranking in medical politics and with Warne and a few others formed an innovative, motivating group.

The file went into details of Margaret's numerous affairs although there were blanks on some of the names. Dave looked at recent photographs. Still a very good-looking woman. Striking. He'd turn his head. Maybe even ... He noted her recent admission to the psychiatric unit at Musgrove Park hospital and the fact that she had discharged herself. The notes indicated that she was still being seen in out-patients. He jotted another note on his pad. More detail needed.

The team had done a thorough analysis of Warne's recent activities; his stroke, time-off for the brain cell stem treatment and recovery and his support for the 'Stop Death by Numbers' campaign. The affair with Maeve Dunlop was raked through and the analysis of her background was detailed. Her mother's file had been resurrected.

As he was looking through the Greenham Common stuff Helen came into his room.

'Still at it?'

'They've done a very good job,' he said. 'Have a look at it when you've got a moment.'

'Can I try this out on you?'

'I'm supposed to meet someone at 8. It's 7 already. Can't it wait until the morning?'

She pouted. 'I'll be really quick.' She shoved a couple of pages of A4 under his nose. He skimmed through them. Pros and cons. Neat summary.

'A Royal Commission would certainly buy time,' he said.

'Yes, I thought that was a good option. They might jump at it. Going anywhere nice? With anyone special?'

'That girl I met at the Lifestyle party. She works in James Fields' department.'

'So it's business ...'

'Not necessarily. I fancy getting into her knickers something rotten. How about you … home to hubby?'

Helen said, defensively: 'And what's wrong with that?'

'Still trying?' He said it sympathetically and Helen flushed. 'Yes, yes, of course. The doctors seem to think there is a chance.'

He said: 'Well … have a good night.'

'You too.'

He thought for a moment after she closed the door and dispatched an e-mail to the investigating team. It said: 'Warne … check … no viable children of the marriage, seemingly no further attempts after the baby's death? Why not? Fern has a child but medical history would indicate impossibility. Check further.' He pressed send and watched the anti-virus window come up and run its rapid check. Then he shut down his computer.

□□□□□

The meeting with the Prime Minister did not get off to a good start. She was running half an hour late, he was told when he arrived. Mike Gladwin was not a man who gladly twiddled his thumbs. He pestered the personal gatekeeper, an obdurate woman whom he did not find attractive, at five minute intervals to know 'how much longer' and received each time a courteous but still obstructive reply.

When he was finally let in it was obvious that Tessa had been in the room for at least five minutes. She looked calm, groomed and there was a half empty glass of whisky on the little table in front of her. Her chief press adviser was sitting on the sofa opposite sipping a glass of white wine.

'Hello, Mike. I'm glad you could come over.'

Instantly she had taken the initiative. He'd asked for the meeting. She said: 'We need to get all this straightened out. I can't say I blame the young man for trying to make the public aware of what is going on. I'm as concerned, ethically, as he is about it but he hasn't assessed the other factors involved. I'm afraid there is no alternative.

'I'm going to give you far more insight into the problem than you have had up to date. I understand that Lifestyle have only briefed you and your team on a minimum 'need to know' criteria and have been doing an enormous 'save our bacon' exercise throughout their department. The shredders have been busy and people have sore fingers from pressing delete. How long have you got?'

Clever lady, thought Mike. It's her time that's so precious. He grinned ungraciously. 'All the time you need, prime minister,' he said.

She continued. 'You can ask questions at the end but let me put all the cards on the table. I can assure you that my office, the prime minister's office, officially or unofficially, had no part in the initial trial and gave it no sanction and no knowledge of what followed. However, we are now in charge and in future you will report here.

'It seems that a think-tank attached to, but not employed by, the Department of Lifestyle has masterminded the research cloning programme. They went far further than they should have, following work done by a group of scientists, medics and actuaries commissioned by the King's Centre, who were exploring a number of issues regarding the nation's survival. They commissioned an eminent reproductive scientist, a chap who has been itching to get going on just such a programme and who took matters into his own hands. There are a number of heads rolling over why he was allowed to get away with so much. An assertive, manipulative individual, I understand. Doctors, again, I'm afraid. There is evidence that he also sold his expertise to anything up to 800 families, through personal contacts, probably through the drugs company he acts as a consultant for.

'The immigration centres were selected for the initial trial because of their isolation from the general population. But, and this is a big but, the programme used willing families, immigrants, who for one reason or another – and we can guess that many of them came from the middle East and eastern Europe – were childless. One parent provided the cell and at first the family kept the children. Later into the programme, maybe from about three years ago when the scientists knew they had got it right, the numbers escalated and the women were used as surrogates for the families which then adopted the child. Although it broke the law, ours and internationally, which, of course, is unforgivable, it seems to me that there are a few positives.

'The immigrant families have been housed in good accommodation in areas of the country where they are most needed to provide service industry back-up. They have employment and the children are growing up, part of an ordered community. It means that with an indigenous population of families we may well not, in the future, have to open the country's doors quite so wide in search of ... well, the people who keep the country running. There have been problems, as I'm sure you appreciate, recruiting at this level. But our biggest concern is for the higher echelons in years to come.

'More important heads will roll, be very sure of that. I have the Secretary of State for Lifestyle's resignation on my desk as we speak but for reasons I'm sure you will appreciate I am holding that in abeyance until a more appropriate moment.

'The last thing I want is for this to become a national scandal. That's where you and your people come in and I shall be relying on your assessment. Here are some more facts.

'In a few months there will be a Cabinet re-shuffle and Geoffrey will go. The think-tank has already been disbanded and those involved know they risk prosecution the minute any of this reaches the public.' She smiled in the way that one political commentator had likened to a wind chill factor of -12. There was no warmth in her pale blue eyes.

She went on: 'Reasons can be given out why the think-tank has dispersed if any reporter gets a sniff of it ... end of useful life etcetera etcetera. And the reproductive scientist has wisely retired, he was near that age anyway and could see the sense of dipping into his pension fund, such as it is. Yes ... there was coercion and yes, there is a signed and sealed binding agreement that he cannot divulge anything. We think, and I want your people to find out, how much cloning he did for himself on a personal gain programme. He had a very remunerative link through a big drugs company. We want the names of the families involved.

'Providing these two currently under investigation, Warne and Fish, can be kept quiet and all the material is secured then we can take our time about how and when we divulge the information. We have every intention of involving the public in the ethical debate but we need to educate them first. Fortunately the legislation brought in to protect government and, of course, citizens, from releasing sensitive material which is against the public interest will work well in this case. We can use it on both of the men in question.

'The immigrant families involved desperately want to be allowed to stay in this country and aren't going to cause any problems. They are delighted to have the children and possibly, in some cases, do not fully realise the nature of the child they have given birth to. Those that have given children up for adoption are also pleased about the change in their lifestyles and the opportunities they have been given. There might be a question mark over fully informed consent to act as surrogates if anyone got pedantic. The adoptions have been carefully controlled ... the parents have been only too happy to sign a document which requires them to maintain silence.

'What we now have, thankfully, is evidence from this unofficial trial programme which proves that human reproductive cloning is viable and that healthy children are being born and surviving in a way that has not been possible before. The children born before the worldwide ban in 2005 only survived a very short time and other claims since the ban have never been substantiated. I understand that we now have six year olds who are responding well to a battery of tests.

'I don't need to spell out why it is so necessary to our survival, world survival, that we now have this option. What we don't have, unless we can contain the information, is time to present it so that the public understands this is the only option. Now, any questions? Better still, any suggestions.'

Mike said: 'I've got two of my people working out a strategy at the moment. Of course, we did not have as much detail.' Drop Lifestyle in it. Then stir it. 'We were given the security aspect, not the overall picture, as you so rightly said. The very minimum of need to know.'

She moved impatiently, putting down her glass. He realised she was not going to listen to any internal criticisms, any inter-departmental feuds or bickering. She wanted solutions and quickly. Her press adviser had kept out of the conversation. Now he spoke: 'We have kept a lid on this so far but it is getting increasingly difficult.'

Mike said: 'I hope to have something for you by lunch time tomorrow.'

He walked back to the office, wondering if Emily would have waited. She was eager but not that eager ... the affair had moved on. Only the security lights were on in the passages and the night-watchman came up with him to his office. On his desk were both Dave and Helen's recommendations. Both must have stayed late to complete them. He would have expected nothing less.

He noted the Royal Commission idea but he was looking for a quicker fix. He noted what Dave had written and picked up the phone.

CHAPTER 2

'I'm sorry, but we will have to keep you in for further tests.' Mac scowled at the doctor, a woman who, he guessed, was about the same age as himself.

'Just give me the pills. If it's that it's not that big a deal nowadays.'

'Your levels are extreme. T-cell count under 10. Viral load in the thousands. We need to find out what is causing the anaemia.'

'I've got things I need to finish at work.'

'You must rest. You must try to rebuild your immune system. It is still serious ... despite all the advances. You'll need blood transfusions.' She had a no-nonsense, no arguments entered into, brusque attitude.

'Shit. Fucking arseholes and shit.'

'We're going to send you to one of the special hospitals. This one is funded by the Elton John Foundation, in the country. It's down in Hampshire. Lovely place. Beautiful water gardens. You'll like it.'

'I've got things I must do.'

'I don't want to get heavy but we can get a court order.'

'Only if I'm threatening to run amok. Make love to every man, woman or child I meet.'

'Far from the case. I'm afraid the balance is now weighted far more in our ... the medical profession's remit ... than in your's. It's in your best interest. You'll start to recover much more quickly and the staff down there are excellent. The counselling is second to none. You'll need it. There are a lot of lifestyle changes to be made.'

She added, somewhat diffidently: 'It's only because of your rank and the fact you work for the Department of Health that you get such a good offer. I'm afraid most of the facilities around the country aren't nearly as good for those who prove positive but they all have to go automatically. You should know the policy given where you work.'

'I'll have to make some phone calls.'

'Of course.' She went out of the room. Mac scowled at his mobile phone, wondering who he should call. He pressed the key for the department and spoke to personnel. The woman in the office didn't probe, just spelled out the procedures he needed to follow to make sure he kept within his contract.

He thought about phoning Fleur. 'The bitch. Had to be her.'

He did phone James but only got his 'I am in the office today but in meetings. Please leave a message.' He didn't. He would have liked to speak to Warne. Out of the question.

The appearance of the two men in the cubicle took him by surprise. One of them said: 'We're here to take you down to Longstock.'

They were big blokes … both of them. The penny did not drop until they were escorting him down the hospital corridor to the lift. He stopped to argue, saying that he needed to go home and get some things. He was told by the guy on his left that it was all under control. Someone would have collected all that he needed during his stay. 'How did they get in?' The man shrugged.

It was in the empty lift that they gripped his arms, one on each side. He tried to struggle but there was no way he could have overpowered even one of them. As they crossed the shiny floor under the big glass ceiling to the front entrance people stared as he shouted that he was being kidnapped. People looked, then looked away. Obvious nutter. There were too many in and around the hospital for anyone to take much notice.

He was put in what used to be called a people carrier when there were still families to be carted around. It was waiting on the hospital forecourt, a woman driver at the wheel. Before it drew away he tried to reach across one of the men to hammer on the window but his arm was held tightly.

His companions kept silent, refusing to answer his questions and eventually he gave up the futile exercise. The woman who was driving never once turned round although he tried to catch her eye in the mirror.

So the government would go this far? He had not envisaged this. His job had given him privileges but he knew that policies, some of which he had worked on, were more than just projects, paper exercises. He hadn't wasted much thought on the logical end game.

He had stepped over the line. He was in new territory. He had thought the gamble was worth it. He had not realised that retribution would be so swift, without reference to the law. Early in the journey he had shouted: 'I want to see my lawyer.'

He began to panic. Sweat dripped off him. He could feel beads of moisture build up, run down his forehead. Drip off his nose. Was this more evidence of his illness? The complete breakdown of his immune system?

The driver swung off the motorway at last and they began to travel through minor roads over the flint flecked, chalky hills of what ... Hampshire, Wiltshire? He wasn't sure. It wasn't an area he had visited. He could not remember if there were any major racecourses in this direction. What would be the closest? He shut his eyes, concentrating. Wincanton ... no, Salisbury, of course. He'd never been there.

They were on the Salisbury road travelling along a long straight stretch that rose and dipped. A Roman road? At the top of a hill, near a building that looked as if it might once have been a pub but was now more than half way to being a ruin, they turned off to the right. They were in wind farm country and once, off to his right, he caught sight of a large dish structure rising above the undulating landscape. Satellite tracking station?

They drove past some run down buildings in what might once have been a village. Part of the relocation programme? He realised what a sheltered life he led in London; office, home, visits to racecourses, visits to the stables. He had never seen at close hand the effects of the stringent planning policies Lifestyle had introduced, or, if he had, he had not fully appreciated them.

The driver stopped the vehicle at some closed gates. A woman, with a big dog at her heels, strong overtones of Alsatian crossed with God knows what, came out of a lodge and looked at the papers the driver thrust at her. She nodded and unlocked the heavy iron gates. Up the drive he could see a large house. The gardens were laid out impeccably and in the distance he caught the glimmer of water through trees, beyond the lawns.

The driver stopped outside the double-fronted main door which was open. Two men in uniform were waiting and his two escorts held his upper arms to take him out of the side opening. They were rough and he protested. The uniforms stepped forward. 'OK lads, we've got him.'

Mac said again: 'I want to see ... speak to my lawyer. You've no right ...' A man came out into the hall from a doorway further back where the light wasn't good.

He was tall, thin, receding hair. Mac knew how donnish he would be before he opened his mouth. He reminded him of a teacher he'd had, a Latin teacher. 'Mr Fish? I'm afraid we have every right. We have an order. Prevention of terrorism. You've been rather a foolish fellow. We have the evidence. I'll come and see you later in your ... room.' Mac noted the slight hesitation with mounting anxiety.

CHAPTER 3

Tanner told Warne: 'You must let her work through this obsession. I can't help her unless she helps herself.'

Then he dropped the bombshell: 'You know I can help her to have the child. She's not too old. Medically ... for her own good ... maybe that's what's best for her. Perhaps for you, too. For both of you. Can I ask why you have no family? From my examinations and from those of the gynaecologist she could have had help after that first death. There were plenty of ways you could have been helped.'

Warne looked at him aghast, outraged at the man's lack of sensitivity. 'It's none of your business,' he said.

'You're wrong. Your wife is 'our' business. There is also the question of healthy children. You must have received the circular from the department in your professional capacity and I can see no reason why you and your wife could not, should not ... you're both intelligent, in reasonable health or at least, not unreasonably unfit. You've recovered well from the stroke and the implants have worked ... you're unlikely to have further problems and are still just about young enough and certainly financially solvent to manage at least one child. You match the majority of the criteria ... apart maybe from your ages and really ... well ... nowadays ... why not?'

'This is madness. That circular didn't mean couples like us. For God's sake. Childlessness isn't a criminal offence. What's the government going to do? Jail?

Fines? This is absurd. I've seen nothing that in any way suggests people of our age ...'

Tanner shrugged. 'Think about it. No, of course I can't force you, nor can anyone else. But it might be the saving of her. I've seen this before. She's at that certain age ... lifestyle choices, sense of missed opportunities, a craving for a way of life that differs radically from the one that has been the norm. It used to be called the menopause. Applies to men as well as women. Usually ends in divorce with the woman shouting that she needs her space. Your wife seems to be having a delayed reaction to the 'nearly too late to have a child' syndrome. She's an unfulfilled mother, not somebody who needs more space. Less, if anything. What was she like five, six years ago?'

Warne shrugged. Involved with a fellow student then? He could not remember. Maybe it was that fling she had had with the golf professional? A man half her age, very good-looking and the only one that he had felt jealous of, not because of what he was up to with Margaret but because he was so confident in his youthful good looks. Fortunately the affair hadn't lasted very long.

He did not intend to enlighten Tanner who continued: 'Momentarily, but not irreparably, this craving for motherhood has disturbed the balance of her mind. She is responding well to treatment and has been able to talk very openly about her feelings to her counsellor. She wants a child. Is that irrational? It seems eminently sensible to me. I am concerned that if she does not get her way she might take her life. She was suicidal when she was admitted and for some time afterwards. I hope, think that, for now that phase has passed.

'I've no idea ... she hasn't told me and you obviously don't intend to ... why you did not attempt another pregnancy. I've been looking back at both your medical histories ... I see in fact that you, in all probability, do have a 'family' except that you have no knowledge of it. You were a sperm donor, weren't you, as a medical student? Does she know that?'

It came out of the blue. Something that he kept battened down, tentatively thought about in the middle of the night. Warne had least expected this attack. He flushed. Why *had* he done it? Persuaded by contemporaries? An easy way to make a small amount of cash when he had been a student? £20 a wank. He'd been going out with a nurse from one of the fertility clinics ... that was it ...

'You're just the kind of donor we need,' she said in her soft Irish brogue when they had been lying in bed after making love. He bent to nibble her nipples, letting his tongue stray round the very pink pimply surrounds which hardened under his caressing. She was a redhead and had the pale freckly skin that went with it. He had always been attracted to redheads.

'Strapping chap like you, good genes, good health ... brainy ...' He'd stopped her compliments and made love to her again but he'd been flattered and had talked about it to other friends whom he knew had been donors. Why not? There had been a couple of donor sessions then he and the girl fell out, she wanted marriage, she was a few years older. He was only 23 and had no desires to tie himself down. He'd not minded the spell in the cubicle ... flipping through the porno magazines. It had been a quiet time in his busy junior doctor day.

It had had its moments. He had come across the photograph of a girl he knew by sight, the secretary of an Ear, Nose and Throat consultant. He'd had to turn the magazine upside down to confirm it was her. Her hands rested lightly on each side of her bottom which faced the camera. She was bending forward, long hair almost touching the floor and her face was between her legs. It wasn't the most erotic bits of her, well exposed, that turned him on but the fact he knew her and that she was wearing only stripy, mid thigh socks. A few weeks later he passed her in the corridor and grinned at her. 'Good job somebody's happy,' she said.

It might well have worked out better if he had married the Irish girl ... better than Margaret ... but his parents had not approved of Bridget and not only because of the age difference. A fast and loose Irish redhead with too thick a brogue for their professional niceties. His mother, with her own Irish ancestry, was most certainly unnerved by the reminder that she was a sister under the skin. Judy O'Grady and the Colonel's lady.

They'd approved of Margaret, praising her elegance and beauty. How short-sighted they had been. She'd never let them find out about the affairs and he'd been too shamed about them and would never have complained about her to his father and mother.

He hadn't gone again to the clinic after he had broken off with Bridget, had failed to keep the next appointment though the clinic's appointments secretary had chased after him for months.

It had always been there. At the back of his mind ... particularly after he'd conceded to Margaret's ultimatum. After the two early miscarriages and then the baby's death she had given up. She said she was not willing to put herself through the agonies of fertility clinics and that she would not go down the IVF route. He must accept that there would be no children. They must please themselves from now on. She said she wanted other experiences outside the marital bed. He could do the same. Hurt by her ultimatum and immediate action in securing a lover he had held back at first, Catholic guilt gnawing at his conscience. Then at a medical conference he had met the girl from Worcester but she hadn't wanted children either. If she had maybe he'd have divorced Margaret.

He'd been comforted by the thought as the years went by that somewhere out there he was the father of children ... how old now ... late twenties? ... how long did they hang on to the sperm? There'd been plenty of it. When they'd brought in the ruling that children could try to contact their biological parents ... his contribution had been before that but he'd wondered if there might be a telephone call, a letter, a knock on the door ... had he wanted it to happen? Part of him had but when he could have volunteered to put his name on the register he had held back. Why?

He had always wanted children. When he embarked on the affair with Maeve there had been the nagging thought that this relationship, too, would never beget the child he craved. Beget. Great word. Maeve was already too old. Or at least he had thought so. Perhaps he was wrong if Tanner was right. There was a brief flicker of thought that he could father a child with Margaret ... and another with Maeve.

If Margaret had not conceived in the past why did Tanner think she would now? He asked the question.

'There is a lot more that can be done. Other methods. The situation ... well, it's thrown up so many more possibilities because of the crisis. The science is proved, tested. The gynaecologist seems to think that she is not infertile.'

Warne nodded. 'I did suggest trying other methods. I don't think she wanted to be hampered by children. It's as simple as that. The failure to carry a child, to have a live child, was her way out, not to have the tests, not to have the treatments. She's very ambitious but she is insecure. I know enough psychiatry to be able to diagnose that. She needed the affairs as a way of convincing herself that she was still desirable to men, still very attractive. She did not want the complications of a family.'

He stopped himself. He did not want to take Tanner, who was leaning forward, interested, into his confidence. He disliked the man.

Tanner said: 'Do I have your permission to pursue this further if she continues to want a child?'

Warne said: 'It takes two to tango.'

'And you won't ...?'

'I don't know ...' He didn't. He thought of
Margaret. The desire still lurked. Could he rekindle it
into the sort of blaze that was needed? Could she? He
looked Tanner straight in the eye. 'I honestly don't
know ... if she ... or I ...'

Tanner said: 'You can be the father but as the donor,
like you did before. That might be by far the best
solution and have far more chance of success. I can
make the arrangements.' Warne nodded.

CHAPTER 4

Gladwin said: 'They're keeping Edward Fish down at Longstock. I think they may have some difficulty with him. He's a very articulate young man and he knows his rights. We've taken precautions within the law. His medical records are watertight. We can easily prove he poses a threat to the population at large. My fear is the girl-friend. What have we done about her?'

Dave said: 'My reports are that they split up in July, August at the latest and that it was acrimonious. We think he may have found out about her little secret. I'm pretty sure she's not been in contact with him since.'

'She was with him at the wedding in June when he met Warne. I think we should take every precaution to make sure they are not in contact.'

Dave grinned. 'She hasn't. Been taking precautions, I mean. She's pregnant again. She's only just got confirmation from the clinic so I guess she's only about six to eight weeks. Another child the same way as the other, we understand. It gives us the hold we need over her.'

'She shows no sign of being involved in any way with what Warne and Fish have been doing. She sounds a self-centred bitch from the reports.'

Dave said: 'The other problem is Maeve Dunlop but Helen's got an interesting proposal on that. I understand the PM has given the go-ahead on her Royal Commission idea. Helen says get Maeve appointed a commissioner. She's high ranking enough to be considered and her leading role in the 'Death by Numbers' business would justify it further. The alternative voice. Keep the public happy. Neat?'

Gladwin nodded, thinking about it, wondering whether it had legs. Dave knew pretty soon he'd start presenting it as his own idea, garnering the kudos, just as he had with Helen's Royal Commission. Poor old Helen. He'd long grown accustomed to his position as number 2, the man who made things work, had his ideas pinched, ran the department during Gladwin's long absences but let Gladwin strut his stuff in high places. Helen still got very upset when she saw her best ideas appropriated. She'd learn ... or move on soon. Maybe she'd be lucky and conceive that baby.

Gladwin said: 'I'll have a think about that. I can see some drawbacks.' He didn't enumerate them. Dave turned away, grinning, ready to leave the room but Gladwin called him back.

'There's something else you should know,' he said. 'It's about Warne. Tanner's come up with an idea. It could be the solution. Really shut him up.'

He looked at Dave. 'I get the feeling Helen might be a touch squeamish over this one. Can you break it to her? You're good at that sort of thing. She's got a few problems in this area. It was borderline whether we'd take her on because of it. Tanner's convinced Warne that the wife will get IVF treatment and that his contribution will ensure he's the Daddy. Seems he's pretty handy in that department.' Gladwin accompanied his words with vigorous action.

'I saw that in the report.'

'Well, it seems Warne was all prepared to do the gentlemanly thing and let nature take its course, close his eyes and think of England, but now Tanner and the gynae have told both of them that the natural way is unlikely to be successful and that IVF is the best bet and he can donate. Warne's keen. Very keen. He wants a child as much as his wife does. Tanner's going to arrange another little surprise, though, when it comes to the crunch. Guess?'

Dave looked at him, trying not to show his real feelings.

'We'll have him just where we want him. A little bundle of joy … spitting image of him. Now that is really neat. I reckon if all goes to plan we should be able to break the news when it's most advantageous. Dr Warne won't have a platform to condemn anything that the government is involved in. I think with a bit of judicious leaking we shall have him by the short and curlies.'

□□□□□

Maeve sent Warne an e-mail at the surgery. 'Guess what … I've been asked to sit on a Royal Commission looking into the population problems. What news on your front???? Love … mean it … Maeve.'

His instant reaction was jealous irritation. Why not him? Why had she had the invitation? He surely had more right to a place on the Commission. He could have had his say, made sure the important ethical issues weren't swept under the carpet in a massive government window-dressing initiative, made the public fully aware of the implications … he picked up the phone too quickly, dialling her number. Then he put it down, giving himself a cooling-off period.

His mind wasn't fully on the next patient, fobbing the woman off with easy solutions to her possibly more serious condition, prescribing pills too quickly with less argument than he would normally have employed.

How was he going to tell Maeve what he and Margaret had agreed with Tanner? That had been uppermost in his mind for a week now but he had shoved it aside, toying with different versions of the conversation he must have. They had not spoken for over two weeks, not since Margaret had returned from the hospital. He had not dared get in touch while Margaret's mind was unbalanced.

He phoned reception. How many more patients? He was told three. He paid more attention to them, ashamed of his treatment of the other woman. The last patient he saw, another woman of much the same age, was a difficult case. He was positive what the diagnosis was but decided to refer her on for rapid investigation. He feared the worst and knew the woman did too.

He took his time, making the arrangements, talking carefully and considerately, making sure the woman understood the options. She was the wife of a local lawyer, a man he had known for a long time in the town and he offered to talk to her husband but she did not want him to. When she finally left his room she had managed to control the tears and as always he was amazed at the resilience so many patients showed when faced with a death sentence. He went to the cupboard in the corner and poured himself a stiff whisky. The bottle was still half full.

When he finally got through he was told Maeve was in London at a meeting. She wouldn't be back in the office until the morning. Was it urgent? Did he have her mobile number? He did but this wasn't a conversation that could be hurried, snatched in Maeve's lunch hour or between meetings.

Margaret was at home and he went there for a coffee and sandwich before going back to the surgery for a clinic. He needed to keep checking on her state of mind. She seemed reasonable, almost happy.

There was a practice meeting later in the afternoon but that evening he was off duty. He debated. He could drive to Bristol, wait at Maeve's home. Take the risk that she would return home that evening.

He said to Margaret: 'Look, something's cropped up at regional HQ in Bristol. They want me to go up and talk through some medical matters on primary health care with the team there and I said I'd go after the meeting. I can justify taking the car and still be home before midnight.' He'd never needed to play these games before. It was understood. She did her thing. He did his. No questions. He could feel himself becoming flustered at the lies.

Margaret said: 'You'd better not be going to see that woman.'

'No, I'm not.' He could feel his colour rising. He turned away. She said: 'Good.' She switched on and found a mid-day news programme. It was on it. The Commission. The names were read out, with shots of the commissioners. Maeve's name was mentioned. God, that would set Margaret off.

Surprisingly she merely said: 'Why's she been picked? It should be you, if anybody.'

'That's what I thought.' He was quite pleased that Margaret felt the same. He grinned at her.

She said: 'The appointment came through today. It's next week. Monday. Can you re-arrange at the surgery when you go back in.' It wasn't a question.

He said: 'There is another way ...'

'I'm not risking that and there is very little chance of it being successful. That's what they told us. Anyway, I can't imagine you want to. You've probably forgotten how ...'

He said bitterly: 'What a passion killer you are.' He slammed the door as he left.

CHAPTER 5

Emery Hambling practised his opening remarks to the press conference to announce the Royal Commission on Human Potentiality as he shaved himself. He was a fastidious man and he was annoyed to find that his wife had re-arranged the contents of the mirrored cupboard above the basin since he had shaved himself the day before. Every so often for some bizarre reason she risked his wrath ... too strong a word ... his disapproval ... and had a tidying up session. She said he sulked.

He still favoured the old style shaving brush, though it was no longer made of badger hair, bowl of soap which he meticulously smoothed out with a piece of tissue after he had used it and safety razor, which he always cleaned carefully, unscrewing it and running the blade under the cold tap, watching the stubbly hairs swirl away.

He was not entirely happy with the format of the day which the over-bearing public relations woman from the Department of Lifestyle had forced through. He had fought for a public relations expert to be funded and attached to the secretariat, one whom he could control, but although his request had been acceded to the man who was appointed was not assertive enough to contain, in any way, Emma Moorhouse from the DoL. She was determined to keep a firm grip on this particularly high profile issue.

It seemed to him that far too much consideration was being given to the media in order to secure a favourable impression for the work of the Commission. He was afraid it smacked of collusion with the government and he wanted to appear more detached. Too much time was being built in to allow interviews by him and selected others, deemed media-friendly. At least two others had their own political reasons for getting over particular viewpoints. The woman he thought of as that damned social worker was one. Maeve Dunlop. He'd told Emma Moorhouse it was her job to keep them quiet, out of the limelight. She hadn't liked him giving the orders and had snapped back that of course, she'd already taken steps.

He was hoping that he would be able to make sensible headlines on behalf of the Commission that might in some way ease the way forward for the government on the cloning issue. He was fully aware what he had been appointed to do.

He anticipated certain groups, certainly many religious groups, would be totally against any kind of formal trial programme. He had been briefed that worldwide there had been at least three children from ill-conceived, badly conducted, illegal experiments in the early years of the 21st century who had died on reaching puberty, some time between 2015 and 2020 and that in Britain there had been some illegal experimentation and that a small number of babies had been born and were surviving well, some now almost six years old. The reproductive scientists were certain that they had perfected the technology and a trial programme would be the only way to ensure that cloning was consistently viable.

That this information had remained secret was surprising given the lengths, pecuniary and otherwise, that the media had gone to in order to secure such stories. He was only privy to the information because the Prime Minister and the Secretary of State for Lifestyle had thought it necessary to inform him when he was first invited to chair the Commission. Now he wished they hadn't.

Hambling was an astute politician - he'd trampled on a lot of other careerists to get to the top. He knew that he had received privileged information in order to tie his hands. There had been a subtle hint that greater things were in store for him if he could steer the Royal Commission to what they, the Prime Minister and Cabinet, believed was the only solution; properly conducted trials with every conceivable scientific safeguard leading to the widespread introduction of a viable reproductive cloning programme. Everyone shied away from the use of the word 'human'.

The reproductive scientists had given categorical assurance that the technology was now in place to allow such a programme to progress and that all the early problems, particularly of rapid ageing, had been overcome.

The Prime Minister, whom he had known as a fellow-student at Balliol and with whom he had once had a one-night stand, had taken him into her confidence and explained that the country was on the brink of disaster. She never gave any sign that she remembered their brief night of copulation and he was too much of a diplomat to remind her. He'd been pretty drunk and didn't remember it that well himself.

The latest population projection indicated that England alone would no longer be viable in 30 years; Scotland, Wales and Ireland no longer viable in 40. There must be a cloning programme.

He had asked about the European option but was told that the union was in even more difficulty since it had brought the population issue, in particular the cloning debate, into the open, had held a referendum and lost.

He had asked about immigration policies but was told that they could in no way sustain the economics of the country and that the birth rate in this previously fecund section had fallen in line with the rest of Europe, Asia, Africa and South America and for many of the same reasons.

The Secretary of State, still in Hambling's view too superficial and immature to have attained such a high position, said baldly: 'We've got more than enough people to do the dirty work but we've got to get the brains back. We've got to have the doers, the thinkers, the achievers, the high-flyers, the innovators. We've got too many civil servants, not enough entrepreneurial types. The bright kiddies know the civil service gives the best chance of long term employment and their salary structure is good – we've got the Blair governments to thank for that.

'There is hardly anybody creating wealth for the country. The birth rate is such that soon there will be nobody left to contribute in any meaningful way to allow this country to keep going. We're already having to pay far too much for the old people who live beyond retirement age and have no pension provision. Somehow we've got to stop all this service industry crap and get back to making things that we can flog to the rest of the world, particularly the American and Far East markets.'

The Prime Minister, frowning slightly, said: 'We've been badly let down by previous forecasts. Environmentally, scientifically, health-wise. Nobody seems to have been brave enough to point out all the consequences to this government or any other since the nuclear disasters .... We've got to grasp the nettle ...' She stopped herself.

Hambling said, rather than asked: 'It has to be reproductive cloning.' He had come to terms with the ethics in the last few years. His second wife, Lynne, desperately wanted a child. She was becoming anorexic again. He had not known her when she suffered from it before, she had been only in her teens. Lynne had been a student when the affair began.

His first wife had pointed out, angrily, when she found out about Lynne that he was old enough to be her father. He had two children by his first marriage, a son, and his daughter was two years older than Lynne. Both of them were living with long-term partners and he hoped for their sakes they could have children of their own. They had been lucky. He had been a visiting professor in the States for five years from 2008, thank God, but his children were only part of the equation. It depended on the partners. He hadn't liked to ask such delicate questions ... he was only just getting back on speaking terms with the daughter although the son had been more tolerant of his new marriage.

The Prime Minister had asked him about his children. He thought about her question while he shaved, taking great care not to cut himself. He had not appreciated how serious the situation was until Tessa gave him the viability figures - so many lives affected and such a devastating prediction.

The press conference was timed for 11.

□□□□□

Press release, October 16, 2021: Embargoed information until 11am.

A Royal Commission has been established to consider human potentiality. Its first report will deal with the viability and ethical considerations of reproductive cloning with particular reference to its suitability in the population adjustment programme already established in this country.

The Commission will advise the King, government, Parliament and the public on the issues. The Commission has been set a tight deadline because of the need for urgency in this important matter and will report within the next three months.

The primary role of the Commission is to contribute to policy development in the longer term by providing an authoritative factual basis for policy making and debate, and setting new policy agendas and priorities. This requires consideration of the economic, ethical and social aspects of an issue as well as the scientific and technological aspects. In reaching its conclusions, the Commission seeks to make a balanced assessment, taking account of the wider implications for society of any measures proposed.

The terms of reference are to examine how reproductive clones will contribute to the long term viability of this country and will have regard to the number of clones allowed in any one year, the potential for such beings to be integrated in society, the long term health of such beings and the cost effectiveness of introducing such a policy. The Commission will take into account all previous research and examination of ethical issues in relation to embryonic stem cells and therapeutic cloning. It will, if appropriate, recommend the repeal of the Human Reproductive Cloning Act, 2001 which made reproductive cloning a criminal offence.

The Commission will give opportunity to all interests likely to be affected by its recommendations to give their views on issues within the terms of reference.

The chair of the Royal Commission will be Professor Sir Emery Hambling, Principal and Vice Chancellor, University of Cambridge. He is former vice chancellor of the University of Sussex (2010-2016); Professor of Bio-ethics of University College, London (2006-2018); lecturer in scientific ethics at the Institute of Education in London (1996-2003). The members of the Commission will be Professor Dame Iqbal Allinson, Professor of Embryology, Queen's School of Medicine, Nottingham University; Sir Anthony Dawes, Chief Inspector of Schools since 2018, chairman of the Greater London Health authority; Sir Philip Trencherman, Former chairman of the European stock exchange and deputy chairman of the Lloyds Barclay banking group; Dr Ian Fenner, general practitioner of the Priory Medical Centre, Oxford and representing the Royal College of General Practitioners; Dr Harold de Sousa, chairman of the Ethics committee, Medical Associations of England, Scotland and Wales; Jasper Goodison, lawyer and director of Provident and Mutual Assurance; Hamoud Hassan, QC, Bencher of the Middle Temple, specialist in family law;

Iris Goodleigh, medical journalist, writer and broadcaster with particular interest in children's welfare, chairman of the British Adoption Society; Professor Idris Hughes, Professor of Paediatrics and Provost for Medicine and Health Sciences, University of Swansea; Maeve Dunlop, chair, Association of Directors of Social Work (England) and a founding member of the 'Stop Death by Numbers' campaign.

For further information please contact Robin Elliott, Freebody Public Relations, 10 Mortimer Street, London, W1T 3JN, Telephone 010 897 6348 or Emma Moorhouse, chief press officer, Department of Lifestyle, 17-24 Smith Square, London, SW1P 3JR, Telephone 010 765 3910.

□□□□□

Mike Gladwin handed the release around the table. 'The press conference, as you all know, begins at 11, in two hours' time. Hambling's taking it. The early press has been good, speculating on the Commission and, wonder of wonders, nobody's broken the embargo. It will be the lead story for the rest of the day, unless there's a mega worldwide disaster.

'I understand that bitch from Lifestyle ... Emma ... is keeping a very tight rein on the show. Maeve Dunlop's the loose canon but I understand Emma's even got her under control. She's very flattered to have been asked on to the Commission. I think it was a good move of our's to get her on side.' Helen and Dave exchanged glances.

'What's the news on Fish?'

'Still at Longstock. They've got him on some tablets that have knocked him out.'

'And who's followed up the girl friend?'

Helen said: 'The latest I've got is that she's had the pregnancy confirmed at the 12 week mark and it's another cloning that looks like being a success. The scans are good. She has been given time to think about whether she ... they ... want to go ahead. Honestly, people like her ...' She reddened, aware of her colleagues' evident interest in her own reactions. 'So we need to make sure there is no contact between Fish and her. He must be convinced by now that she infected him. Let's keep it that way.'

Dave asked: 'This guy Hambling ... how impartial is he?'

'Hand-picked,' said Gladwin. 'There are enough free spirits on the Commission to keep it honest ... but not enough to upset the outcome. These things take a bit of time but there's a three-line whip on this one and it's being rushed through. It should report in early spring. They're allowing James Fields, from Lifestyle, to work on the figures for it. He's had a fright, he knows he's been under surveillance, his wife is pregnant, it's a way of keeping him on side. I thought he might be more of a risk but Tessa's henchmen think it's better this way. We'll wait and see.'

'And Maeve Dunlop? She's obviously going to take an independent line.'

'Again we'll wait and see. I think she will get sucked in ... Hambling's a very skilful operator. And if she doesn't ... well, she'll be the voice crying in the wilderness and she'll soon find she's being pushed in all directions by the loony fringe organisations. No, our main concern now is keeping Warne and Fish contained until after the Commission reports. I think we're probably OK now the medics have done their job with Mrs Warne.'

Helen said, more shrilly than she intended: 'This is totally unethical.'

Gladwin replied: 'If you don't like the heat, get out of the kitchen. You knew what you were getting in to when you applied for the job.'

He turned to Dave. 'I'm leaving Fish to you and your bods. I'll keep control of the Warne situation. Helen, any assistance Emma Moorhouse needs with the commissioners ... that's down to you. Now you can both bugger off and get on with things. I'm a very busy man. We'll meet again at the end of the week.'

CHAPTER 6

Mac opened his eyes. There was someone in the room but he could not make out who it was. His first instinct was that it was Fern, she had been real in his dream, but then the figure moved again and he could see it was a man. He felt so fuzzy, blurred, out of his body, out of control.

He had been sleeping, it felt, for weeks. He had lost all sense of time. Each time he came to, felt strong enough to shuffle to the bathroom or move around the room, he had quickly become exhausted and, gripping on to the furniture, crawled back into bed.

They shoved the pills at him at six hourly intervals, shaking him awake. It seemed it was a different nurse each time. Men and women. Who was the person in the room now? He thought he had spoken but perhaps he hadn't. It was a struggle to move his lips, to get enough air into his lungs to allow him to speak. His throat felt paralysed. What the hell was going on?

The man didn't speak. He tried again. The man turned. It was his father ... no, his father was dead ... in any case that man hadn't been his father. He knew that. He'd known that for a long time. Not his real father. His mother had told him that. When he was twelve. Told him. Much wanted. Both of us wanted you. Sometimes it happens with a man and woman. The man can't but the woman can. Daddy's lung condition meant he couldn't ... I had some treatment. Then we had you. We both love you dearly. Your father does, loves you to bits ... just like as if he was your real father. You're our son.

They had tricked him. The man whom he had called Daddy ... he wasn't really his father. Some other man. Somebody his mother didn't even know. A donor. Somebody who had been kind enough to give what was needed to help her have a baby. To fertilise the egg that was him. 'We should think of him as a very kind man,' she had said.

He'd gone on the internet straightaway. Sperm donors. The idea appalled him. The boys at school joked about masturbation. Bashing your meat. Just wait. It'll come. That's the stuff that makes babies. He'd come from that. Put in a test tube and then put inside his mother. But his father ... he wasn't his father. He'd never felt close to that man, had always found him an embarrassment, he was so uncool. It was a relief to find that Jim was not, after all, his father. They'd tricked him, though, and he resented that he had spent so many years believing their lies. He was breathless from the deceit. He couldn't bear it. He looked at the mothers with their children. How many of them? Or was he the only kid in St Albans. How many were there like him? The memory of that time flooded back, as it did most days when he woke. He screwed up his eyes to focus on the man in the room, to see his face.

The man said: 'You're properly awake, are you? I've been coming in to see you at regular intervals but you always seem to be asleep. I'm going to ask the nurse to give you something that will help you keep awake ... the pills are working well but maybe you could have something which won't make you so woozy.'

Mac mumbled, hesitated, then spoke more clearly: 'I don't want any more damn pills. What are they? Something that's going to get me to say things I don't mean? I'm not bloody daft. You're here to trap me into saying something that I'll regret, aren't you? I want my lawyer. It's my right.'

'Don't get excited. My name's David Melhuish. My friends call me Dave. I'm here to help you out of the mess you're in. We don't want you to ruin your career for the sake of a bit of nonsense. We know all about what you've done. Taking the information and then telling Dr Warne about it. Where's the disk? With Warne? It doesn't actually matter to us because we've already got enough evidence to pin this on you.'

Mac didn't answer. He sat up, swung his legs over the side of the bed and stood up, grasping the duvet around him.

'What are you? Secret Service? MI whatever it is. 5?'

Melhuish nodded. He said: 'You signed the confidentiality contract when you got the job with your department. You're in big trouble already but we can see you through this without it ending in a trial if you'll play ball.'

Mac said: 'You don't want the publicity of a trial, do you? I can force it through. What have I got to lose?'

'Possibly your life,' said Melhuish. He said it quietly, looking at Mac. 'Who knows you're here? Your mother? Your girl friend … the lovely Fern? Warne … your employers know what you're suffering from … colleagues won't be surprised … a dose of pneumonia and with your condition … curtains, eh? Quiet funeral in the grounds … just who would kick up a fuss about you? You're a gambling man. What do you reckon the odds are on you getting out of here alive?'

Mac didn't answer at first. He looked at Melhuish. 'About 11 to 4 against, I'd say.'

CHAPTER 7

The taxi drew up and Maeve got out, dropping keys into the gutter in her haste to find the money to pay the driver. Warne watched from his car parked further down the street. It was unlike her not to have planned in advance, found the money during the journey from the station.

He felt very unsure of himself, unsure of her reaction. He had been on the point of driving off, aware that it was too late. Quarter to ten. There was no way he would be home until after midnight anyway. Should he phone Margaret? Better not. With luck she might be asleep by the time he got home.

He waited until the taxi drove off then got out, slamming the door. He hoped the noise would make her turn round but the light went on in the hallway of her house so she had presumably not paid any attention to the sound in the road.

She had shut the front door by the time he reached it and he had to ring the bell. He waited, wondering whether to ring again but then heard the sound of the lavatory flushing. He could see her shape, distorted by the glass, coming to the door. 'Who is it,' she said, opening the door narrowly on the chain.

'Me, John.'

She said, opening the door: 'What on earth ... you're the last person I was expecting ... I mean, I wasn't expecting anyone but well ...' she giggled. She had obviously been drinking on the train home. It explained the fumbling with the taxi money.

'Can I come in?'

'Of course. You'll have to excuse the house ... it's in a bit of a mess. I left in a hurry yesterday to go up to London to stay with a friend ... last minute decision ... and then ... well, you'll know ... I've been at the Commission meeting all afternoon which followed on from the press conference. I wish you'd phoned ... I'd have caught an earlier train if I could. It's a bit late.'

'Nearly ten.'

'Can you stay ...what's up?'

He said: 'Look, can I have a whisky and sit down for a minute. I can't stay long. I wanted to see you ... talk to you face to face. I ...' he hesitated for too long.

'It's Goodbye isn't it?' She didn't sound angry, not even resigned. 'I've been through too many not to know the signs. I've known, anyway, since your wife had the nervous breakdown. You're not the sort to up-sticks in a crisis, worse luck. I think you're a fool, because she'll just go on blackmailing you for however long it suits her and I think ... I think you and I would have been good together ... long-term good. Old age good. We could have had a better time. And we could have made a difference too ...we work well together.'

'You'll make the difference,' he said. 'You've got the power now. Make the most of your position on the Commission. I saw it on the lunchtime news. Congratulations.'

She handed him his drink and looked at him hard. 'You'd have liked it, wouldn't you?'

'Yes, I'd have liked to be a commissioner.' She sat down beside him on the sofa. He pulled her towards him and she did not resist and after a moment murmured: 'Why not? As good a way as any of saying goodbye.'

Later, much later, later than he dared think about in relation to returning home, they talked. She told him about the first meeting of the Commission. Her impression of the others, particularly Hambling, whom she thought a smooth operator. Her first impression had not been favourable. 'I know there is a problem. A big problem. But I got the impression that decisions have been taken already and we are wallpaper. Grist to his ambitions.'

He said, risking it: 'I know they've already begun cloning, there have been experiments which the government has connived at. Don't ask me how. I can't compromise my source. You must be the voice of reason. You must bring ethics to this discussion. Don't let them ride this through rough-shod.'

She tensed in his arms. 'Look, it's going to be down to me how I handle this. I have to be impartial. Listen to the evidence. I don't like the idea of cloning. I've always thought it's creepy, totally unethical, unnatural, but they gave us some very clear instructions about how we handle the issues. We have to take into account the position the country ... well, the world, really, is in. I shouldn't even be talking to you about it. Everything we are given is going to be numbered, secure ... and we've sworn an oath of confidentiality.'

He changed the subject, seeing a way to tell her about Margaret, about him and Margaret. He said: 'Would you not have liked to have a child? I'm sure it was possible for you. Do you regret not having one?'

'It's still possible,' she said. 'Everything is still functioning. How about it? I'm only 46.'

She giggled, looking at his face. 'That put the wind up you, didn't it? I don't know ... yes ... at one time I desperately wanted a child. Late thirties, early forties ... not that long ago, really, that's pretty normal isn't it? And once before ... mid twenties when I thought I was going to marry somebody that I'd been living with since uni. I got very hurt by that. He married my best friend in the end. I was godmother to the first child.

'Now ... no, I don't think so. I don't think I can, anyway, medically speaking. Not from the gender bender business, something else. Too late. Elderly

single mum. Too much hassle. No … not the hassle.
Being tied down … and for years. I'd be such a
responsible parent. That's my nature. And I'd be so old
for the kid when he … she … was a bloody-minded
teenager. No thanks.'

He said: 'What about a couple … two elderly people
coping with a teenager?'

'Is this an offer?'

He flustered. 'No … no … look, I'll … Margaret's
doctors think she … we … should, could, have a child.
They think that's what's causing all her grief and that
we're not too old … they almost make it seem like it's
our duty, given the present circumstances.'

She shot away from him, sitting upright and staring
down at him.

'Bloody hell. You can't seriously be considering this?
You must be out of your mind. You as well as her. You
are, though, aren't you? Go on, get out … get out of my
house. I can't believe you can do this. That's what you
turned up to tell me, isn't it. All the rest about the
commission was bullshit.'

She stood up and grabbed a beige silk dressing-gown
that wrapped its folds clingingly around her body, tightly
to her legs. She looked wonderful … red hair flaming over
her freckled shoulders … Warne groaned and buried his
face in the pillow. Completely wrong … why was he such
a failure with women. What a bloody idiot. And he still
had to face Margaret's wrath when he got home.

He said: 'I knew it would be like this. I'm … sorry,
truly sorry. But I've got to go through with this. Say she
commits suicide … I won't be able to live with it. And
…' He didn't need to finish what he was going to say.

She said it for him. 'You want a child, don't you?
That's what you really want. Well, good luck to you …
but don't ever come creeping back here expecting
anything more from me.'

He got up, dressed and left without another word.
The long drive home was on auto-pilot, the events of

the night churning in his head. By the time he got home dawn had broken and he shivered in the cold chill of the breaking morning. He left the car further down the road, walked carefully to his front door and tapped in his code. The door sprung open silently. As he reached his bedroom he thought he heard movement in Margaret's room but she didn't call out. He lay down, fully clothed on the bed, and fell asleep.

CHAPTER 8

'What do you mean he's gone?' Gladwin was turning purple in the face.

Dave said: 'They've just phoned me. Went up to his room this morning and he wasn't there. Nobody's seen him. They're wondering if they should dredge the lake. He's got so much dope in him he can't have gone far.'

'Oh for God's sake. Look, this has to be kept under wraps. There has to be containment. Get back to them. Then get a team down there. He can't have got far. It's not possible. The place is pretty well cut off from civilisation. What's the nearest ... Andover?'

'No, Stockbridge. That's still viable but no communication. Oh, actually there might be a bus link. And there's Winchester. Andover and Winchester both have railway stations. And Basingstoke. That's a bit further. In his state, on his drugs, I should think we'll find him asleep under a haystack if he hasn't drowned.'

Gladwin swore. 'You stupid mother-fuckers. Why am I surrounded, always surrounded, by bloody imbeciles. I'd like to shove broken glass up all your arses. Heads are going to roll. He's got to be found and quickly. The last thing we want is him contacting the girl. She'll soon put him in the picture and then we've really got problems.'

'I've stepped up surveillance on her,' said Helen. 'We can move in swiftly if necessary.'

'Good.' Gladwin spat out the word.

Dave said: 'I've done Warne. He can't move without us knowing. Fish is more likely to try and contact him.'

'Yes.'

Dave and Helen left Gladwin's office together. In the corridor outside Helen said: 'I've got a sneaking admiration for the guy. I wonder how he did it? Security is pretty tight there, isn't it?'

'Never had any trouble before. When I saw him he was practically incapable of having a pee by himself. My visit obviously spooked him. Well, got lots to do. See you later.'

□□□□□

The adrenalin rush from achieving his escape from the house and grounds had subsided. Mac found himself on the edge of a golf course. He had no idea where he was. He was wet, his shoes and legs soaked by the grass on the river bank. He was cold. The early morning temperature was very low and the frosty grass crunched beneath him, leaving tell-tale footprints. He began to shiver uncontrollably. Somehow he had to get back to civilisation, somewhere he needed to find more clothes. He'd found a nurse's uniform hanging on a rack near the kitchens. He was wearing the uniform over his pyjamas and some trainers that were too small for him, probably a woman's, which he had found outside the kitchen door. His right ankle hurt where he had tripped over brambles, his feet were pinched and sore. He skirted the greens in the pale light of dawn.

He was finding it a struggle to get across fields, over gates and across a couple of ditches. He had done some karate as a boy and been forced onto the rugby field in winter and the cricket field in summer but he'd specialised in playing the duffer using his dilettante mode to great effect. The sports master had soon dismissed him from any serious involvement, glad not to have his disruptive influence.

He'd stopped the pills the night after Melhuish's visit, without anyone noticing that he had not swallowed them. Although the nurses presumably doubled as guards they were not that efficient, he noticed. He was allowed to walk down the corridor by one of them after he had charmed her and said he must stretch his legs, he was getting cramps in them and was afraid of deep vein thrombosis. He noticed that other rooms seemed to have ordinary occupants, an elderly woman sitting in a chair in the autumn sunshine by a window. He glimpsed, through a door near the stairs; old people gathered round a television set.

He had experienced 48 hours of increasing clarity and had timed his escape for two in the morning. It was surprisingly easy finding his way down the stairs to the ground floor and making his way through the passages to the kitchen. Trays were set out on a big table with breakfast things but there was no sign of anyone on duty. The first door he tried was locked but he found his way through to another door which opened with a yale lock to a back vestibule. This is where he had found the uniform and the door beyond that into an inner courtyard was open. He lifted the latch nervously expecting an alarm but nothing happened. Getting out into the grounds was easier than he thought it would be - there was an archway from the courtyard and he looked through it to a long path and lawns. It was cloudy, with fitful moonshine, but he got more accustomed to the light and went across the lawns towards the water and followed its edge away from the house. He could see a dim light coming from a window at the side, up on the first floor but apart from that the house was in darkness.

He'd thought at first that he would have to cross the river that fed the water gardens but he'd followed up stream along the bank, scrambling over gates and ducking through wire fences. He'd finally reached the car park of a pub. He went into the road beside a bridge. On the far side of the bridge was a sign post and he went nearer and picked out the direction to Andover. He re-crossed the bridge but as he looked back across the river and through the trees he could see the lights of a car. He dived into the field opposite and made his way through. He'd stayed there, going through the fields, finding his way over gates or gaps in hedges until he'd come to the golf course.

There was a hut off to one side. Perhaps he could find something else to wear. It was locked tight and he spent useless minutes trying to find a way in. He could see more traffic now on the road. A car pulled in to the golf course and he watched from a bunker. The greensman? A woman got out. Greenswoman? She went towards the club house and he could hear her unlock the door. She went inside. He broke cover and went towards the car ... if only ... she was still in the building and although she had put lights on he felt he had some time.

He opened the passenger door. Maybe she had left keys ... he sat in and reached across to feel. No. He moved into the driver's seat ... wondering. There was a handbag on the floor. He riffled through it. There was a spare key in a zipped pocket at the side. He tried it and the car started up. He threw it into gear and spun it round on the forecourt. The woman came running out of the club house door. He saw her startled face as he revved past her.

He found the slip road to the motorway less than a mile up the road. The first slip road showed Exeter, the second London and the sign ahead was Andover. He passed the first turning and headed for the second, thinking hard. No money, no clothes. He passed the second turning as well and found a cul-de-sac of semi-detached older houses. People were already up. A man slammed his front door and started walking towards his gate. Mac drove past and turned at the head of the close. He came back out and followed the road back towards the Exeter turning. Somehow he had to get to Warne. He was his only hope.

He headed down the motorway. The petrol gauge showed quarter full. He saw signs to Salisbury at one roundabout, took it on the spur of the moment. It was now nearly 8. As he approached the city the workers' buses were filling up at the stops. There were signs to a hypermarket and although not as near as he had hoped he finally found it. In the car park he had another look through the woman's bag which seemed to be crammed with cosmetics. In the central zipped pocket he found two store credit cards. He looked around. One of the stores was on the site.

He looked in the mirror. He needed a shave. He badly needed a shave. His hair was hanging loose. He always took the rubber grip he used for his pony tail off before he went to sleep, not that he'd had any sleep last night, but he'd forgotten to pick it up. His hair was about four inches lower than his shoulders. He shook his head, looking all the time at the mirror. Maybe.

◻◻◻◻◻

Margaret called Warne at the surgery. 'I'll pick you up at 12 and we're catching the 12.30. The appointment's at 3. That should give us plenty of time.'

Shortly afterwards the receptionist phoned him and asked him if he could fit in an extra patient at 11.00. A woman who used to be a patient of his? The receptionist giggled. 'She's rather a peculiar woman. Looks a bit like one of those whaddyacalls - trans what nots. You know.'

Warne said: 'I'm sure I'd remember somebody like that. Can't you get rid of her … or whatever. What's she called.'

He was told Edwina Mack. 'Ring any bells?'

Warne said no. He gave himself a break between his last patient who had been quicker than his allotted time and poured himself a Scotch. Then he spoke into the internal paging system and called the name.

He stood up and went to the door, watching for the woman to walk down the corridor. She walked awkwardly towards him. He looked at the face. 'Oh my God. Quick, come in.'

Mac said: 'I didn't know what to do. They'll be watching you. What have they done to you?'

'Nothing so far as I know.'

'They will have. They locked me up in a so-called AIDS quarantine centre in the country. Sort of hospital. Somewhere near Andover. I escaped this morning. They say I'm positive, danger to society, standard practice ... but one of the goons from the secret service came to visit me yesterday ... no day before. I'm having difficulty remembering things. They doped me up to the eyeballs. I'm not sure what I've been taking. I don't know ... I'm beginning to wonder if the whole thing isn't trumped up. Can you do a test? See if I am positive? I think it's just another con by them. Since I stopped the drugs yesterday I've been feeling much better.'

Warne thought Mac had had some kind of nervous breakdown. He said: 'Well, I can. Won't have the results back for a day or two. Nice disguise. My wife's coming in for me quite soon and we've got to go to keep an appointment in Bristol. Catching the train. We'll be back later this evening but I daren't have you at the house. I can't trust Margaret and in any case they will be watching me, too, now. Have you got some money?'

'Some, not that much. I'm going to be on the wanted list in a big way ... I stole a car, forged a credit card ... What were you thinking? B and B in the town? I could do that. Might need a bit more if I'm going to pay cash. What do you think ... two or three nights? Maybe I can come and see you here again at the surgery?'

'Look, here's some cash.' Out of his window he could see Margaret parking the car. She would be early. 'There's a pub called the Cross Keys in Gold Street. I'm pretty sure they do b and b and they're not the sort to be nosy. Not like your average landlady. Just calm down. Look, take some of these.'

He grabbed a handful of pharma samples from the drawer. 'They won't hurt you, just keep you a bit sedated. Take them when you've got a room and stay put. I'll see you in the morning. You go first and then I'll come through to reception.'

As they drove off towards the station they passed him on the road. Mac was walking awkwardly in the skirt.

At the clinic they went through a battery of tests and consultations. He was surprised at the skin sample but the nurse said it was routine. Finally he was taken to a room on his own. 'It's OK, I remember the drill,' he said taking the flask.

Margaret travelled home elated. 'They're certain it will work,' she said. 'You heard what they said. I go back again at the end of the week. It's what I've really wanted all these years.'

He looked at her. 'Bloody hell, Margaret, you never wanted this. It was me who wanted a family.' How could she turn everything upside down?

'Well, maybe to begin with I wasn't very interested … we wanted the money to spend on other things. But when I lost …' she faltered. Then after a minute or two spoke again: 'Then you lost interest … had that affair with that blonde bimbo from Worcester … and then … I don't know … we just drifted apart. Dr Tanner says …'

'I don't give a fuck what that jumped up, squat arsed trick cyclist has to say …'

Margaret smiled serenely. 'You just cannot concede that others have a point of view. That's what Dr Tanner says. You need to be in control. I had to do the things I did just to retain my own sense of self …'

'Oh my God, don't start on that self-analysis mumbo jumbo. At least when you were off on your non-stop shagging career I gave you credit for not getting tied up with a lot of guilt-trip psychoses or basically giving a bugger about anybody else. Particularly me.' They finished the train journey in silence then drove home. As they turned into their road they could see car outside the house.

'What the hell ...' Warne's belligerence began to evaporate. Mac. Silly sod. It had to be.

He parked the car in the drive and got out. 'Dr Warne ...?' He nodded. The taller of the two men said: 'I wonder if we could have a word inside ...' He nodded his head at the front door.

Warne said: 'What's this all about?'

'I believe you know a man called Edward Fish. He's also known as Mac?'

Warne said, keeping it calm: 'I met him ... at a wedding ... way back in the summer. Who are you?'

The other man flourished identity under his nose.

Margaret by this time had got out of the car and joined them. She tapped in the numbers on the keypad and the door sprung open.

'Do come in,' she said. 'I'll get us a drink. We need one. What an exciting day.' Warne could see that the taller man was eyeing Margaret. She'd soon be playing to the gallery. He sighed and followed the men into the house. What the hell had Mac got him into?

CHAPTER 9

James Fields kept his head down. Hambling was in full flow and it wasn't pretty. His principle target was Emma Moorhouse but she seemed well able to stand up for herself and so the flak became indiscriminate. It was the guy Hambling had insisted on employing as press officer on the Commission who was getting the brunt of it.

Hambling used his well-honed sarcasm effectively and Robin Elliott, sallow, border-line effeminate, reeled from the lashing, unable to defend himself verbally and reduced to stuttering out explanations that lacked any cohesion. It was an humiliating performance and neither Hambling nor Elliott did themselves any credit.

James caught Emma's eye. She raised one eyebrow eloquently and picking up her papers said: 'Well, Sir Emery, you've made yourself very clear. I've got things I need to get on with and I am sure Robin has too. The press conference starts in an hour. We have had the press non-stop on our backs since Warne's statement and it's not going to be easy to pat all this back into place.'

James made a move to go too but Hambling said fiercely: 'I need you. There are things I want explained. I'm not facing the media without every fact and figure I need at my fingertips. And you Gladwin. Stay.'

Gladwin looked as if he'd explode. His sidekick Melhuish caught James's eye and gave the glimmer of a wink.

Three quarters of an hour later Hambling drummed his knuckles on the table. 'That's enough.' James had to hand it to him. He mastered a brief quickly and efficiently.

Hambling said: 'I want you in the room … no not you Mike.' He had softened just enough to use Gladwin's name during the course of the briefing. He gave a wry smile: 'I could do with you and your mob a million miles from here. Are you any closer to nailing this guy Fish?'

Melhuish answered before Gladwin could. 'He seems to have been very effective so far but we got a lead very quickly. A man who keeps a pub in the town told one of our team that a woman had stayed the night that we were asking about but that he'd wondered whether she was a he. She'd signed the register as Edwina Mack and she left the next morning, paying in cash. That was a week ago and Warne's pre-emptive strike has not helped us any. We're having to keep the operation very low key. But we are now looking for a woman as well as a man with Fish's appearance.'

Emma Moorhouse came back into the room. 'They're ready,' she said. 'I've told them, Sir Emery, that you will give a short statement and that you are prepared to answer ten minutes' worth of questions but that's all. The whole pack is there … tv, radio and the papers. I've lined up the tv interviews for afterwards but they are champing at the bit. Their producers want it back and ready for the noon bulletins.'

Hambling said: 'I need a pee first. I shan't be a minute.' He went out of the room and they heard his footsteps retreating up the corridor.

Emma looked at Gladwin: 'I hope he can bloody well handle it. I've had a hell of a time from the PM's office. Tessa is going to cut up very rough if he gets it wrong.'

James said: 'He's well briefed. Not many can master a brief as quickly as he can.'

Melhuish asked mischievously: 'How's Robin? Changed his trousers?'

Emma gave him a withering look and didn't reply. They heard Hambling's footsteps again, walking briskly back up the corridor. They all moved towards the door and as he opened it they had the satisfaction of seeing a glimpse of momentary alarm on his face at the sight of them en masse. He gathered himself rapidly.

'All right. Let's face the music.' They followed him out and down the corridor to the meeting room where Emma had set up the press conference. He sat down at the table with Emma at his side. Robin was somewhere at the back of the room and James sidled into a chair in the front row. One of the television reporters was sitting next to him and asked him where he was from. James said brusquely: 'Staff.'

'He'll need some protection on this one,' the man muttered. 'No doubt the lovely Emma will keep it all under control.'

Hambling asked for silence before speaking, holding up his hand to emphasise his request. He was treating the whole thing as if the press were a bunch of unruly schoolchildren. Surprisingly they settled down.

He said: 'I understand you all want some clarification after what Dr John Warne has told the Sunday papers and subsequently repeated on television and radio last night. As chairman of the Royal Commission on Human Potentiality the prime minister has asked me to put what he has said into context. First of all let me say that if any cloning of a human being has already taken place then it is illegal and the perpetrators will face the consequences of the law as it stands.

'I believe he has described the Commission I chair as a rubber-stamp for actions already carried out. I categorically deny this and will explain the function of the commission.'

There was an audible groan from the Guardian's medical correspondent. Hambling fixed him with a glare before continuing: 'Not all this audience will be as well-informed as some of you specialist writers and I think it is important to reiterate the brief the Commission has been given and the work that has been done up until now. Emma has got fact sheets and figures for you which will be distributed now ...' he paused while Robin came forward, fumbling the delivery of two sets of papers.

Bad move, thought James. He'd got their attention. Now he's in danger of losing it while they look at the papers. He looked down at his own crib sheet, aware that his moment was approaching.

Hambling waited until all the papers were handed out. Then he said: 'Right. Now I will go through this and I may call upon the Department of Lifestyle economist, James Fields, for further explanation of particular figures.'

Only may. Maybe not. He might be let off the hook.

Hambling marshalled his facts well but James was aware that the reporter beside him was getting increasingly agitated. 'Cut the crap,' he muttered. 'I'll miss my slot if this goes on much longer. Look, can I take you outside and do an interview. You could give me the figures. I don't need all this background.'

'No way,' said James sotto voce. At that moment Hambling said: 'Right James, I need you to go into these details.' Blast the guy. He fumbled with his crib sheet. 'Er ...'

'The numbers of impotent males,' said Hambling. Emma intervened. She'd obviously seen James distracted by the reporter. She said: 'It might be better if James talks individually to those of you who want to expand on the statistics that Sir Emery has just given you. I'm sure you're going to want to clarify a number of points.'

It threw Hambling for a second but he rounded up his spiel and opened the conference to questions. The guy from the Guardian jumped in first. He knew far more about the subject than Hambling and showed off with a tricky ethical question that he had already hammered in a couple of features on the work of the Commission. The guy from Sky got to his feet and walked up to Emma.

'Look, we need to get this back if we're going to make the noon bulletin. I'm speaking for all of us ... can we do the interviews first and then the rest can ask the questions.' The rest of the television, radio and internet reporters began to surge forward.

It was at this point that those at the back began to get to their feet. At first James thought they were protesting at being upstaged but then he was aware that someone had come into the room. The press thronged around, ignoring Hambling. Emma was moving rapidly now, to the left of the chairs.

James got up on his chair. In the open doorway, being jostled by the reporters, stood John Warne and Mac.

Chapter 10

James Fields - Via Voice

I phoned Steph immediately after the conference. 'You're not going to believe this.'

'I am, I am. I've just seen them on t'telly. Warne did well. What a star. Your lot must be shitting bricks.' She was so partisan about her bloody doctors.

'No, it's not just that. It was when they burst in the door. I suppose it was because Mac had had his hair cut short, really short ... to be honest it took me a minute to realise it was him. Warne's greyish, of course. They just looked so alike. The chap beside me from Sky who'd never set eyes on them turned to me and said: 'Is that Warne's son?' I said no. It was really weird.'

'Why? Lots of people look alike without being related. People quite often mistake my mum for the Countess of Wessex.'

I said and regretted it: 'That's just because she's so bloody stuck up and la-di-da.' Steph said: 'Actually she ... the Countess ... is pretty down to earth. I meant looks.' There was a bit of a silence.

I said: 'Well Warne and Mac looked alike and it wasn't just me who thought so. What's weird is that you get two guys on this mission to stop cloning who look like clones themselves. That's all. All hell broke loose when they came in.'

'I could see that. What was all that about being HIV positive and that he'd been somewhere illegally.'

'Warne says he did a test and that Mac isn't positive. Mac's threatening to sue for being taken off to some place in Hampshire on the pretext that he'd got full blown AIDS and needed to be quarantined and treated. He's got a legal case, I should think. He had not given consent to procedures, for sure. Gladwin's lot had something to do with it.'

I stopped. Of course that lot would be listening in to me now. How bloody daft could I be?

I said: 'How are you feeling ... how's Algernon?' She'd felt the first movement the week before.

'Algernon's well. Little butterflies. It's so exciting. I just keep praying ... just hoping everything will be OK. We are so lucky.' I said I'd be home by 6.

Later, after a meal, I said: 'When we were going through the figures, briefing Hambling today ... I can quite see why the government is trying to find a way to get cloning accepted. I hadn't realised how many men and women have been affected. The human potential is really scary ... not just here, worldwide. Not all for the same reasons but the outcome is the same. There have been too many catastrophes. Famine, Africa wiped out by AIDS ... the flooding and India and Pakistan also facing the AIDS epidemic and the other sexually transmitted diseases like chlamydia. All the countries who copped the fall-out from Iran's nuclear explosions. The Far East is now catching up with Africa in terms of AIDS. Even China ... they must be regretting that limit of one baby per family in the last century. Too many boys and now ...'

Steph said: 'You realise that the sci-fi scary stuff about cloning isn't right? It doesn't mean exact replicas of the donor. Lots of people looking the same. I've had a full briefing on this ... the office has been inundated with press calls since Warne opened his mouth on Sunday. I haven't been able to track down the chap who carried out the cloning illegally ... I mean Warne obviously hasn't got his name or he'd have said but I'm retty sure who it is though Hislop won't budge and confirm the name to me. The real inner sanctum among the medics know but they're not going to say.

'One of the editors on the Medical Journal put me on to this high-up medical research prof. Top drawer. He was bursting to tell me that the guy who is most likely involved has retired early and gone to ground. Probably being held somewhere by the goons who locked up Mac. He wouldn't give me the name but he gave me a very good briefing ... how it can be done etc. Very simple, actually. Just fiddling accurately with needle, cells, test tubes. They'll probably be doing it for GCSE biology next.

'The actual business of emptying a donor egg and filling it with the DNA of the would-be what ... clonee? ... really isn't that difficult. Of course it has been done and nobody will know how many times, the records will all be missing. This country ... worldwide. There are always people willing to pay and doctors willing to be paid. But I am pretty sure there has been no watertight research, because of the illegality question, into what the survival rates really are, what the abnormality rate is, whether there is rapid ageing. But if Warne and Mac are right it sounds as if somebody may have got the science right.'

I wasn't really listening to her while she rabbited on.

I said: 'Did you see what I mean about how alike they are?'

'To be honest, I was so intent on what Warne was saying and then what Mac said about being locked up in some kind of hospital in the country and the threats that MI5 made to him that I didn't notice. Are you sure Mac can be trusted? You know how he lies ... OK, fantasy world. Walter Mitty was a novice compared to him. I wonder if he's caught Warne up in something that won't hold water when the journos really start digg'

I bet in a week there'll be another deno'

Hambling looked sick as a parrot. He d'

across that well. I thought you thought h'

'Well, I've got a certain amount of respect for him. And actually he handled the hi-jacking of the press conference pretty well. Emma was very impressed by him. He got up, brushed the rat-pack aside, swatted them out of the way, and invited Warne to join him at the table. He sort of shoved Mac into a seat near the front ... the other end of the row from me.'

'And did Mac stay put?'

'Almost. Right at the end he butted in and Hambling let him have his say. He said he knew somebody who had had a cloned kid. Then it was hell. All the TV crews grabbing him and Warne for interviews, the tabloids going bananas that they hadn't got him and getting blasts down their mobiles from their news desks. Quite funny for me, just hanging around, semi-detached. I might have had my own starring role but nobody really wanted to know. They weren't interested in figures. The trouble is it has blown the whole carefully laid plans for getting a sensible public debate out of the water.'

Steph started thinking with her public relations hat on. She said: 'They ... government, Hambling, departments, your department ... somebody's going to be all out to discredit Warne or Mac, preferably both. That's what will be going on. Mac's easy. They can arrest him for breaking the official secrets act but they'll have to be careful. They need to produce some medical records showing they had good cause to take him to that place but despite Warne's tests they've probably stitched that up. Warne's trickier. The public like him. They think he did a good job getting the QALY targeting stopped. They need some dirt on him.'

She was thinking through the problem. She was very, very good at it. Spin doctoring of the highest order.

I said: 'I'm going to try and meet Mac. Maybe not today. I've got to talk to him. No ... I don't mean a late night session. Emma's just asked me to because I know him pretty well. They want me to talk him round, stop him taking this whole thing much further. Stop them having to take the thing so much further, more like. You're right, they can prosecute. They've already threatened it. They want Warne isolated. I think they've got something else on him. You're right about that, too. I don't know what it is but I don't like what's going on. They are ruthless.'

I met Mac in the same pub in Putney the next day. He was already there with a half drunk pint, sitting in a corner. The evidence on the table showed it wasn't the first. He introduced the girl and four men who were sitting with him. They were all from the popular tabloids and looked a pretty hardened crew. Their talents didn't lie in their writing skills but in sticking to their victim like a burr, in asking questions, getting enough information to piece together the story their editors wanted - and trying to do each other down and buy him as an exclusive.

Mac was probably an unusual victim because he seemed reasonably capable of heading off their questions. They were zizzing about him like a swarm of mosquitos asking for the name of the family he had said had had a cloned child. It probably wasn't long before someone would get the answer they wanted. They could outdrink him any day. There were a lot of cash offers with some fancy zeros being made but he had obviously stood firm so far. It looked as if Mac was enjoying himself, enjoying the notoriety and the intellectual game he was playing. One of the men was obviously beginning to lose his cool at Mac's evasiveness.

I said: 'You want to talk here?'

He said that it seemed fine to him. Nobody was going to disturb us. He waved his hands at the rat-pack. 'Just bugger off for a minute, will you, and let me talk to my mate. I'll talk to you later.' They didn't budge and so we did, outside by the river although it was absolutely freezing and perhaps that was why they didn't follow us.

He said: 'They've been following me about all day. I think they need a bit of time to contemplate their next moves. I feel a bit like Dr Livingstone or someone, trailing through the jungle with my band of native bearers.'

I said: 'This is hopeless.'

He said: 'If this is about what I said at the press conference, forget it. I'm not retracting anything. I know the papers are saying that I made up all the stuff about the place down in Hampshire. All they've come up with is an old people's home where most of the inmates are ga-ga but I promise you it wasn't that at all. I was detained, locked up in a bedroom. They drugged me. I don't know what they intended to do with me in the long run but one of the goons told me that I could disappear and not be missed. Buried quietly in the grounds. And I'm not HIV positive. No way. Warne's done all the tests. I'm in the clear. I had some sort of virus but it wasn't that.'

He added, lowering his voice: 'So I can stop blaming Fern now for that particular little surprise at least. The bitch. That's why I haven't ...' he didn't finish the sentence.

I didn't know then what had broken them up and made him so bitter. I looked at him but he shook his head. 'Off limits.'

I said: 'Are you OK for money? Where are you staying?' We had moved back into the Putney house. 'I'm sorry but we just don't have ...'

'Well, you have the room but your wife wouldn't like it, would she?' He laughed. 'Your wedding. A real highlight. Her mother ... what a pill. Fern did brilliantly that day. That's when I got to know Warne, of course.'

I thought about it momentarily, then blurted it out anyway. 'You know that you two look tremendously alike?'

'Really? You really mean that.' He got very animated.

'We all noticed it. The bloke from Sky asked me if you were his son. I guess getting your hair cut has made you look more normal ... anyway, more like Warne. What is he? Some relation?' I was joking.

He got even more excited. Over-excited. It hadn't occurred to him. The guy from Sky had mumbled something but he hadn't paid much attention. Now I'd said it ... he started firing off all this stuff about him having been the result of a sperm donation. How he'd asked his mother a long time ago what she knew about his biological father. Medical student. She didn't know where.

He knew Warne had trained in London. He'd come about through the good offices of a north London clinic. He said it bitterly then added. Could be, could be. He felt so close to the guy. He was sure it was true. He started speculating about their future together. He'd be exactly the kind of father to have ... the one he'd had, not his real father, ... what a misery, what an anorak ...he was getting up and jigging about with excitement like a little kid.

I was astonished. He said his parents had told him when he was about 12. He'd registered to see if he could find out about his father as soon as he was 18 but nothing had ever come to light.

I asked if he would say anything to Warne. 'What do you think ... maybe ... maybe not yet?' Of course, this wasn't my brief. I was supposed to split them up not bring them closer together.

'You could have DNA tests done. That would prove it one way or another.'

I tried to get back on track but he was really high and only calmed down when he realised the scandal merchants had finished their beers and were about to join us. In that, he wasn't at all like Warne who from the little I'd seen was a more reserved, much more calculating political animal. Maybe the doctor's training. He'd blurted out the cloning stuff, though. They did share this liking for being centre stage, in the limelight. Warne with his media career as your first-choice friendly family doctor and Mac ... well, Mac couldn't stop himself being centre stage. He was enjoying his entourage of hacks.

More people were going into the pub now, skiving off work early or maybe the job sharers, flexi workers, home workers.

He stopped jigging around and got serious, keeping his voice low. 'This Warne thing ... do you seriously think I ought to ask him to have DNA tests? What if ...' He stopped.

'You aren't his son?'

He nodded. 'I'd be devastated. Ever since my mother told me I've wanted to find out who my real father was ... is. You wouldn't know what that feels like. It gnaws away at you. I guess from the moment I was told I decided I was going to be completely different from old Fish face, my stand-in Dad. I mean, I wasn't like him anyway but I just threw all his values out the window from that moment on. And what a name he'd landed me with. Fish. Fish-paste, fish fingers. I got the lot at school.'

'Well, you got through it OK. You're a gambler. You'll have to take a gamble on this.'

Maybe this was my contribution to splitting them up. If Warne wasn't happy with Mac's 'are you my daddy' question he might be less keen on the campaign they'd embarked on, were knee-deep in, wading and splashing around, causing havoc. The telly was going strong on the cloning issue. There were big ethical debates, talking heads, rights and wrongs of it all and quasi-scientific documentaries. The churches, all the religions, were getting in on it too, big time.

That evening there were more headlines. Mac had been arrested on charges of treason. It must have been not long after I left him. Was I under suspicion too? I had a strong feeling that I was.

Chapter 11

James Fields - Via Voice

Mac was jailed on remand but his lawyers argued the case for him being bailed and a week later Warne stood surety. It was a lot of money. I only learned what difficulties he'd had when I was looking through his stuff which included his bank statements. His partners wouldn't let him use the practice in anyway as collateral and he'd had to remortgage his house to the hilt. I should think he had some mega fights with his wife over it.

It was that week they learned that she had conceived. Warne was going to be a Daddy at the age of 50. His files give no indication that Mac had broached the subject of their relationship and he doesn't mention anything about his donor sessions in his youth, not in anything I've seen any way.

I knew I was under surveillance and Steph was adamant I must not get involved in any way again. Emma Moorhouse, of course, was really pissed off with me. She regarded the fact that I'd failed to quieten everything down as total incompetence and she blamed me for Mac getting even more publicity. It was no good my saying that it was the intelligence services ... Gladwin and company ... who had made everything worse.

The public were beginning to swing behind Mac although nobody likes treason. It's one of those crimes that brings out patriotism and not just among British chauvinists or the far right. They weren't too keen on David Shayler when he was tried and sent to prison at the beginning of the century. His whistle-blowing on MI5 didn't go down well and then his running off to Paris for a couple of years with the connotation that he must be having a good time in a city like that and being paid for it by the newspapers. It's not just the Colonel Blimps who object. People don't like the UK being betrayed. That's got even stronger since we joined Europe lock, stock and barrel, oddly enough. Try as the politicians will they can't make a European of Joe and Josephine Public.

I did contact Mac, despite Steph's diktat. I tried Warne at home and his wife answered.

'He's here. I've told John that if he's put up that sort of money then I'm going to make bloody sure that he doesn't rat on us and leave us in the cart. John's squared it with the police. I suppose we're landed with him until the case comes to court. Do you want to speak to him? He's still in bed. I feel like I've got a cuckoo in the nest. And I don't like cuckoos.'

It was then she told me that she was pregnant. Not so much a cuckoo, more a bun in the oven. I didn't say it. I was surprised, very surprised, but managed to gabble some congratulations.

'Yes, we got the confirmation the day before yesterday. John's really chuffed about it. So am I. We've always wanted a family.'

I mumbled something about Steph being pregnant too and that we were delighted. Couldn't stop her then. She'd got some pretty strong opinions about it being everybody's duty to have children if they could. Now having read Warne's documents I can see what a hypocrite she was. Finally she went off to call Mac but when he came on the phone I could hear straight away that he didn't want to talk to me.

I ended up by saying lamely that he was to give me a ring if he needed to talk ... he said abruptly that it was good of me but that I ought to have the bloody nous to realise that everything he said, we said, was being recorded. Then he shouted down the phone ... 'got that, you bastards' and hung up on me. I felt a complete fool. Steph would be furious if she found out that I had put myself right back in the frame.

I remember talking to Steph that night about the Warnes and asking her about a pregnancy at Margaret's age. She said that it was not that unusual. She'd met two people in the ante-natal clinic she was going to who were late forties and one of them said they knew somebody who was in their early fifties.

What were their reasons for such late pregnancies? Steph wasn't sure. One of the women had said it was a lifestyle choice. She'd put it off earlier because she hadn't wanted children, then she'd met a man who had already had a family, there had been a divorce and now she was living with him and they'd decided to see if they could have a family. The doctors had been keen to help. She understood there was government funding to help with the fertility clinic they'd attended.

She looked down at her own bump and patted it. She was doing well, really well. I was getting a buzz out of the thought of being a dad now that I could feel the baby kick. I still wasn't too sure about the crying and dirty nappies. I'm a bit squeamish about that sort of thing. I could imagine that Warne would feel the same. Pleased about having a baby, I mean. Of course at that time I knew nothing about his affair with Maeve.

The case against Mac was going to be at least three months coming to court I was told. It was unlikely before Easter. In the meantime plans were rushing forward to hold the public meeting of the Commission. It was being set up to take evidence from the main professional bodies who had responded - the doctors, the lawyers, the social workers and of course all the ethical lobby groups who wanted to have a say. It was scheduled for early December. We're still in 2021, here. So much happened that year and so quickly.

The lawyers had been called in to make sure that the Commission's activities would in no way affect the court case. I don't think any rules were bent but it must have been a close call. I went to only one of the commissioners' meetings in the run-up to the public inquiry and it was then that I saw Maeve at close quarters, although I didn't realise her relevance at the time. I remembered her from the 'Stop Death by Numbers' campaign and I can quite see why Warne had been bowled over by her. A very striking woman with her flowing chestnut hair and her assertive personality.

Hambling quite obviously hated her guts. She was not a rational thinker in the way these academics preen themselves on being. The way I am, come to think of it. Economists don't rush into things. She was emotional. Emotive. Heart on her sleeve. Very keen on exploring how a cloned child might feel, the ethics of creating a child that perhaps wasn't perfect. All the awkward questions. There had been a mountain of evidence from different groups, interest groups and research groups. There had been nearly 3000 letters from members of the public. Of course, none of us knew then how far advanced the science was, how there had been a conspiracy of silence for so many years while the scientists and medical research people had perfected the techniques. I'll swear that Hambling had not been told the half of it.

Over the next couple of weeks I knocked all the statistics into shape with my team and we made a presentation video highlighting the problems in this country and worldwide of the population decline and the serious imbalance.

Hambling wanted me at the inquiry. It was a cold, cold day and walking across Parliament Square on my way to the Queen Elizabeth Hall I could feel dewdrops forming on the end of my nose. I used my sleeve then had a bad feeling I might have been caught on camera. It was too cold to rummage in my trouser pockets for a handkerchief.

The television cameras were out in force. Hambling was on the steps being interviewed. He told me later: 'I kept it short, just a few pertinent words'. He is a self-satisfied prat. Competent, but a prat.

Out of the corner of my eye I saw Maeve Dunlop being interviewed by a household name woman television reporter. Inside the other members of the panel were gathered in the small committee room off the main hall.

Emma said brusquely: 'Now James, let's keep this tight and under control, shall we?' I was obviously still enemy numero uno for my failure to keep Mac out of the headlines.

Hambling came in then. 'You've all had the papers but another set, with the agenda, has been laid out for you at your place.'

The secretariat knew it was a dead cert that half the commission members would mislay their papers by the time they reached their seats.

Hambling was businesslike, I'll give him that: 'I propose, first of all, to introduce the day and outline the agenda to the representatives of the public who are attending today. I hope we can all benefit positively from our first chance to hear what the people of this country think about this emotive, ethical issue. Thank you all for attending.'

The hall was crowded. Hambling opened the meeting fluently. I was sitting in the first row of the audience, out to the left, poised to run up the steps if there were any hitches with the video or when the awkward questions began on the statistics.

I imagine the room, holding probably about 200 people, were impressed at his introduction.

'Good morning and welcome to this day of hearing for the Royal Commission on Human Potentiality which will specifically address the viability and ethical considerations of reproductive cloning. Let me say at the outset that we ...' and he indicated the panel 'are completely open-minded. The government wants the public to make the choices on the evidence that we have. We appreciate this large turn-out and that there are so many groups here today to give evidence on this important and difficult subject.

'I want to introduce the debate by showing a short film ... a video presentation ... which gives you some idea of the very real problems facing the world. Yes, it is as serious as you are about to see. We appreciate that many of you have already presented evidence, some strong arguments for and against and we hope today will be an opportunity for us to build on that very strong platform of evidence ...'

He carried on with some facts and figures that I'd put together in an audience-friendly way before winding up: 'Today is a crucial day for us in, as I say, putting some of the issues back to the groups who have given substantial evidence, asking if there are amplifications now that they wish to make and helping us as we approach what I can only call 'make up mind time'. We have not quite reached that stage yet but we shall do shortly as we are duty bound to report before the end of January. That is less than two months and Christmas and New Year fall between.' He paused to let that sink in.

'Can I just tell you something about the running order of the day, following the video? We are going to run this as if it were a Select Committee Hearing in Parliament. That is to say, lead individuals from the groups on the list that you have been given will present their evidence, the panel of commissioners will then have the opportunity to ask detailed questions, but I am afraid it does mean that those sitting in what I have to refer to as 'the general audience' will not have that opportunity. You will, however, have the opportunity perhaps to speak to commissioners over lunch and at the end of the day. It is important that we hear the evidence of the groups that have come specially prepared.'

He explained that the timetable had built in ten-minute slots for groups to speak and that the commissioners would then question. He also said that individual commissioners might come and go for media interviews. There was enormous media interest and some concessions had been made so that the much wider public could be kept informed as the day progressed. The groups, too, would come and go. It was only then that he referred obliquely to the court case and said that those giving evidence should disregard anything that they had seen on television which might influence their views. Easier said than done, I thought.

The video worked well. I was pleased with it and at the end there was a ripple of clapping from somewhere near the back of the hall which was shushed. The Royal College of Obs and Gynaes were the first lot to speak.

The morning session was just drawing to a close. I'd been up on stage a couple of times to explain some points but I was back in my seat when the disturbance began.

One of the commissioners, the lawyer, Jasper Goodison, had put some very good questions of an actuarial nature to the Pro Life chairman, tying her in knots over whether the survival of a nation was preferable to a diminished nation of mentally defective and physically handicapped people for whom there were no longer, in any case, enough carers. There had been a swollen murmur of disapproval at the lawyer's use of the word defective. Maeve Dunlop had spent most of the morning out of the hall giving interviews so was not around to weigh in with the condemnation as she surely would have.

I wasn't sure where the shouting was coming from. The acoustics were slightly odd. It seemed like a few rows behind me.

I craned my neck round a big man from the Paediatricians lot who was sitting next to me. The interrupter was Warne.

He spoke even louder: 'Am I allowed to make a statement? This is a public hearing, isn't it?' Out of the corner of my eye I could see that Emma was on the move towards Hambling on stage.

Hambling repeated what he had already said, about there being the chance to talk to the commissioners at lunch time which was now only quarter of an hour away. He said: 'It's Dr Warne, isn't it? You seem to like disturbing my meetings.' There was a slight ripple of laughter that died away almost as soon as it had begun.

Warne said: 'I have some important information that this commission should take account of and which the general public should be aware of. From all I've heard this morning it seems that the most important finding of this commission is likely to be that a human cloning trial programme will be implemented - and yes, we are talking about humans - and the act that expressly forbade human cloning and made it a criminal offence, punishable by imprisonment, will be repealed.

'I think you should all know that human cloning has already taken place and on a large scale. I made this clear a few weeks ago and a young man is now awaiting trial for treason. He believed it was important enough to break his contract with the government, his employers, who I have proof have connived at these experiments. He is being called a whistle blower by the media. I don't see it as that. I hope you won't. At the time we did not have strong enough evidence of what has occurred. I have that evidence now.

'The first clonings, using the immigrant population, took place in 2015. Of these there are at least 400 cloned children aged six years old. Overall, since that starting date, there are probably some 2000 clones in this country. Some have been dispersed throughout the country through adoption procedures; others remain with the families of their one genetic parent. A secret government experiment has already taken place ... is still taking place ... we are only one step away from cloning babies in laboratories.'

People had turned to stare at him and there were one or two shouts of: 'Sit down.'

Emma was whispering in Hambling's ear. A crescendo of noise took over the hall.

Hambling said, icily: 'I made it very clear that there could be no questions from the floor in this way. I would be very pleased to meet you, Dr Warne, in the lunch break but I'm afraid that we must ask you to sit down now and let the Pro Life group continue to answer questions from the commissioners.'

Warne looked round the hall and addressed the audience. 'Is that what you want? It seems to me that this whole proceeding is a farce. It is another case of this government trying to keep secret quite unethical policies regarding population. You may remember that I have been involved before ... and so in fact has one of the panel ... Maeve Dunlop ... she ...'

I don't know quite what he was going to say because at that moment Maeve reappeared on the platform and shielded her eyes, looking to see who was speaking. She sat down rather abruptly when she realised it was Warne.

Warne was still talking to the audience, rambling on about population adjustment and cloned children, as I heard Hambling say to Emma: 'For God's sake get that idiot out of here. The whole hearing is about to be shot down in flames. He must not be allowed to grab the headlines.'

Emma acted swiftly and I have to say I for one revised my opinion of her and her professional capabilities. She approached Warne from behind, having signalled to two men to join her - I thought at first they were from the secretariat but later realised she had planned for such an eventuality by hiring security guards.

Before Warne had any time to resist they had taken him by the elbows and steered him promptly out of the hall. Lifted him by the elbows. He was a tall man but they were taller and bigger. He looked like a rag doll, with his feet trailing behind him as they heaved him out.

Emma walked behind, calming down the audience as she went and, before making her exit, turned to make a circular movement with her arms indicating that Hambling should pull the meeting together and continue with the questions. I just caught sight of her silhouetted in the doorway pointing her fingers, cocked like an imaginary gun, at the back of Warne's head.

Hambling was aware that the press bench was stirring, ready to evacuate the hall en masse in search of Warne. He snapped, authoritatively: 'Nobody is to leave the hall at this moment.'

There was the beginning of a clamour from the press benches with journalists scrambling to get out of their seats and the television reporters scrambling to get to their camera crews but Hambling made an announcement that riveted their attention.

'Dr Warne is himself about to become the father of a cloned child. His wife underwent treatment at a clinic in Bristol in September, with his full consent, and is expecting a baby. An egg was emptied and the DNA taken from Dr Warne has resulted in a viable foetus. It is due to be born in late June. The matter has been reported to the Human Embryology Authority and the clinic itself is under police investigation. Now if you can bear with me for ten more minutes while the Pro Life group finishes answering questions I will then meet you in a press conference arranged in meeting room Number 1, that's right as you go out those doors and down the corridor to the end. Now please be seated.'

He immediately asked a particularly difficult question of the Pro Life spokesman. To my surprise the journalists, to a man and woman, shot back into their seats and the hearing continued for another ten minutes when he promptly closed it and gathered up his papers.

'Follow me,' he commanded the press. They trooped off behind him.

CHAPTER 12

Mac watched the lunchtime bulletin and his recently eaten breakfast rose back into his gullet with an acid surge. The 'on the hour' bullet points trumpeted the news that the doctor campaigning against cloning was himself to be the father of a cloned child. A shot of Warne being dragged from the conference hall by two burly men opened the lead item. He listened and watched with disbelief as the morning's events at the public forum on cloning unfolded and old footage of Warne at different times of the 'stop death by numbers' campaign were run.

He could hear Margaret in the kitchen. She had already said she was going to get a snack lunch. Did he want something? It had been said icily because she was fed up with him lying in bed all morning. Her question expected a negative response. She wasn't a good cook, didn't like cooking, but she begrudged him any time in the kitchen. Any time in the house, really. It was only the threat surrounding the bail money that made her keep him there.

He didn't feel happy at being left alone with her. He hated the way she treated Warne, who didn't seem able to stand up to her. He'd been concerned about Warne going off last night, determined to force his way into the forum and make the statement. He had gone off with hand-outs for the press, a statement, statistics. They had got evidence together just in time and Mac was nervous about it standing up to scrutiny.

The starting point had been the clinic Fern had attended. He didn't tell Warne but he phoned her at work and told her that if she didn't tell him the name of the doctor, the name of the clinic, he'd give her story to the papers. He was being offered a lot of money for her name and it was amazing that it hadn't leaked already. She screamed at him down the phone. Blackmail, blackmail. He repeated his threats and finally she gave in. She said that other cloned children had been born as a result of the clinic's work.

She said: 'You won't make me feel guilty about this, you know. I think it should be made legal. That's what this inquiry will do, isn't it? These children are surviving. William is absolutely fine now. That's what you should be telling this inquiry, commission, whatever it is. The government's right. It's the only way forward. Your squalid problems of who your daddy is are nothing to do with this. We have to survive. We have to have children.'

Mac did not tell Warne how he had obtained the information but Warne was able to verify it. Then he leant on contacts, friends from university, Medical Association colleagues, scientists. He had come across a lot of useful people in his medical political career and gradually he had pieced together the history of the recently surviving cloned children. Much of it was hearsay but it seemed Fern was right. There were children, about 1600, born to individual couples. The rest, over 400 in the early experiments, had been born to immigrants at the centres. A high percentage had survived. Some of the immigrants' children had then been adopted. It was these Mac had doubts about being able to verify.

Mac and Warne worked in Warne's study in the evenings when he came home from the practice, keeping away from Margaret.

'I've told her we're working on your case,' Warne said. 'Better she doesn't know.'

Mac's conviction grew stronger. Warne was his father. He wanted him to be. They got on so well but still he held back on asking the question. He thought of it all the time but what if the answer was not the one he wanted?

He had been waiting until this big day was over, waiting to say: 'Would you have a DNA test?' He was sure Warne would. Sure of it.

Through discussing the ethics of cloning he was able to bring the conversation round to other infertility measures. He quizzed him about his thoughts on AID. Good thing, really, said Warne. I was a donor in my students days. And now again for our child that's on the way we've used in vitro fertilisation but with my sperm. Margaret and I ... he didn't finish the sentence. He explained why he thought AID was good, giving the chance to a couple to have a child. The mother is genetically the child's parent. She gets a chance to produce her own child. Before Mac could ask anything else he went on to say that he wasn't sure about the law which gave fathers and children the right to register their interests in finding out about each other.

'I don't know how I'd feel if a son or daughter found me. Not now. Not so long after. Medically speaking, it's probably right for the individual to know their genetic make-up but I think there could be a lot of emotional baggage and what about the poor sod who's suddenly denied his position as father? After all, he's the one who had the sleepless nights, borne all the costs and expenses of bringing up a child he regarded as his own.'

Mac, for once, held his tongue. Later he'd grill him about it. Explain how it had felt to him. The shock and grief when he had found out. The longing to find his real father.

Once he'd said, in a joking way: 'Come on Dad.' Warne had grinned. None of your cheek, young man. But he'd looked pleased.

Mac went to the downstairs lavatory and knelt in front of the bowl. Nothing would move. The toast and coffee he had consumed sat leadenly in his stomach. He sat down on the seat. He heard Margaret calling. 'John's on the television. Do you know what they're saying ... they're saying I'm having a cloned child. I haven't given permission for that to be announced. They can't do that, not without my permission.'

He got up and went back into the sitting-room. She was standing looking at the television although by now the newsreader had moved on to another story. He said: 'What do you mean, you haven't given permission. Is this true? Is it true?' He was shouting at her.

'Of course it is.' She turned to look at him. 'And John knows it is. He signed the agreement and gave his permission.'

'He said he'd donated sperm. You lying cow.'

'Don't you speak to me like that. He's the liar. He said he was going to a medical conference in London. He butted into this forum on cloning and has made a complete idiot of himself. I suppose you knew all about it. Is this what you've been hatching up together? John told me it was about your case, that you were working on the evidence. Now he's dragged me into this. I can't cope with this. I'm getting really upset. I may lose the baby. It's a bad time, three months, I could lose it. If you make me miscarry ...'

The phone rang. Mac went to pick it up but she got there ahead of him. 'Yes, it's me. On the telly ... yes, I saw it. No, of course it's not true. How could it be? It's not legal. You can't imagine John doing anything that wasn't legal. No, no, I'm fine. Yes, we still have our house guest.' She glared at him. 'I'll talk to you soon.' She put the phone down.

'Who was that?'

'A friend.' She saw his look. 'A girl friend.' She left the room and a minute later he could hear her moving about upstairs.

Mac zapped from one news channel to another. It was the lead item everywhere. The story moved on at each bulletin. By 2 the headlines said that Warne had been arrested for a breach of the peace. There was more coverage of his campaigning career. A red-haired woman who was on the commission gave an interview. She said she was horrified to hear that Dr Warne had apparently agreed to clone himself. Her name came up on screen and Mac realised she was the woman Warne had campaigned with, Maeve Dunlop. He was watching her when Margaret came back into the room.

She pointed at the screen. 'That bloody woman. You know he had an affair with her? Yes, he was thinking of leaving me for that bitch. He didn't but it was a close run thing. She's evil. Look at her. I expect she's still angling for him, probably wants to have his kid too.' He watched amazed as Margaret advanced to the screen jabbing her finger at it even though Maeve was no longer on it. 'It's me that's having his baby. It's me he wants.'

Mac said: 'Why don't you just shut up and listen. John's been arrested for a breach of the peace. Look, I'm going for a walk. I'm not running away, not jumping bail but I've got to get out of here and think. I'm going mad trying to work out what's going on.'

She screamed at him. 'Found your hero's got feet of clay, have you? You make me sick. You're gay, aren't you? You're in love with John, aren't you? You make me sick you lot. I've wondered about you from the very first moment you came in the door. All that long hair and earrings. At least that was one thing I got John to make you do, get that all cut off.

' I wouldn't wonder if you haven't got AIDS. That's what they said, didn't they? Don't you come near me. I'm going to make sure you only eat off one plate, one mug, one glass, one knife and fork and spoon from now on. And don't you go near my bathroom, do you hear. Go on, get out. But you'd better be back by 7 or I'll call the police.'

As he walked out the door he heard the phone ringing. If it was Warne he knew he could not speak to him, not now, not yet.

He walked through the town to the leisure centre. Some women were playing tennis on the courts near the road. It was windy and there was a lot of shrieking as the ball veered off at impossible angles. He stood and watched through the fence but the next time they changed sides they stood at the net and talked, looking at him. He moved off.

He walked back up the hill to the town and into a newsagents and bought the Sporting Life. He went into a café and bought some coffee and a scone, with cream and strawberry jam. Bad choice, he realised too late and left the cream and jam.

He turned to the section with the following day's racecards. The horse he had owned was running at Uttoxeter. All that seemed a lifetime away, a different life. It was only last summer that he and Fern had been going to race-meetings together. When they split up he had sold his share in the syndicate. He'd split with her because of her cloned child. He hadn't been able to stomach that. What was he going to do about Warne, if it was true?

The café shut at 6.30 and by 6.15 the waitress, a woman with a series of chins that ran down into the v-shape of her jumper, was making his life a misery. There was nothing else to do. Reluctantly he started back towards the house.

Turning the corner into the cul-de-sac he saw the crowd. Cars parked anyhow, some up on the kerbs, one blocking an entrance to a house where the woman owner was out on her doorstep shouting at the driver at the top of her voice. There were a couple of television camera crews set up on the lawn outside the Warnes' house and a posse of photographers right up against the windows of the sitting room. The curtains were drawn. He glanced upstairs. All the windows had their curtains drawn.

He could see somebody coming out of the side gate which led round to the back and the main part of the garden. It was a woman, small, with red-blonde hair and a rather open, cheeky freckled face. She called: 'She's in all right. I caught sight of her in the kitchen before she pulled the blinds down.'

'Good girl, Sally,' said a short fat bald photographer. The rest of the group moved towards her and he could not hear what else she said.

Stupid, stupid. Of course this was going to happen. How was he going to get into the house? He turned to go back down the road but at that moment another car drove up and two men got out, one a photographer who immediately took his picture on his mobile.

'Who are you? Do you live here?' The other man asked.

Mac said: 'No, just passing, just delivered something.' He quickened his step, reaching the end of the road and heading on up the hill, but the man kept pace with him.

'Are you a neighbour of Dr Warne's? Hey, I know who you are ... you're the guy out on bail for whistle blowing. Newsdesk said you were living here with him. Something Fishy ... Fish. Edward Fish. That's you, isn't it? You are living with them, aren't you? Look, we can do a deal. It'll be better in the long run for all of you. Give us the story and the rest of the pack will go, leave that poor woman in peace. She doesn't want trouble now, does she? What is she ... three months up the duff? Bad time. My wife had a miss at that stage. Bad news.

'There's a fair bit of money to make on this. I'll ring my editor. Daily Mail. There's obviously a lot of interest so that will push the price up a bit. This is Bob, who's just taken your pic. I'm Jerry. Jerry Goodall. Give us a break and we can help you. Help your friend, the doctor. He's going to get crucified by the media if what that idiot Hambling said is true. There has to be another side to the story. He couldn't have been campaigning against cloning as he has if it were true, could he?

'You help us. Get him and his missus to help us tell it. It won't do you any harm, either, though we'll have to go a bit carefully. There's a case coming up with you, isn't there, so that's going to be sub judice ... hey, but who cares about the sub judice law nowadays. Most journos haven't got a clue what it is. It's obvious to me that MI5 is tied up in all this. Dirty mean buggers, they are. Lot of dirty tricks and you aren't the first threatened with their kind of 'no evidence' death. Others have disappeared without trace. Our political guys are working on that aspect.'

Bob, who had a Brummie accent, said: 'Watch your back. They've seen us.'

As he spoke the crowd came surging round the corner. The woman they'd called Sally and whom he had thought kind-looking was in the lead. She had a look of pure fury and hate on her face. Back off, Jerry, she said. Just back off and fuck off, you cunt. We've cut a deal and I'm the front runner. I'm going to do the business and get the lady to talk. She'll talk to me, you know she will. Woman to woman. Just my line. You know I can make it happen. Gentle chat up and then we'll share.'

Jerry said: 'Meet Sally Bishop. The Sun. Lovely lady, just lovely. Come off it, darling. There aren't any deals to be done on this one. I heard your news desk is anti, very anti. No nice words for Doctor Warne and his missus there. Every man for himself. Now just fuck off yourself and let me talk to my friend.'

He put an arm round Mac, who shrugged it off. The other photographers by this time had all taken his picture. Suddenly they heard the sound of a car starting up and with one accord, except for Jerry and Bob, they raced off back down the hill to the cul-de-sac where the Warnes' house was. A car came speeding out of the road. Mac thought he saw Margaret in the passenger seat.

'Is that her? The missus?' Jerry said, obviously not needing an answer. 'That'll teach them all a lesson. I bet they didn't leave anyone sensible keeping a look-out. All too anxious to get their hands on you.'

At that moment Mac's mobile rang. He got a clear picture on it of Warne and he walked away. Jerry followed him. 'If that's Warne tell him we can cut a deal that will give him a chance to tell his story. Let me speak to him.'

'Fuck off,' Mac said.

Warne said: 'What's up? I'm on the train, nearly home. I've had a hell of a day with police, press. Arrested then bailed. They hounded me all the way. I know there are at least two guys on the train with me. They've already tried to get me to talk.'

'They're here. The press. All of them, waiting for you,' Mac said. 'I've got a guy with me right now. Daily Mail. The house is surrounded. They'll be back here after me in a minute. I'm up the hill from the house.'

'How's Margaret? Is she OK?'

Mac said: 'She's just this minute left. Somebody's given her a lift. The chap in number 12, I think. I don't know where she's gone. I'm stuck with the news mob. I need to talk to you but I don't know if I can throw them off.'

Jerry stood in front of him and the burly photographer Bob was at his back as the rest of the door-steppers advanced up the hill.

Mac said: 'The Daily Mail guy wants to speak to you. His name's Jerry Goodall. Here he is.' He handed the phone over. Bob moved his position to shield Jerry as he backed into the thick hedgerow.

Jerry said: 'Dr Warne. At last. Jerry Goodall. We've been trying to reach you. You need some help. We gave you a sympathetic hand last time over the 'death by numbers' thing. Remember? I've talked to you before a few times. Medical stories. No, well you may not remember but I do. We can give you a platform on this. If this is some stitch-up by government we can get to the bottom of it. And your views on cloning. We can help. Can I ask you just one thing?'

But before he could ask Warne either switched the phone off or lost the signal. 'Bugger, bugger piss and shit.'

Mac noticed he hadn't mentioned cash yet. Clever. Warne would have run a mile. Or maybe not. Did he know him, really?

The girl, Sally, was pushing forward. 'Who's that you've got? Is it Warne? For God's sake Jerry play ball and we can all get our news desks off our backs. It is Warne, isn't it?'

Closer too Mac realised she was even older than he had thought. And a lot harder-boiled.

'Here listen,' Jerry thrust the phone forward. 'Nothing, see. Nothing. And you stupid pillocks have let the missus escape.'

Sally said: 'Jim let her go. Or rather he didn't see that she'd somehow got over the fence at the back and then down to the house next but one. The man came out first and started up the car and then someone with a jacket, trousers and a baseball cap came out. He didn't realise it was her until the car started up. I hope she hasn't done any damage to herself climbing over fences. Not a good idea when you're preggers and her age.' She didn't sound as if she meant it.

Mac thought: 'That's the guy Margaret's been chatting up.' He'd seen her in action a couple of times, stopping to admire something in the garden and turning the conversation flirtatiously. What a bloody awful woman. Warne deserved something better. No, maybe they deserved each other.

'What are we doing next?' Sally asked. 'Are you going to share him or not? Look, sonny Jim, have you got a deal on with the Mail or not and don't play the innocent. You know the score. You've been through this already and very fucking bloody clever you were too, my mate Charlie ... remember him ... tells me. We know it can't be you because of the court case. You're the untouchable but you can get to Warne for us. Look, ring him back. If he'll talk we'll all give him a fair crack of the whip.'

Mac said: 'I'm not doing it. Look, just piss off. I'm going back into the house and you can all bloody well leave me alone.'

Jerry said: 'Sal, old gal, you've lost your touch. I don't suppose even taking your knickers off this time is going to swing things. Quick screw, Mr Fish? No, didn't think so. You're just too old, these days, darling, and you've lost the few looks you used to have.'

'Charming.' She turned on her heel and the gaggle around her burst into laughter. Mac went down the hill and turned into the road. As he did so a car roared past him. It was a taxi which turned into the Warnes' driveway and he saw Warne get out and race for his front door. He must have been nearly at the station when he had called before. The flash bulbs went off from the waiting photographers, sharp light in the darkness.

Mac broke into a run. 'Wait for me, let me in.' He hurtled through the door, just as Warne was about to shut it. The journalists set up their baying clamour behind him. Dr Warne, Dr Warne, just a word, speak to us.

Warne turned and put the chain up across the door. As he did so an envelope dropped through the letter box.

Mac picked it up and handed it to Warne. 'For you.'

Warne said: 'This is intolerable.' He opened the envelope and took out the note which contained a cheque. '£100,000 for the story,' he said. 'God, they are just so sick.' He stuffed the envelope back out through the letter-box.

He went into the kitchen. Someone was rapping at the window on the other side of the blind. He turned to Mac.

'I suppose you are wondering what has happened. Well, so am I. What did Margaret say if anything?'

'She said that you knew, that you gave permission for a cloned child, that the DNA came from a cell of yours.' Mac was guessing, trying to force Warne to come clean.

'I gave sperm. I donated sperm, that's all. That's what I signed for. For IVF. Nothing else. They duped us. That bloody doctor, the psychiatrist, Tanner. He's in this.'

He went into the sitting room and switched the television on. Maeve was on, her interview being repeated. 'Oh God,' he said. 'Oh God.'

There was more noise by the front door and the letter box snapped open and shut. Mac went to collect the notes.

'Shall I open them,' he offered. Warne nodded.

'No cheques, just offers, £200,000 from the Sun and the Express. The Mail's upped its offer but only to £150,000. There's a note from the girl at the Sun. Sally. She says that unless you play ball the other papers are going to do a really big hatchet job on you. She says that the Guardian is going to do a big feature on your affair with Maeve Dunlop and she says that there is an allegation that money went missing from the accounts of the Stop Death by Numbers campaign. Apparently some butcher in Bristol has put the knife in. He's accusing you and Maeve of taking money from bereaved people under false pretences and misleading others over what you could do to get the government to stop the death targets. That you're a charlatan.

'He's also saying that he was tricked into letting you have a shop of his and no rent was paid for it although he asked over and over again for it. Sally's suggesting that it would be far better for you to speak to her than let all this get out with just a one-sided account. Oh, by the way, she also says that Maeve is talking to the Guardian, putting her side. She says if only you could give her an exclusive then you could get a much more sympathetic press.'

Warne groaned. The phone rang and he picked it up. 'Margaret, where are you?' He listened, saying nothing. Margaret had plenty to say which Mac could not hear. When Warne put the phone down, he looked at Mac and then the tears rolled down his face and he bent over, trying to control the sobs that shook his upper frame.

'I can't stand this,' Mac heard him say.

Mac gambled. He said: 'We could get out ... you and I ... get away. They can't arrest us and we could give them the slip. If Margaret can do it, so can we. How about your boat?'

Warne looked at him. 'Why do you want to risk everything? You're in enough trouble. I'm standing bail for you to appear in court. You can't leave the country. This is my mess, mine and Margaret's. Somehow they tricked us. She's just told me that she didn't know it was a cloned baby. She thought they used IVF.'

Mac said: 'That's not what she said to me. She said she hadn't given permission for them to release the news that it was a cloned baby.' He saw Warne's face cloud over with despair. Something else too. Shame?

'You want a child, don't you? Desperately? Were you desperate enough for cloning? I don't think so. I think that was Margaret. Maybe in cahoots with MI5. She must hate you. You didn't know, did you?'

Warne shook his head.

Mac took the plunge. He said: 'You know you told me that you had donated sperm when you were a student? What would you say if you got to know one of the children that had resulted from that donation? You said before you thought that would be tricky. But now ... in all this mess ... what would you honestly say if you got to know a child of your's?'

Warne said: 'I suppose if I could get used to the child ... well adult by now. I suppose I'd like it. Well, for Christ's sake, of course I would. Interested to see if he or she carried any likeness, facial, mannerisms, how the child had turned out. My biggest regret has always been not having a child with Margaret. The donor episode ... that was when I was breaking away from my church, from my Catholic upbringing. I did a lot of things then that I now feel guilty about. I was a late developer. I suppose it was my teenage rebellion delayed a few years. I was in my early 20s.

'And later ... when I had affairs. I feel guilty about those too. And about Maeve. I get more and more guilty as I get older. Weighed down with it. That's why I could never leave Margaret, no matter what she did ... does. Do you never feel guilt? You strike me as someone who probably doesn't. That's not a criticism. You are self-centred but, whether you like it or not, you do have some kind of ethic. Why else did you get so embroiled in this cloning business? It wasn't just because of Fern, was it?'

Mac said: 'It was because I was the result of AID. I hate the idea of children being manufactured. Off the peg children. They told me when I was 12 and it shattered me. I said then that I would find my real father. I think I have.'

He looked at Warne. 'I think it is you.'

Epilogue

James Fields - Via Voice

I knew first hand a bit of all that went on that evening because Mac got Warne to speak to Steph at some point. After all he was a member of the MA and doctors expect to get their money's worth. She was careful, very careful. Hislop had already told her not to get involved but she gave Warne a lot of very good advice about handling the mob that was door-stepping him. He didn't take her advice.

Most of what I now know comes from the newspapers and much later from what was said at the inquest. It seems Mac and Warne made their plans very carefully. They called Jerry Goodall in from the Mail and Warne signed a deal. Goodall got them out of the house and away and I think, at this point, Warne insisted on going to a hotel up on the estuary near Bideford, The Commodore, at a place called Instow.

It must have been after midnight when they arrived. Jerry Goodall wrote later that Warne was very protective of Mac that whole evening but whether that was written with hindsight I don't know. They obviously did talk in detail to Goodall about the possibility that they were father and son and all that they had said, of course, went into his paper.

When and how they managed to get out of the hotel isn't clear. I think Goodall had to save his bacon with his editor so some of what he wrote probably isn't true.

Anyway, at some point before 7 in the morning

Warne and Mac got away from the hotel and got on board Warne's boat which he kept anchored just up stream in the estuary, very near the hotel.

It was just after high tide. We're talking December now so it certainly wasn't ideal sailing conditions. There was a strong wind coming into the estuary off the channel all the reports said. The experts said it was a foolhardy thing to do, to take a 26ft yacht like his Contessa out on an ebbing tide into a north-westerly gale. By the time they left the shelter of land it would have been something like gale force 6, maybe 7, by lunchtime it was 8. He would have had to take the boat out without the customary checks a sailor would normally make and the boat had been laid up for two or three months. That came out at the inquest too.

By the time they were missed at the hotel, Goodall and the photographer having dropped off to sleep, they were already out into the Bristol Channel and heading presumably for Ireland. Maybe Warne had other ideas. He might have thought he could head west, round the Cornish coast and then across the channel to France or Spain. It would have been suicidal but then they were both up against it and what they had already done was foolhardy enough.

Goodall must have panicked, more afraid of what his news desk and editor would say than the police and so he did not report them missing until lunchtime. They had certainly been gone over 6 hours by then. The storm that day grew worse. There was an inboard motor on the yacht but even that would have been pretty useless in those conditions.

I don't know if Mac had ever sailed before. I'm sure if I had asked him the question he would have boasted about this or that experience, something that put him in a good light. I can hear him spinning just such a tall story about sailing on a tall ship. Now I shall never know.

The story of their disappearance broke first on

television. Then the media went mad. Goodall did well. He had the upper hand, of course, with the interviews he had carried out that night. There was a lot of sob content in his stuff. Anyone reading the Mail would have had a lot of sympathy for both Warne and Mac. And it was Goodall, of course, who more or less confirmed that Mac was Warne's natural son and went into the past history of Warne being a sperm donor in his student days. Photographs were published showing how alike they were. Who was there to refute it?

It was the Sun which had Margaret's story. They had one of their headlines which passes into newspaper lore. 'Hypocritic Oaf' with a half page picture of Warne. Margaret had obviously sold out to them and they weren't going to spoil her story with too big a showing of the escape by boat.

She now said categorically that Warne had been party to the agreement to have a cloned child. He was the villain of the piece and she went into a lot of detail about their marriage, making out Warne was some kind of control freak who had stopped them from having children earlier in their marriage when she had gone through the trauma of miscarriages and then a baby that had lived only a few hours. She said that she had always wanted to find out what was going wrong for them but he had refused.

Maeve Dunlop as the betrayed mistress had a good showing though the Guardian, who had signed her up, concentrated more on her views about Warne's deception and combined this with the more distasteful facts about cloning children. She managed to get a lot in about the whole ethical question of cloning from the point of view of the child. I knew later from Hambling that he had been pretty sickened by the fact that she had been given that sort of unopposed platform. He felt it helped to skew the inquiry's eventual findings which ruled out the trial programme though it did absolve any families from prosecution who had already broken the law.

By mid-week the media had moved on to other things. The public was no longer interested in Warne or Mac's disappearance although there were small paragraphs for a day or so about the sea and air search that went on and was then finally abandoned.

So on the following Saturday it was a complete shock when Warne was reported to have turned up in a pretty bad way on the island of Lundy. He'd managed to crawl ashore some time within a day of setting out but had not been found for over a week. There was little left of the boat, some splintered planks on the rocks near where he was found.

How do some people manage to survive in the most awful conditions and elements? The weather had been atrocious the whole of that week and he was shipwrecked on jagged rocks and the place he crawled to, under a steep cliff, was lashed by spray, wind and rain. He was alive, but barely alive when one of the very few islanders spotted him and called out the air-sea rescue boys. They winched him up and packed him off to hospital in Bristol.

That first night in a hospital bed he had another stroke which took away his power of speech. There was no sign of Mac around the coast of Lundy and nobody could ask Warne what had happened to him.

The story faded until just after Christmas when Margaret lost the baby. Then the media raked it all up again for a day or so.

It was February when a body was washed up much further along the Bristol Channel. It came ashore on the muddy flats at Weston-super-Mare. It was in a pretty terrible condition, headless, and it must have been knocked about by tankers en route for Cardiff but they took DNA samples and proved it was Mac. I hated to think of him dying in such a way, disintegrating, destroyed and his drowning still haunts me.

The Daily Mail campaigned to get a DNA test of Warne to prove whether or not he was Mac's father but it wasn't allowed. He couldn't give his consent to the procedure and Margaret wouldn't, probably because she hated Mac so much, and so the doctors would not allow it. They said it wasn't ethical. Somehow that seemed the final irony.

And cloning? The first Royal Commission came down against the trial programme but left the door open for more discussion. The projected population figures are even more dismal and now this second commission has been set up. That is what I am working on now. There is no doubt that this time cloning will get the green light. I can't in honesty see what else the country can do. Other countries have already overturned the ban. The families who have participated in cloning children, and that includes those who have adopted, have been given immunity from prosecution. The government ruled that it was in the children's best interest that the families should not be penalised.

Many of the few children who are being born are handicapped, mentally and physically. Mostly the problems are because of the radiation fall-out. The food supply chain is still the biggest culprit with caesium causing long-term poisoning and affecting water and crops and then onwards into milk, meat and vegetables. Whatever and whenever it is detected it is always too late because damage has been done.

Our own little girl, Elizabeth, Lizzie ... she is, of course, absolutely lovely and we both love her dearly but her spine is crooked and probably she will never walk properly. She's having more tests at the moment and there might be operations. She's bright as a button, though, mentally and we must be thankful for that.

The most extraordinary sequel to all this is that a week ago we were in Kingston-upon-Thames at a big out-of-town toy shop. We wanted to get Lizzie something for her birthday which might help her with her movement.

Walking through the store I saw them first. I wasn't sure whether to say anything to Steph but at that moment she caught sight of Fern and pinched my arm. Johnnie was pushing the push-chair and William was talking animatedly to his mother, a very blonde good-looking little boy, very like his father. He must be nearly 4 now.

I said as we came up to them: 'Hello, didn't expect to bump into you again.'

Johnnie seemed really pleased to see me. He had never met Steph, of course. He looked into our pushchair and tickled Elizabeth under her chin and she giggled happily.

'She must be about the same age as Eddie,' he said. I looked into the pushchair and there was a little boy, dark eyed, dark curly hair, with a pixie-like delicate little face.

We didn't talk for long, Steph and Fern hardly spoke. When we got back to the car Steph said: 'Well, what do you think?'

'I guess Mac must have looked very much like that when he was the same age,' I said.